# Finding Lucy
## The Dream Traveler
## Book Three

Ernesto H Lee

## Dedication

If I have learned nothing else in my life, I have learned that no matter how dark your life may seem, love and hope are always possible.

At a dark time in my life, a beautiful friend gave me the greatest gift that one person could give to another.

I couldn't see it and I couldn't hold it - but I could feel it. It wasn't the most unique, the most expensive, or even the most elaborately wrapped gift - but its value was immeasurable.

Love and hope have the power to brighten the darkest days.

By giving these things, we lose nothing and gain everything. Love and hope knows no limits. Give generously.

M, you are my candle in the darkness x

Ernesto H Lee
13th March 2019

# Preface

It's been almost two months since my joyride in the back of a police van with sergeants Huntley and Bellmarsh, and I think it would be fair to say that a lot has happened since then.

In the two weeks following on from the arrest of Detective Superintendent Clive Douglas, the remaining members of 'The Network' were systematically rounded up and most were only too willing to spill their guts and pass the blame on to others in return for a lighter sentence. I say most, because two very senior individuals chose to follow the example of Assistant Chief Constable Maurice Butterfield. Rather than face the shame of arrest and imprisonment, one former magistrate took a nose dive off the balcony of his swanky Mayfair penthouse apartment and a serving chief inspector stepped in front of a speeding train at Kings Cross station.

Call me prejudiced, but the only real loss in my opinion is the fact that, like ACC Butterfield, they will never be held accountable for their crimes. Many others will, though. And due to the scale of the corruption and seniority of the players involved, the story of 'The Network' was front-page news for the best part of a month.

Each passing day brought a fresh slew of revelations and arrests to keep the public and the press hooked, much to the annoyance and embarrassment of those in power. At one point towards the end of the first week, questions were even asked in parliament about how such corruption could go undetected for so long within the senior echelons of the Police, the Judiciary, and Local Government. I suspect that some of those asking the questions were possibly trying to divert attention away from themselves, but only time will tell if I am right.

Regardless and, suffice to say, the level of concern within the government was enough to push the senior leadership within the Police Service to accelerate the investigation and to apprehend the remaining suspects as quickly as possible.

By the end of week two, the final suspects had been taken into custody and eventually public interest in the case, or lack thereof, pushed the story further and further towards the back pages of those publications still interested enough to cover it.

Before this, one particularly satisfying moment for me was the arrest and return to the UK of Mr. Desmond Carter. With the police diverted looking for other high-profile suspects, he had managed to slip out of the country to Spain. His freedom was short-lived, however. With his photograph circulated to every hotel and boarding house throughout Europe it was only a matter of time before he was recognized. After just twelve days on the run he was found hiding under his bed in a cheap Magaluf hotel.

Rumor has it, that he cried and pissed his pants when the cuffs were going on his wrists. I know about this rumor because I started it and as far as anyone else is concerned now, it is a hundred percent true and that suits me just fine.

And what about my old friend Detective Superintendent Clive Douglas? After his arrest, he was remanded in custody to Meerholt Prison, but unlike me and for exactly the reasons you would expect, he opted for the supposed safety of solitary confinement.

Unfortunately for him, he seriously underestimated the power and influence of Frank Butler and after a particularly unpleasant encounter with a razor blade stuck into the end of a toothbrush, he was quickly transferred to a maximum-security prison in the north of England – minus half of his left ear and with twenty-seven stitches in his face and neck.

I took no particular pleasure in the news of his injuries, but neither could I feel any sympathy for him. For a man that has spent the best part of his life dispensing his own particular brand of justice without compassion or remorse, this was in my opinion a long overdue reckoning. I am only thankful that he is still alive and will hopefully have many years of happy isolation in which to reflect on his actions.

As for myself, I was kept in hospital for nearly four weeks. Just after my discharge, I paid a visit to Darren 'Daz' Phillips at his home to thank him. God only knows what this man is made of. Despite taking both barrels of a shotgun in the chest and only being released from hospital a few days before me, he was already up on his feet and having a kick-about with his son in his garden. As you can imagine, he wasn't exactly pleased to see me. My arrival was initially met with a barrage of expletives and threats of violence from both Darren and his missus Karen. Thankfully, my news that all the pending burglary charges had been dropped calmed the situation, and when I mentioned the possibility of a fat compensation check all was forgiven, and I was duly invited in for a couple of cold cans of Stella.

I don't think I can exactly describe us as best friends now, but I did leave their house with the distinct feeling that this wouldn't be the last time that our paths would cross.

I also visited Billy a few times in his bail hostel and, with the help of Jean Monroe, we were able to have his sentence reduced to six months of community service. As of now, he has managed to keep himself out of trouble and has even started a part-time job stacking shelves in a supermarket. In a few weeks' time he will be moving back in with his mum and dad and I am hopeful that he has turned a corner in his life.

For the rest of the time, I have been playing an increasingly difficult game of avoiding Ben Pinto at all costs.

Finding out I had a son just a few years younger than myself was a kick in the guts. Finding out that he is also a dream traveler and that he knows I am his father was a kick in the guts with steel-toe-capped boots on! He has been calling constantly for the past few weeks and no doubt wants to discuss his plan to be my partner. Thankfully, between my recuperation, physiotherapy, interviews with internal affairs, DCI Morgan and the serious crimes squad, along with visits from my mother and a serious of unfruitful dates with the lovely Nurse Samuels, I have thus far managed to put off this inevitable conversation with him.

It's a conversation that we need to have, though, and it's going to come soon. I have absolutely no intention of letting Ben get involved in my investigations. If my experience from the last few months has taught me nothing else, it has taught me that even with my own experience of dream travel and police work, I still have a lot to learn. There is no way on earth that I am going to allow a complete novice like Ben to tag along and put both of us at risk.

My only issue is that even if I turn his offer down, I have no real way of stopping him and perhaps not knowing where or when he might turn up might be even worse than allowing him to help. It's a question I don't even want to contemplate. So, as usual, I will bury my head in the sand until I need to confront it again. For now, I have other more immediate concerns to think about.

Today is the first official day back at work for me and Cath after our recovery. The investigation into 'The Network' is far from over. In all likelihood, given the depth of the conspiracy, it could take years to complete and bring all the suspects to court, but life goes on and there are many more unsolved cases that deserve our attention. I have been out of action for nearly two months and now I am ready to sink my teeth into another juicy case.The office can wait, though – there is somewhere else that I need to be first.

Sean McMillan
17th April, 2018

# Present Day – Tuesday, 17th April, 2018

Until this morning I had still been using a walking stick to help take the pressure off my right leg. There is no way, though, that I will be using it today, or indeed on any day from now on. If I am honest with myself, I haven't needed it for at least two weeks. It was more just the comfort of knowing it was there if I did need it.

Today is my first day on the job as a Detective Sergeant and I have no intention of letting the team see me as anything less than fully fit.

By 9 am, I am up, showered, shaved, and dressed in a new made-to-measure suit, hopefully befitting of my new rank and status. Just before 10, my taxi drops me off at the entrance to Hounslow Town Hall.

Apart from a few other people going about their normal business, I am pleased to see that the only person waiting for me at the top of the stairs is Catherine.

Over the course of the last two months I have met up with Cath many times to catch up and quite a few of our physio sessions have been at the same time, so there is no awkwardness in seeing each other today. This is the first time in quite a while, however, that we have seen each other suited and booted, and I can't help smiling at how glammed up Cath is.

"Wow, Cath! Anyone would think you were here for something special. Don't tell me, you're getting married? Who's the lucky fella?"

"Well, it's not you, Sean," she replies. "Not after leaving me standing here on the stairs for ten minutes. That's not a good start to married life. Nice suit, by the way. Primark have really raised the bar with that one."

We both laugh at her killer sarcasm and I am halfway through a comment about her concussion returning, when the main door to the Town Hall opens and Detective Chief Inspector Morgan steps out immaculately dressed in his best uniform.

"If you don't mind, let's not keep the Assistant Commissioner waiting. This is one of those rare occasions in your career that you might be able to get away with it – but let's not push it please. Just to be on the safe side, a bit of a limp might help, Sean."

It's a great feeling to be back and this bit of light humor from Morgan helps to diffuse the nerves we were both trying unsuccessfully to hide. Morgan leads us into the main civic hall and the gathered crowd stand and applaud us all the way to the stage where we are greeted by the Assistant Commissioner of the Metropolitan Police, Sir Greville Stanley.

The Chief Constable of the Bedfordshire Constabulary and the Lord Mayor of Hounslow are also in attendance, and after a brief introduction, we are guided to our seats.

The Assistant Commissioner remains standing. Following a short pause to check his notes, he moves forward to a lectern, adjusts the height of the microphone, and starts the delivery of his carefully prepared speech to the assembled audience.

"As police officers, there are many difficult and stressful times in our careers, so when I am asked to attend an occasion like this one, it does of course give me immense pleasure and an immense sense of pride in the Police Service and the officers that serve within it. When a police officer willingly puts him or herself in a position where their own life is at risk, it demonstrates beyond all dou …"

At this point my mind starts to wander and I turn my attention to the audience, the vast majority of whom are police officers. It looks like every available officer from the Cold Case team is in attendance. There are also a large number of civilians, including councilors, my friend and solicitor Jean Monroe, reporters, and some of the nursing staff that helped with my recovery.

It's no surprise that I can't see Karen Samuels amongst them. We had a few dates after my discharge from hospital, but any spark of romance quickly fizzled out and whilst we parted on good terms, it's probably for the best that she is not here – less embarrassment all round this way.

I am surprised, though, to see Billy sitting next to Darren and Karen Phillips in the front row. I am of course happy to see them, but I had no idea that they had been invited. The invitation I did know about was the one extended to Maria and Ben Pinto. Maria is looking as glamorous as ever sitting to the right of my mother, but it is Ben that has caught my attention and not because of anything in particular he is doing. Seeing him reminds me again that I can't avoid him forever.

I am so wrapped up in thoughts of how to handle Ben that I don't notice that Sir Greville has finished his speech and has asked me and Catherine to stand up. A sharp dig in the ribs from Cath brings me back to reality and we both move towards the front of the stage.

"It gives me great pleasure to present the Chief Constable's commendation for exemplary service to Detective Sergeant Sean McMillan and Detective Constable Catherine Swain."

The applause from the audience and the flash of cameras seems to go on forever and we are both hugely relieved when it finally dies down and we can step off the stage and relax slightly. What follows next is a short reception with lots of hand shaking, pats on the back, and requests for quotes or pictures from the press with Cath and me holding our commendation certificates.

Unused to such attention, Catherine looks almost as relieved as I feel when DCI Morgan finally excuses us and ushers us outside to his waiting car.

"Well then, you pair, now that we have that out of the way, let's get back to some real police work, shall we?"

"Absolutely, sir," I reply.

"Great – back to Blackwell Station please," Morgan tells the driver. "Go easy, though, we have a couple of celebrities on board."

With a knowing smirk to DCI Morgan, the driver pulls away and heads towards Blackwell. "Right you are, sir. I will have you and this pair of celebrities safely there in fifteen minutes."


By the time we arrive at the station, most of our colleagues are already back at their desks and we once more must run the gauntlet of handshakes, congratulations, and welcome-back speeches.

This new-found celebrity status will probably last only as long as our next failure or screw up, but we might as well milk it for now and Morgan waits patiently as we both soak up the praise. I can tell, though, that he is keen to get to work and after ten minutes, I nod to Cath and we follow Morgan to his office.

Detective Sergeant Sarah Gray is waiting for us and she stands up and smiles when we enter the room.

"Sean, really great to see you back. You look well and congratulations on a job well done. Your commendation and promotion were both very well deserved."

My promotion hasn't really sunk in yet, so Sarah addressing me by my first name causes me to flush slightly with embarrassment.

"Thank you, Sarah. It's good to be back."

Then she turns to Catherine and adds, "DC Swain, you're also looking well. Your commendation was much deserved. Personally speaking, though, I think it should have been a medal for what you did. Perhaps if you had been a man ... Don't you agree, sir?"

Now it's Morgan's turn to be embarrassed and he looks like he is unsure if DS Gray is joking or not.

"Um, yes, perhaps, but a chief constables commendation is not something that is given away lightly, DS Gray."

Then turning to Cath and me, he adds, "Both of you are a credit to the force and to this team. Now, please, let's get down to business, shall we?"

Morgan takes his seat and removes a thick manila folder from the top drawer of his desk. I can see already from its condition that it is much older than anything we currently handle. This is confirmed when Morgan drops it in front of me.

Handwritten on the front of the folder is the name 'Lucy Partington-Brown' and surprisingly the date: March 14th, 1972.

I reach over to take it, but Morgan stops me.

"Is that name familiar to you, Sean?"

My face gives away the fact that the name means nothing to me. Morgan speaks again before I can answer.

"No, I guess it wouldn't. This case was a bit before your time. I was only a youngster myself, but it was headline news in 1972."

"Is it a murder case, sir?" I ask.

"That's what I need you and DC Swain to find out, Sean. It's currently still classified as a missing person case, but pressure from surviving family members looking for answers has resulted in the case been handed over to us to take a fresh look."

The longer a case has been cold, the less likely it is for any new investigation to reveal any new evidence, so after a break of forty-six years, making any progress on this case under normal circumstances would be extremely difficult. It must be a particularly significant or high-profile case for it to be re-opened now.

"After more than forty years, sir, that must be some significant pressure from the family, or have they provided some new information?"

"No new information, Sean. It's the Partington-Brown name that has been the influencing factor in bringing this case to our attention. Lucy Partington-Brown is, or was, one of the daughters of Sir David Partington-Brown. At the time of Lucy's disappearance, he was the Member of Parliament for Spalding in Lincolnshire."

"So, the sister has been applying pressure, sir?" I ask.

"No, Sean, it's Sir David himself that reached out to the home office to have the case re-opened."

"The father is still alive? Wow, he must be cracking on a bit. He must be at least a hundred by now, sir."

Morgan is not impressed with my comment and lets me know it.

"A little respect please, Sergeant McMillan. Sir David is ninety-three years old and in extremely poor health. This is his last chance to find out what happened to his daughter. I realize that after this length of time, it is going to be difficult to give him the answers he is looking for but, given that you and DC Swain are the flavor of the month currently, the Home Secretary has personally requested that this case be assigned to you. What do you think, Sean? Are you up for the challenge?"

Morgan has only given me very limited information and I haven't seen the contents of the case file yet, but it makes no difference. I am a newly promoted Detective Sergeant and flavor of the month apparently. It's not like I am in a position to say no.

"Yes, of course, sir, we will give it our best shot."

Morgan stands up and smiles. "That's great. I will let the Home Secretary know that you are on the case. I suggest that you both head home and get your things together.

DS Gray has made arrangements for your hotel. You can make a start on reading through the case file on your drive up to Lincolnshire."

Before I can say anything, Sarah Gray hands me two copies of the case file and then passes me a white envelope.

"The hotel details are in there, Sean. It looks nice enough. I have booked you in initially for two weeks. If you need longer just call and let me know. If you make a move now you should get there by five or six this evening."

I had expected my first day back at work to be interesting, but I had not been expecting to be shipped up north to investigate a nearly half-century old missing person case. My look gives away what both Cath and I are thinking, and Morgan reads our minds.

"Don't look so shocked, you two. You can't investigate a Lincolnshire case from down here in London. All of your leads, suspects, and surviving witnesses are in Lincolnshire. No need to worry, though, I hear that they stopped human sacrifices in the north of England years ago. Now, go on, time is ticking on this one.

"Sergeant McMillan, DC Swain, good luck and keep me updated on progress."

Without another word, he turns to DS Gray and they start to discuss another open case, which is our less-than-subtle cue to leave.


In the lift down to our office, we don't speak until the doors have closed and then I ask Catherine what she thinks.

"I think that we have just been handed a big bloody ticking hand grenade, Sean. That's what I think. If we solve this case and find out what happened to the missing girl, the Home Secretary gets to help out one of the old boys' club and we get to put the pin back in the grenade. But If we get nowhere, I have a feeling that this big bloody grenade is going to go off with one almighty bang in our ears," she says, adding sarcastically, "Like you said, though, we will give it our best shot, Sergeant McMillan."

Her nervousness at taking on this case is completely understandable. Very few of my other colleagues would be keen to go anywhere near a forty-six-year-old missing person case and particularly not one that comes with the added pressure of the involvement of the Home Secretary.

The role of Home Secretary is a senior-level government position within the British Cabinet and, amongst other things, is responsible for policing in England and Wales, matters of national security, and the Security Service MI5. Little wonder then that she is nervous.

Being given this case also worries me, but our recent success in bringing down 'The Network' makes us the obvious candidates to take on this one. It's too late to worry now anyway – we have accepted the case and we need to get moving on it.

"Let's not worry about that grenade just yet, Cath. Maybe after forty-six years the mechanism will have seized up."

She doesn't look impressed at my poor attempt at humor, so I try another.

"So, do you think that they have booked us twin beds or a double? A double would probably be better if we want to go undercover. Do you prefer Mrs. Smith or Mrs. Jones?"

"You bloody wish, Sean. I am way out of your league and if these tight bastards haven't paid for two rooms, I will be turning the car around and heading straight back to civilization."

By the time the doors open at our floor, we are both smiling and ready to get moving. Catherine collects her laptop computer and a few other pieces from her office and then we head down to the garage to collect our cars. Before we separate, we make arrangements to meet up later.

"Okay, Cath, it's just after 1 pm now – how long do you need to get ready?"

"By the time, I get home and get a few things packed, I think an hour should do it, Sean."

"That's perfect. Pick me up at my place at two-thirty," I tell her.

She looks confused, so I fill in the blanks.

"Oh, sorry, Cath. I thought I had mentioned it already. You're driving. It will give me a chance to go through the case file on the way up."

Less than impressed, Cath turns up her sarcasm levels to full.

"And will I make you some sandwiches and a flask of tea for the trip, Sergeant McMillan?"

"Aw, that's a lovely offer, Cath, but there's really no need – although if you're making some for yourself, ham and mustard would be perfect. Just don't skimp on the mustard!"

With a parting, "Cheeky bastard!" from Cath, she gets in her car and heads home. Twenty minutes later I arrive back at my own place and pick up the folded sheet of paper that has been pushed under my door. Without even needing to read the note, I can guess already who it is from.

The handwriting is by now all too familiar and this note is one of many that I have received at home and whilst I was still in hospital. Along with the numerous calls and visits, Ben is determined to speak to me.

Hey, Sean,

It was good to see you at the ceremony this morning. You were looking well, and it is good that you are getting back to work. I know that you have been busy, but it has been nearly two months since we met in 1994. We need to talk about our situation. I have tried calling and have left you notes. I know that you must be getting them. I know that this is a messed-up situation that neither of us asked for, but let's not forget who caused this. Like it or not, you are my dad and because of you I am also a dream traveler. Please call me and let's meet soon. I can't talk to mum about this, but maybe I should?

Here is my number again – 07767 44534921.

Your loving son,

Ben 'McMillan' Pinto ☺

The cheeky little shit hasn't just inherited my ability to dream travel, he has also inherited my sarcasm and straight to the point attitude. I can live with his sarcastic reference to McMillan in his name, but I can't have him talking to Maria about us.

I don't have time to talk to him, but I send him a WhatsApp message to say that I'm going away on a case but will call him as soon as I get back.

Naively, I hope that this will keep him off my back for a few weeks, but within seconds my phone beeps to signal a new message.

How long will you be away for? We need to talk about this, Sean.

For a second I consider ignoring the message, but then I think better of it and send a reply.

Possibly for a couple of weeks. We have been assigned a case in Lincolnshire. I promise that as soon as I get back, we can meet up for a pint and talk about how to handle this.

My message is read immediately, and I can see that Ben is typing his reply. It is a few minutes before his message comes through and I am surprised when it just says, Okay, thanks. I will wait to hear from you.

He must have reconsidered and deleted whatever it was he was typing for so long, but I am just happy to be able to end the conversation and I put my phone back in my pocket.

Forty-five minutes later I have packed a bag, showered, changed suits and cooked myself a frozen pizza. I am halfway through it when Cath calls to say that she is waiting outside for me. I stuff another slice of pizza in my mouth, pick up my bag, and head down to join Catherine.

"So, where exactly are we going, Sean?"

"Hang on, let me check the booking confirmation, Cath," I reply. "Okay, it's called the Winchester Hotel in a place called Tyevale on the Wold."

"That sounds a bit fancy, Sean."

"Yep, it does Cath, which as we both know, probably means that it is a complete shithole. Wonderful."

Cath punches the address into the GPS, and we set off towards the M1 motorway. If the GPS is accurate, it is 102 miles and two hours, twenty minutes away, so we should get there comfortably before five.

With Cath concentrating on the road, I get to work and open the file. It is jam-packed with interview notes, witness statements, photographs, newspaper cuttings and, helpfully, a short summary of the case provided by the lead detective prior to the case being closed in August of 1974. Keeping a missing person case open for more than two years in the seventies would have been highly unusual and this alone speaks volumes for the influence that Lucy Partington-Brown's father must have had back then.

I had been wondering why we were being sent to Tyevale on the Wold and not Spalding, but it makes sense now. This is where the Partington-Browns were living at the time of Lucy's disappearance and this is in fact where they are still living.

As Cath reaches the outskirts of the town, I am still working my way through the file, but I close it and put it away.

Far from being a shithole, Tyevale on the Wold is almost picture postcard perfect and has a name that wouldn't be out of place in the medieval Domesday Book commissioned by William the Conqueror in 1085 AD to record, amongst other things, all the towns and villages in England for the purpose of confirming accurate tax collection.

Whether Tyevale was or wasn't included in the Domesday Book, it is a lovely looking town and is surrounded by lush countryside and farmland made all the better by the beautiful spring weather.

A few minutes later, Catherine brings her car to a stop in the courtyard of the Winchester Hotel and we are met at the entrance by a well-dressed young woman who escorts us to the reception to check in.

When the young man behind the reception desk confirms our reservation and hands us the key cards for two rooms on the fourth floor, Cath smiles and looks at me with puppy eyes.

"Aww, boss. So sorry about that, you really were hoping for just one room, weren't you … Mr. Smith!"

The guy on reception looks both bemused and slightly embarrassed at Cath's joke, which has gone right over his head. To save him any further embarrassment we head straight up to our rooms. In the corridor, we make plans to meet later.

"Okay, I have a couple of calls to make, Cath. Let's meet in the bar in about an hour. I'll take you through what I know already. Sound good?"

"Yep, sounds good, I might just grab a shower and get changed. I'll see you down there around 6, Sean."

"Great, just call me if you need anything. Maybe I could hand you a towel or some extra shower gel," I joke. "You sure you don't want to go undercover? It might help the case."

"Yep, I'm sure, Sean. I also think that once we get back to London, you need to get yourself laid. I'm guessing that nothing happened with your nurse friend?"

I ask her what she means.

"You're a man, Sean. If anything had happened with her, you would never stop talking about it. Even I could see how hot she was."

Cath laughs as my face turns red with embarrassment and I turn away to put my key card in the slot, but Cath hasn't finished punishing me yet for my towel and shower gel comment.

"So how long has it been, Sean?"

"Sorry, how long has what been?"

"How long since you got laid? Don't go all coy on me now, not after that feeble attempt to see me in the shower just then. If I was easily offended, I might easily interpret that as sexual harassment from a senior officer."

I may be a detective, but Cath is incredibly smart and now has me completely flustered.

"No, no, I didn't mean anything by it, Cath, I was just joking."

Catherine bursts out laughing and takes the card from my hand and uses it to open the door for me.

"Sean, calm down, mate, I'm just messing with you. Jesus, the look on your face is priceless."

I can hear her laughing all the way down the corridor to her room and I feel like a prize twat as I close my door.

She is right, though; I do need to get laid. It's been way to long since I was last with a woman. From my recollection, the last time was in 1994!

The room is nice enough. From the fourth floor it has a pleasant view across a beautifully manicured garden. At most other times of the year it would probably be fairly grim and deserted, but in the middle of April the weather is starting to warm up and the flowers in the garden are in full bloom.

The ground-floor bar opens out onto a paved terrace area and I can see that four or five of the tables are already occupied. Regardless of cracking this case or not, there are certainly worse places I could think of to spend the next couple of weeks.

I unpack my bag and hang up my spare suit and shirts and then I call my mother to let her know where I am and that I won't be home for at least two weeks. Under normal circumstances, we would generally only speak once or twice a month and it would be a rarity for her to visit my apartment, but since the shooting, she has gone back into overly protective mother mode. We talk for five minutes and then I grab a quick shower and change into jeans and a t-shirt. It's just past five-thirty and Cath will be expecting to see me in the bar at six, but there is something I need to do first.

I want to dream travel tonight, but my clothes would stick out like a sore thumb in 1972. I should of course have thought of that before I left home, and I had been wondering what to do about it when a possible solution presented itself on the way into Tyevale in the form of a couple of charity shops on the high street.

The high street is just a two-minute walk from the hotel. With twenty minutes to spare until closing time, I push open the door to a mid-sized branch of Oxfam and am immediately greeted by an officious-looking woman with silver hair who looks to be in her late sixties or early seventies.

"We shut at six, young man. Is there something that I can help you with?"

Looking around the store at the numerous racks of suits, dresses, shirts, and other items and given the fact that I am not an expert on seventies fashion, I am grateful for her offer of assistance and I flash her my best smile.

"Thank you, some help would be wonderful. I have a fancy-dress party coming up soon and it's a seventies theme. I'm looking for a suit and some shoes with a matching shirt and tie if possible."

My mention of the seventies makes her smile. If I am right about her age she would have been in her late teens or early twenties at the time. Perhaps then the reason for her smile is fond memories of her youth. She steps from behind the counter and guides me towards a rack of men's clothes. I am hopeful that she will be able to help me out, but then she turns back towards me.

"Oh, no, I thought that we had a nice three-piece suit from the mid-seventies, but I just remembered that we sent it across to our local theatre group last week. I could call around to some of our other branches for you, but that might take a few days. How soon do you need it, love?"

"I was hoping to have something today if possible," I reply.

She thinks about if for a minute, then she smiles again and asks me to wait. "We don't have any suits in stock at the moment but let me have a look in the back to see what we do have. What are you, a 34-inch waist and 46-inch chest? Am I right?"

I confirm that I am, and she smiles at me again. This time there is more of a twinkle in her eye and it is blatantly obvious that she is flirting with me.

"Yes, I thought so, I'm not usually wrong about men's sizes. I'm generally correct, give or take an inch."

For the second time in as many hours, I find myself blushing and I am thankful when she turns and disappears into the stock room.

A few minutes later and with the color of my cheeks nearly back to normal, she reappears holding a pile of clothes, a pair of brogue shoes, and a pair of platform boots, which she lays out on the counter. I am truly lost for words, but she is extremely pleased at her selection and is keen for me to try them on.

"Well, what do you think, young man? This look would have got you all the girls back in the seventies. Would you like me to help you try them on?"

"Actually, I think they will be okay. To be honest, I'm in a bit of a hurry," I reply.

Being in a hurry is not a lie. It's nearly 6 and knowing Cath, she will already be in the bar waiting for me.

Looking slightly disappointed, but accepting my explanation, my new-found admirer folds and bags the clothes and then asks me about the footwear. "Which do you prefer, the boots or the shoes?"

In truth, both are absolutely ghastly, but I tell her I will take both.

"I can wear the boots with this outfit and if it's okay, would you mind calling around to see if you can track down a suit for me that I can wear with these shoes?"

She agrees, and I jot down my name and number on her notepad and then I hand her a fifty-pound note for my items. Despite the bill only coming to thirty I tell her to keep the change in the hope that she will find me something decent that I can wear on a later trip. She hands me my bags of shopping and I swear that her hand deliberately brushes over mine longer than is needed. If I am in any doubt, there is more than a hint of flirtatiousness in her last statement and the unnecessary way that she draws out my name.

"Before you go, Sean. Take one of my cards and don't hesitate to call if you need anything else. Anything at all that is. It's really no problem."

Like a teenage boy caught looking at the top shelf magazines in a newsagent, I blush for the third time today. I leave as quickly as I can and make my way back to the hotel.

From the reception, I can see Catherine sitting at the bar. Fortunately, she has her back to me, and I am able to make it to the lift without her noticing. I head straight to my room and drop my bags onto my bed and then I take the man-eater's business card from my pocket.

Ms. Abigail Whitchurch, Chairwoman, Tyevale on the Wold, Women's Institute.

I think for a moment to cross out the word 'Chairwoman' and replace it with 'Cougar' but decide not to be so childish. I drop it on the bed next to the bags and head down to see Catherine with the file under my arm.

In fairness, it's only a few minutes past 6, but I can see that she is not impressed at my lack of punctuality.

"That's twice in one day that you've kept me waiting, Sean. I hope it was for a good reason?"

"Sorry, Cath. Mum was stressing about me being away. Let's grab a table over in the corner where it's a bit quieter and we can talk over what we need to do over the next few days."

I order a pint of Stella and another glass of red wine for Cath and we move away from the bar to the table furthest away from the bar. As soon as we sit down, one of the waitresses comes over and hands us the bar-food menu and I suggest to Catherine that we order a few bits to nibble on as we go through the case file. We order and, as soon as the waitress is gone, I open the file and lay out the contents on the table for Catherine to see.

"Okay, so our missing person is Ms. Lucy Partington-Brown. She was last seen at the O'Hanlon Brothers Carnival here in Tyevale at around 11 pm on Tuesday March 14th, 1972. At the time of her disappearance she was 22 years old.

"As you know from DCI Morgan's briefing, she was, or is, the daughter of Sir David Partington-Brown, the former Member of Parliament for Spalding. She has one sister, Joanna Partington-Brown. Joanna kept her maiden name when she married a guy called Edward Wells. Her mother, Beatrice, passed away of natural causes in 1974."

I pull a creased black-and-white photograph from the file and hand it to Catherine. "The date on the back is December 25th, 1971 – Christmas Day – so this is quite possibly one of the last photographs of the family together."

The image of the two girls with their parents standing in front of a Christmas tree screams of aristocracy and old money. All are formally dressed as you would expect from the times and their social status, but what strikes you most of all about the picture is the sisters themselves. They are both tall, slim blondes and both are incredibly photogenic.

Your eyes are almost drawn to them and while it's horrible to even think such a thing, it would be easy to understand what a would-be kidnapper would be attracted to. We both stare at the photo for a few seconds and then Cath breaks the silence.

"Are the sisters twins, Sean?"

"No, but you might think so looking at this picture," I reply. "Joanna is a year older than Lucy, but you're right, they are very alike."

"And what about suspects, Sean?"

I hand Catherine the case summary from 1974.

"Flip to page 3, Cath. Quite a long list of suspects – I've made some notes next to the names."

I give her a few minutes to read it through and then I take the summary back.

"Okay, so top of the list, as always, are the close family, primarily the father and sister. Next is the sister's boyfriend at the time, Edward 'Eddie' Wells, a local farmer. As I said earlier, He's now married to Joanna. They married a year after Lucy disappeared.

We also have the owners of the carnival, two Irish brothers, Jed and Tighe O'Hanlon – both provided identical statements. They say that Lucy was with them until just after 11 pm but then she left and didn't say where she was going. Unfortunately, both are also now deceased, so no chance of us exploring that avenue.

"Then we have a group of local lads. It seems they had a gang thing going back then and were known for causing a bit of bother around town. One of them, Paul Oliver, was an ex-boyfriend of Lucy's. Her father didn't approve, of course, and he forced Lucy to end it."

"And where is he now?" Cath asks.

"Unfortunately, we have no idea. According to the file notes, he skipped town a couple of weeks after Lucy went missing and nothing has been heard of him since."

"Wow, so is he our prime suspect then, Sean? This must surely have raised a flag back in 1972."

"Yep, you would think so. He was pulled in for interview three times, but in the end, it looks like he had a firm alibi for that night and was ruled out."

"So why skip town then? That doesn't make any sense."

"That's why we are here, Cath," I reply. "To try to make sense of this and to find out what happened to Lucy."

Cath nods and points down to the case summary.

"I guess so. And the last suspect, Sean?"

"Oh yes, finally, and the most unlikely, is this guy."

I pull out another black-and-white photo of a young man in his mid-twenties and I hand it to Catherine. The picture has been taken during the winter and his overcoat is pulled up close round his neck, but you can still see the top of his white dog collar poking out over the top.

"Jesus, he looks about 14-years-old and butter wouldn't melt in his mouth," Cath says. "Pardon the reference to Jesus, no pun intended, Sean. So, what's the connection with this guy, are the family Catholic?"

"Nope, that's the interesting part, Cath. The Partington-Browns are Protestant Church of England through and through. The interview notes seem to indicate that our young Father James Beale was working on Lucy to convert her some time before she went missing. Also, possibly some romantic attachment, but there is nothing conclusive to indicate that anywhere in the file."

Cath smiles and then says, "It wouldn't be the first time that a young woman has fallen for a handsome young priest. So, where is he now? I don't imagine he is still in Tyevale. The Catholic Church would have moved him quicker than a woman un-tagging an ugly picture of herself on Facebook at the first whiff of any scandal."

"You're right, Cath. After he was interviewed by the police, he was moved to a parish in Scotland. For the last two years, though, he has been responsible for another parish here in Lincolnshire: the Parish of Beckhampton. It's just twelve miles away. We passed a sign for it on the way here."

"Okay," Catherine asks, "apart from the close family, what ties all of the others to her disappearance?"

"The carnival mainly, Cath. Lucy was at the carnival with her sister and Eddie Wells. The last confirmed sighting of her was by the O'Hanlons just after 11 pm. Prior to that, there was a disturbance involving the three of them – the O'Hanlon brothers, Paul Oliver, and a few of the local lads. It seems that Lucy might have been having a bit of a thing with one of the O'Hanlons while still flirting with Paul."

"Wow, she sounds like quite the slut," Cath exclaims. "Do you think there is anyone in this town that she wasn't shagging?"

We both laugh and then I give Cath a fake look of disapproval that DCI Morgan would be proud of. "Detective Constable Swain, a bit of respect if you please."

This causes even more laughter and after we finally compose ourselves, Cath asks me what the plan is for tomorrow.

"We start with the family. Joanna and her husband Eddie live with Sir David now on his estate just outside of town. Sarah Gray has already made an appointment for us to visit them tomorrow morning at 10."

"Okay, that sounds like as good a place as any to start. So, what about this evening, what's the plan, Sergeant McMillan?"

I call the waitress over and then I turn back to Cath. "I think a couple more drinks, then we get an early night and regroup over breakfast tomorrow to discuss strategy for our meeting with the Partington-Browns."

Cath smiles and after two more glasses of red wine for her and two double Jameson whiskies for me, I pay the bill and we get up to leave. Whilst I head towards the lift, Catherine turns towards the garden and the outside terrace to stretch her legs and I wish her goodnight.

It's still only around 7:45 pm and I can't risk traveling until I am sure that Cath is asleep, so I use the next few hours to research life in 1972 and to try on my outfit.

Although I am feeling tired, I also drink two beers and another whisky from the minibar as a precaution against insomnia. At just after 11 pm, I shave, shower, and get dressed ready to travel back to March 1972. I must hand it to the Oxfam Cougar, she wasn't wrong when she said she was a good judge of sizes.

The clothes and the shoes fit well apart from the blue flared trousers being a little snug around my groin. The rest of my outfit consists of tan leather platform boots that add at least three inches to my height, a white woolen turtleneck pullover and a checked polyester jacket with the widest collars that I have ever seen.

To finish the look, I smear a generous portion of Brylcreem into my hair and then I stand back to admire myself in the mirror. According to the cougar, this look would have got me all the girls back in the seventies. Looking at myself now, it does make me wonder exactly what kind of girls she was talking about.

If you want my opinion – I think I look like a massive bell-end and the boots feel like lead weights strapped to my feet. If it helps me blend in, though, so be it. If the girls go wild for the look – well, that's just a bonus.

My plan tonight is to travel back to the week before Lucy's disappearance. The O'Hanlon Brothers Carnival was in town from the middle of February until the third week of March in 1972, so my intention is to start there. At just past 12, I drink the last miniature bottle of whisky from the mini-bar and lie down on my bed with a crumpled photograph of Jed and Tighe O'Hanlon standing next to one of their carnival rides in a field on the outskirts of Tyevale.

I stare at the photograph for a full minute to memorize as much detail as I can and then I close my eyes and begin my chant.

"Seventh March, 1972, Seventh March, 1972, Seventh March, 1972, Seve …"

# The Past – Tuesday, 7ᵗʰ March, 1972

The first thing I notice is how bloody cold it is. Even in this thick, wooly turtleneck and jacket, I am still shivering slightly, and I'm surprised to see a light covering of snow on the surrounding fields and a thick wall of dirty brown slush on the side of the roads to indicate a recent snowfall.

The next thing I notice is how quiet it is in comparison to 2018. The O'Hanlon Brothers Carnival is spread out across three fields in front of me and two hundred yards behind me is the start of Tyevale high street. The lack of cars and general hustle and bustle compared to modern life is striking.

My intention had been to take a look at the carnival first, but it is only just after 2 in the afternoon and it looks completely deserted. Instead, I turn back towards the high street and carefully take my first steps in platform boots. The boots themselves are hard enough to walk in, but the addition of the slush-covered streets makes it all the riskier for a novice such as myself. After a few close calls, I make it to the top of the high street unscathed.

This is the furthest that I have ever traveled back in time and standing here now I can't help but wonder if we were better off in the past. The high street is full of shops, but every single one of them looks like an independent.

There is a butcher, a greengrocer, and a baker and I don't see anything wrapped in plastic or prepacked. There is a small supermarket, a fish and chip shop, a post office, a bookmaker's, and a small branch of Barclays Bank where no doubt the manager will know the name of every one of his customers.

I can see two pubs, a church, a scout hall, and a police station with the front door open.

The streets are clean; there is no graffiti. There are far fewer cars and I don't see anyone staring into the screen of a smartphone as they walk along.

I know of course that life in 1972 was far from perfect and had its own share of problems, but looking around at the people passing by, they seem to look generally happier and healthier than they do now. McDonalds and KFC have a lot to answer for.

Halfway down the high street I step into a small newsagent's and pick up a copy of the Daily Mail to check the date. I had been hoping for anytime between 7th and 9th March, so I am pleased to see that it is Tuesday 7th.

I browse the store for a few minutes, trying not to look like a geek in a museum before I take the newspaper to the counter and hold out a ten-pound note to the young girl serving. From the look she gives me, you would think I was handing her a human head, but I can understand why when she speaks.

"It's five pence for the paper. Don't you have anything smaller? If I give you change for a tenner, I won't have anything left and the bank only gives out change first thing in the morning."

The whole point of doing my research is so that I don't make such basic errors as this. Now I look like a right flash bastard and in a town like this, word soon gets around. The average weekly wage in 1972 was just thirty quid and here I am flashing ten-pound notes around like they are going out of fashion.

I awkwardly check my pockets for change, but I know that I don't have any. I take out my wallet again and pull out a five-pound note and sheepishly hand it over. It's not much better, but she reluctantly accepts it and then takes unnecessarily long to fumble in the till and hand me back four pounds and ninety-five pence in coins.

As I turn to leave, she shouts back to someone else in the stockroom that I can't see. The comment is clearly meant for my attention though.

"Beryl, I need to pop out for change. Some bloke just paid for his paper with a fiver. Watch the shop for a few minutes while I check with the supermarket."

Keen to get away, I cross the street and head into the closest of the two pubs, the Tyevale Arms.

Inside there are half a dozen middle-aged men chatting and supping on pint pots of dark bitter at the bar and the air is thick with cigarette and pipe smoke. Four young guys in their late teens and early twenties are gathered around a juke box listening to 'American Pie' by Don McLean and two pairs of old age pensioners are sitting at a table in front of an open fire playing dominoes.

The young guys barely give me a glance, but as I pass the pensioners on the way to the bar, they look me up and down with disgust. One of the old fellas doesn't even bother to keep his voice down when he comments on my appearance.

"Look at the state of him! It's a bloody disgrace, I tell you, men wearing high heels. I blame the parents myself."

The barman hears him clearly enough and probably agrees, but he doesn't say anything himself. After looking me up and down suspiciously, he asks what he can get me to drink.

Unlike the many choices in bars today, my options in The Tyevale Arms are decidedly more limited and comprise of John Smiths Bitter, India Pale Ale, Guinness, and Carling Black Label Lager.

Generally, I drink Stella Artois, so the Carling should be the obvious choice, but teenage memories of drinking the piss that is Carling Black Label preclude that as a choice and I opt for a pint of John Smiths.

The barman carefully fills the pint pot from the tap and then places it onto a beer towel to allow the head to settle and I hand him twenty pence. It's almost a shame that none of my friends can dream travel. With prices like this, we could get trashed for less than the cost of a movie ticket in 2018.

Apart from the music from the jukebox and the chatter of the customers, the pub is eerily quiet in comparison to a pub in 2018. There are no screens blasting out MTV or SKY sports and you can hear the crackling of the log in the fire when the record in the jukebox finishes playing.

The other thing that is noticeable in its absence is the lack of menus and chalk boards announcing the day's special offers. UK pubs in 2018 make a significant chunk of their profit through food sales. If I get hungry in here, I think the best I could hope for would be a bag of nuts or a packet of pork scratchings.

I pick up my pint and take a seat at a table close to the fire to warm up and to read my newspaper. From my earlier research I know already that Edward 'Ted' Heath is the Prime Minister and has been in power with the Conservative Party for nearly two years.

The country is rocked by unrest in 1972 and the big stories are the recent ending of the miners' strike and unemployment that has topped the 1,000,000 mark for the first time since the 1930s. There is also a lot of coverage about the bombing of Aldershot Barracks by the Official Irish Republican Army on February 22nd.

This bombing was in retaliation for the killing of fourteen people when troops from the Parachute Regiment opened fire on demonstrators in Derry, Northern Ireland on 30th January.

Even today, the story of 'Bloody Sunday' is well known by nearly everyone in the UK as it has been in and out of the news constantly for nearly fifty years.

The sports pages at the back are dominated by horse racing and football. Three days ago, on March 4th, Stoke City beat Chelsea 2-1 at Wembley Stadium to win the 1972 Football League Cup Final and, sadly for them, this is the one and only time that they have won a major trophy or competition.

I finish reading the newspaper. Just as I stand up to get another pint, the door opens, and three young women walk in and head towards the bar.

The sisters, Lucy and Joanna, are instantly recognizable, and in the flesh they are even more stunning than they were in their photographs. I had not been expecting to see them today, and for a second I stand there like an idiot staring as they walk towards the bar. Thankfully, I am not the only dribbling fool held captive by their beauty. The young guys by the jukebox are also looking at them. One of them wolf-whistles and calls out, "Looking good, Lucy!"

Until now, I hadn't been exactly sure which of the girls was Lucy, but her smile makes it clear. It's obvious she heard the comment from her admirer, but she doesn't turn around or break her stride. At the bar, the barman greets the girls with a smile.

"Good afternoon, ladies. I'm just about to call last orders. What can I get you all?"

Lucy orders two half pints of lager and lime for herself and Joanna and then asks their companion what she wants.

"What about you, Abigail? Do you want the same or something else?"

Abigail is around the same age as the sisters and looks familiar to me. I think at first that perhaps I may have seen her name or picture in the case files, but the answer comes to me when she answers Lucy.

"Unfortunately, they don't serve what I want here, so for now I'll settle for a gin and tonic."

Then with that same look in her eye that she gave me earlier today, she adds, "Maybe one of the lads can sort that out for me later."

Well, this is convenient, my cougar friend, Ms. Abigail Whitchurch, Chairwoman of the Women's Institute, is a friend of Lucy and Joanna Partington-Brown. I think that perhaps I need to have a chat with her soon.

The barman turns to get the drinks for the girls, and I am snapped out of my obvious staring by the same young man calling over to Lucy again.

"Hey, Lucy, this one is for you. Come and join us."

The mechanical arm in the jukebox lifts a new record into position and 'Sweet Talking Guy' by the Chiffons starts to play. The music selection has the desired effect and Lucy turns around to face her admirer.

"Is that the best you can do, Paul? You will have to work harder than that if you want to get me back. My father has threatened to send his gamekeeper after you with his shotgun if he sees you with me. Doesn't that worry you?"

Wow, this just gets better and better. I am now looking at Paul Oliver and his gang, although they look more like a 1970s boy band then a gang, as you would define it today. All four of them are smartly dressed in made-to-measure suits and have the look of MODS about them.

Paul flashes Lucy a smile and she picks up her drink. All three of the girls join the guys next to the jukebox and I'm pulled back to reality once again by the sound of a hand-bell ringing incredibly close to my ear.

"Last orders please, ladies and gentlemen. Order your last drinks if you want any or start supping up. Doors close at 3 pm."

This is another major difference between now and 1972 – no all-day drinking. In 1972, pubs open at midday for three hours and then close again until 7pm.

I order myself another pint of bitter and then I take a seat nearer to the jukebox in the hope that I may pick up something useful.

At 3 pm exactly, the pub landlord moves from behind the bar and moves towards the front door. He is just about to pull the bolt across when the door opens and a uniformed police sergeant steps in and stamps his feet on the doormat.

"Afternoon, Donald, get me a pint in and a large scotch. It's bloody brass monkeys out there."

He is clearly well known, and Donald smiles and locks the door, "Right you are, Henry, grab yourself a seat by the fire."

I am surprised that nobody seems in any hurry to leave or seems bothered by the arrival of the local bobby. Quite the opposite in fact. After pouring the drinks for the sergeant, Donald resumes his position behind the bar and continues to serve drinks for the rest of the customers.

I am so lost in taking in the scene of a uniformed police sergeant drinking his pint by the fire after the permitted licensing hours that I don't notice that I have been joined at my table by Abigail Whitchurch.

"Penny for your thoughts, handsome."

Whilst she is not in the same league as Lucy and Joanna, Abigail is still a very good-looking young woman and I am momentarily taken aback.

"Um, sorry, what did you say?" I finally reply.

"I knew it as soon as I saw you – you're a London boy. You are way to flash to be from around here. What's up, don't they have lock-ins in London?"

I must be looking confused again because she explains what she means.

"A lock-in, after hours drinking, it's no big deal. Relax and get us another drink. My name's Abigail by the way and mine's a double G&T."

I ignore her comment about the drinks and point towards the sergeant. "And is that normal?" I ask her.

My question makes her laugh and she points towards the landlord.

"The guy behind the bar is Donald Cuttler and the policeman sitting by the fire is his brother Henry Cuttler. Welcome to the countryside. What's your name, handsome? Why haven't we met before?"

For a young woman in the seventies, I imagine that this obvious flirting would be considered incredibly forward. But with the experience of Maria and Ben still fresh in my mind, I have absolutely no intention of letting anything develop of a romantic or sexual nature. For now, though, it suits me to sit and chat with her. I hold out my hand and give her my best smile.

"It's Sean. Nice to meet you, Abigail."

I order a fresh round of drinks and whilst we chat, I do my best to make it not look too obvious that I am listening in to the girls and guys chatting at the jukebox. For a while this is easy enough, but as the drinks flow, Abigail makes it increasingly obvious that she fancies me, and I am forced to concentrate most of my attention and effort in fighting off her wandering hands.

By 3:30 pm and with nothing useful picked up from the conversations, I once more push Abigail's hand away from my crotch, and I stand up to leave. Abigail follows suit, but in her haste and obviously the worse for wear she knocks the edge of the table and sends her drink crashing to the floor.

"Where are you going, lover boy? It's still early," she says, slurring her words.

The breaking glass and her comment draw dirty looks and murmurs of disapproval from the pensioners by the fire and the police sergeant looks me up and down with suspicion, but he doesn't get up or say anything. I am surprised, though, to see Lucy staring at me and smiling.

Yet again I find myself blushing and Lucy smiles and blows me a kiss before turning back to her companions. Either Abigail was right about my outfit, or maybe it is something to do with the upper classes and the fresh country air. Whatever it is, these girls are going to be a handful and I need to be careful if I am not going to mess things up.

As I reach the front door, Donald has already unbolted it. He holds it open for me to leave, but before I can step through, I am pushed to one side by a well-dressed middle-aged man coming in. For a second, he scans the room clearly looking for someone, then he makes his way towards the jukebox and pulls Lucy and Joanna to one side.

They are talking quietly, but it is clear that he is agitated about something. Joanna shakes her head and walks away, but Lucy reaches into her handbag and hands him two ten-pound notes, which he snatches and thrusts into his jacket pocket. I notice that he is wearing leather driving gloves, so I assume that he must have arrived by car.

Without another word, he leaves as quickly as he came. My intention had been to pay a visit to the carnival next, but intrigued by what has just happened, I step outside to follow whom I assume to be Sir David Partington-Brown.

Parked outside on the pavement there is a green convertible MG sports car and as I turn I am just in time to see the back of Sir David disappearing down an alley at the side of the pub. Before I even get to the top of the alley, I can hear raised voices and it is easy enough to imagine what is going down.

"Twenty quid! Are you bloody serious? That doesn't even cover my time and trouble getting out to this bloody shithole."

The voice is aggressive and distinctly cockney. I carefully put my head around the edge of the pub wall to try to see what is going on. Sir David has his back to the wall and there are two well-built thugs penning him in. The one doing the talking is around forty years old, smartly dressed in a suit and polished brogues, and from where I am standing, I can see a thick ugly-looking scar on the back of his close-cropped head.

His companion looks slightly younger, possibly in his mid-thirties, but he is much bigger and is carrying a leather cosh in his right hand. It doesn't take a genius to work out that they are loan sharks, but if any further confirmation was needed, Scarface gives it.

"You don't seem to understand just how serious this is, your lordship. You're into the boss for nearly twenty-grand and his patience is wearing thin. Just tell me if you can't pay and perhaps we can work something else out."

I'm no mathematician, but even I can work out that twenty thousand pounds in 1972 was a huge sum of money. It's no wonder he is shaking like a leaf. He has a huge country estate and is a member of parliament. To go to a loan shark, he must have serious money problems.

I move slightly further forward to try to hear better and when Sir David doesn't immediately answer him, Scarface nods to his companion and the cosh slams into the side of Sir David's head.

My first inclination is to call out or rush forward to help him, but I hold back in the hope of finding out more of what is happening.

Both thugs lift him to his feet and push him back against the wall. There is a small cut on the side of his head, but otherwise he seems okay and after a few seconds the lead thug asks him again.

"Well, do you have the money or not? The boss is running out of patience and if you can't pay, then we need to work something out."

"I don't have it right now, just give me a few more weeks, a month at the most. I can get the money, I just …"

Sir David's words are cut off by a burly hand around his throat and Scarface pushes him down onto his knees and screams in his face.

"You don't bloody have a few more weeks, you toffee-nosed bastard. I want my bleedin' money now, or we make a deal for that car and house of yours."

I can see that he is struggling to breathe, and it is all I can do to hold myself back until the thug releases his grip on his throat and lifts him up again. Scarface takes a moment to compose himself and then he leans menacingly towards Sir David.

"I'm a reasonable man, so let me tell you what I am going to do for you. I'm going to go back to the boss and I'm going to tell him that I have given you another month. If you don't have the full twenty-grand by then, you are going to sign over that house and that flashy car to us. How does that sound, Sir David?"

In his position, he is likely to agree to anything just to get away, but he nods anyway, and the thugs release their grip on him.

Scarface smiles and then he suddenly grabs Sir David by the lapels of his jacket and pulls him forward.

"That's good, but just in case you're thinking of trying to do the dirty on us, don't! If you try and fuck us over, then me and Frankie boy are gonna be paying you a visit and after we have finished with you, we are gonna be taking those two princesses of yours for a little walk in the woods."

At the mention of his daughters, Sir David pulls back and tries to take a swing at Scarface. Years of street brawling allows

Scarface to easily dodge the punch and he lands his own fist in Sir David's stomach, who drops to his knees again.

"Give him something to remember us by," Scarface growls. When he nods to Frankie boy, I know that I can't stay quiet any longer.

As Frankie raises the cosh above his head, I step forward and shout out, "Oy, what's going on?"

Surprised by my interruption, Frankie lowers his weapon and both thugs turn to face me. Scarface has another huge scar running down the left-hand side of his face and he is as intimidating as any one I have ever met in my police career.

"Nothing for you to see here, son. If I was you, I would turn around and walk away while you still can."

His voice is calm, but the intent in his words is obvious. In this time and in this scenario, Sir David must have taken a beating, but my conscience won't let me walk away, even though I know that it cannot have been too serious.

I am about to answer when a voice behind me interrupts.

"I think that's good advice, son. Walk away and keep your nose out of what doesn't concern you. Be a good lad and move along."

The voice is vaguely familiar, but I can't quite place it and now I am conscious that Scarface and Frankie are moving closer towards me. Weighing up my options, I decide to brazen it out and I reply as I turn to face the newcomer, "Sorry, but I can't do that. Three against one is just not fai ..."

My words are cut off before I can finish, and something hard strikes me a vicious blow on the bridge of my nose. I can feel the bones in my nose and my cheek shatter, and my mouth, nose, and eyes fill up with blood. A second blow lands on my shoulder and I fall face forward onto the cobbled alley.

The last thing I remember is a kick in the head from a heavy boot and the same mystery voice telling me that I should have walked away.

# Present Day – Wednesday, 18th April, 2018

The alarm on my phone wakes me at just after 7 am and my first reaction is to reach for my nose to check for damage. I'm not sure what I was expecting to find, and it is a completely irrational reaction given my experience of dream travel, but nonetheless I am relieved to find that everything is as it should be. I'm never fully sure what to expect when I travel, but last night was completely unexpected and now potentially gives us a new line of enquiry to work on.

Sir David was clearly in massive debt and the threat to his girls just one week before Lucy's disappearance surely can't just be a coincidence. I shower and dress and then scan through the case file to see if there is any mention of the loan sharks, the threat, or any indicator of Sir David's financial difficulties.

I find nothing and this in itself is worrying. Why would he not have mentioned this to the investigating detectives? Another question nagging at me is: how did he get himself out of debt? He is still living in the same house on the same estate as he was in 1972.

Loan sharks don't make idle threats. It is bad for their reputation. Either Sir David found the money to pay them off, or something else happened to clear the debt. My gut feeling is that if we can find the answer to this question, we will also find out what happened to Lucy. I close the case file and head downstairs to meet Catherine for breakfast.

For once, I am there before her. I order myself a full English and a cup of tea. Cath appears just as my breakfast is arriving and gives me a mock look of disapproval.

"You need to watch yourself with those fry-ups, boss. You're looking a bit chubby lately."

I instantly suck in my stomach, realizing too late that Cath is winding me up again.

"That's twice in two days, Sean. Bloody hell, mate, did you lose your sense of humor when they gave you that promotion? Don't worry, the Sean McMillan fan club is still alive and kicking."

Then with a small smirk on her face, she adds, "Seriously, though, maybe you'd better just have a slice of toast. Having more chins than the Chinese telephone directory is not a big turn-on for most women."

Once again, Cath has got the better of me and I see there is no point even trying a sarcastic come back. Instead, I spear a sausage on the end of my fork and hold it out to Cath.

"And good morning to you to, Detective Constable Swain. Sausage?"

"Tempting, Sean. But I think I will stick to my coffee, thank you."

"Great," I reply. "Now, if you don't mind, I have this great big plate of calories to finish."

Ten minutes later, we head out to the car and I check the directions to Sir David's estate. This morning I am driving, and I hand Catherine the case file.

"It seems to be no more than a ten-minute drive, Cath, but have a quick read through the interview notes for Sir David, Joanna, and her husband Eddie Wells. There may be something useful that we can pick up on."

Cath opens the file and asks, "Was there something in particular you were thinking of, Sean?"

"Check for any references to Paul Oliver. He's the boy that went missing a couple of weeks after Lucy. That has to be worth digging into. And see if there is anything on the priest that might give any more clues as to his relationship with Lucy."

Cath nods and starts to sift through the interview notes. I start the engine and after taking a couple of wrong turns, ten minutes after leaving the hotel, I pass through a pair of ornate stone columns that mark the entrance to Colevale Manor.

The graveled driveway looks like it has seen better days, but after about forty yards we arrive at a central landscaped roundabout in-front of a grandiose Manor House. I wouldn't have been at all surprised to have been met by a line-up of immaculately dressed maids, gardeners, and butlers assembled on the stairs. But the front of the house is deserted and the front door is closed.

I park the car just off to the side of the roundabout and shut off the engine.

"Anything interesting in the notes, Cath?"

"Not really, it's all pretty much what we discussed last night. Joanna and Eddie both confirm that the last time they saw Lucy was at the carnival. Sir David says that he saw her at breakfast that morning. The priest and Paul Oliver only get brief mentions and it is all in the same context as the case summary from our predecessor. Paul was an ex-boyfriend but still on friendly terms with Lucy and the priest was possibly trying to convert her. Sorry, Sean, that's about it."

I wasn't really expecting Cath to find anything new. I have already been over the notes in detail myself, but it never hurts for a fresh pair of eyes to take a look. From my trip last night, I do know that Paul was still on very good terms with Lucy and might not have been as 'ex' an ex-boyfriend as people thought.

They seemed very close when I left the pub last night and it is certainly a line of enquiry worth following.

"That's okay, Cath. It was worth a try. Come on, let's go and see what the family have to say for themselves."

Before we reach the top of the stairs, the door opens and a well-dressed woman with graying blonde hair steps out to greet us. For a woman approaching seventy, Joanna Partington-Brown still cuts a striking figure and her bearing and manner pay homage to her aristocratic heritage as she reaches to shake my hand.

"Good morning, you must be Detective McMillan. I am Joanna Partington-Brown. It's my pleasure to welcome you here to Colevale."

"Thank you," I reply. "It's actually Detective Sergeant McMillan, and this is my partner, Detective Constable Swain. I hope that it's convenient for us to come in and ask some questions about your sister and the circumstances around her disappearance?"

She moves to the side to allow us inside and then politely nods to Catherine, but we both pick up on her obvious disdain. I'm hoping that it's the fact that Cath is female in a male-dominated career and not that she's black, but I suspect that it's probably both. Joanna Partington-Brown is from a less tolerant generation and social class, with entrenched attitudes that are hard to shift.

To make a point, Cath reaches out to shake Joanna's hand. Joanna shakes Cath's hand, but she doesn't make eye contact with her and quickly turns back to me.

"Please, come inside. My father and husband are in the study."

We follow behind. Although it is only just after 10 am on a warm spring day, inside the study there is a log burning in an open fire and Sir David is sitting in a wheelchair next to it with a blanket around his shoulders.

Eddie Wells is sitting on a brown leather sofa next to him and he stands up to greet us as we enter the room.

Unlike Joanna, Eddie looks like he has lived every one of his seventy-two years and has a noticeable stoop as he shakes my hand. His dress and general demeanor also give away his more humble beginnings as a farmer and his voice is trembling slightly as he speaks. Joanna then introduces her father and after the usual pleasantries, Cath and I take a seat on another leather sofa opposite Joanna, Eddie, and Sir David.

Joanna pours us all tea from a silver pot and whilst I am keen to press ahead with my questions, I can see that it is better to ease into things slowly. Joanna doesn't appear to be in any hurry, and these are not the kind of people that are used to being rushed.

"This is a beautiful house, Sir David. Has it always been in your family?" I ask.

His home and estate are clearly a source of pride to him and my question makes him sit up in the wheelchair and smile.

"Colevale has been the home of the Partington-Browns since the early part of the nineteenth century, young man. It was built by my great-great-grandfather in 1821. The land was given to him by King George the Third as recognition for his service under the Duke of Wellington at the Battle of Waterloo."

"Wow! That's very interesting. I suppose then you would do anything to keep the house and the estate in the family?"

This completely random question leaves Cath looking confused as to where I am going, but despite his age I am sure that Sir David has understood. I am hoping that even after so long, his eyes might give something away.

Unfortunately, Joanna interrupts and it is clear that she is not happy with me.

"What is that supposed to mean and how is that relevant, Detective Sergeant? This is our family home and will remain our family home as long as there is blood in my veins. What a stupid question!"

Cath kicks my foot under that table, and I apologize.

"My sincere apologies for the way in which I phrased that. I wasn't suggesting that you would ever sell up or leave. I was merely making the point that a house with such historical ties and family history must be very precious to you. I'm sorry if it came across in any other way."

Sir David looks gracious and accepts my apology in good faith, but Joanna looks less convinced as she speaks.

"Yes, well, if we could kindly move along please. My father is not a well man and he tires easily. Please ask what you came to ask, Sergeant McMillan."

I nod to Cath and she takes out her pocketbook and a digital voice recorder.

"Thank you. If it's okay, I would like to ask each of you some questions about Lucy, her last known movements, and what you might know about her disappearance. This is not a formal interview, but DC Swain will be making notes in her pocketbook and, if it is okay, she will also be recording our conversation."

"Is a recording really necessary?" Joanna asks.

"It's not necessary, but it might be helpful to our enquiry. It's often easy to miss something the first time around. Having a recording ensures that nothing gets missed. It really is nothing to be concerned about."

Joanna thinks about it for a few seconds and then nods her agreement. "Very well, please proceed, Sergeant."

Cath turns on the voice recorder and I turn towards Sir David.

"If it's okay, sir, would you mind telling us why after all this time you have asked for your daughter's case to be reopened?"

I am surprised again when it is Joanna that answers.

"I tried to tell him that it was a waste of time after such a long time. He wouldn't listen though. We tried to tell him, didn't we, Edward?"

Apart from saying hello to us, Eddie Wells has said nothing else up to this point and the sudden question from Joanna has him looking like a rabbit caught in a headlight. When he doesn't answer quickly enough, Joanna continues.

"Well we did, but he is a stubborn old man. It's a waste of all our time and no good will come of it. If you have any sense at all, Sergeant, you will tell him that it is a waste of time."

I look back to Sir David, but the earlier spark has gone. He once more looks like the frail ninety-three-year-old man that he is. Joanna's outburst seems to have frightened him and I know that it would be pointless to ask the question again. I turn my attention back to Joanna.

"Why do you think that it's a waste of time, Ms. Partington-Brown? What do you think happened to your sister? Do you think that she is dead? The first statement you gave in 1972 suggested that she was, and you pointed towards the owners of the carnival, the O'Hanlon brothers. Later, though, you suggested a connection to an ex-boyfriend of Lucy's. Why did you change your opinion on what had happened?"

Joanna is now sitting ram-rod straight in her seat and she takes an audible deep breath and smooths down her skirt before answering.

"The last time I saw my sister alive was when she went off with those awful brothers. No doubt you have read my statement in detail. Lucy and I were at the carnival with Edward, minding our own business, when the O'Hanlon brothers and a few others showed up. One of the brothers, Jed O'Hanlon, was coming on to Lucy and when Paul Oliver showed up with his friends there was a minor scuffle between the two groups. It wasn't particularly serious, but Paul was furious with Lucy and demanded that she go home."

"And what happened next?" I ask.

"Well, she certainly didn't go home. My sister was not the kind of girl to take orders from anyone, and particularly not from an ex-boyfriend. She went off with the O'Hanlons and that was the last time that I saw her alive."

"If it's not too sensitive a point, may I ask if your sister had been seeing one of the O'Hanlon brothers previously, Joanna?"

Her face hardens, and she surprises me with her response and use of an obscenity. "Do you mean was she fucking one of them, sergeant?"

Sir David protests, "Joanna, please, there is no need for that kind of language."

"Oh please, let's not beat around the bush, Father. It was well known by all, including you, that Lucy was fucking Jed O'Hanlon and, not just in the weeks before she disappeared. Sergeant McMillan. The O'Hanlon Carnival had been visiting Tyevale once a year since the early sixties and Lucy and Jed had been at it like rabbits for at least two years on and off whenever the carnival was in town."

"So, because of this you thought that the O'Hanlons had something to do with your sister's disappearance?"

"Yes, I did at the time."

"But not now?" I ask her. "What do you think now? What do you think happened to your sister?"

She doesn't answer my question immediately but looks towards her father for support. He doesn't say anything, though, merely dropping his head again as if embarrassed by what is coming.

"I believe now that either my sister is alive and living somewhere with Paul Oliver, or that Paul Oliver killed her out of jealousy and that's why he left town so soon after her disappearance. Why else would he leave and why has he never been seen since?"

The look on Sir David's face suggests that he doesn't agree with his daughter's theory. I am about to ask him for his theory when Cath kicks my foot again and nods towards Eddie Wells.

Eddie is now visibly shaking and sweating heavily, and so I direct the question to him instead.

"Mr. Wells, do you agree?"

My question catches him off guard and when he does answer he is clearly flustered.

"Um, I mean, sorry. Agree about what?"

"Do you agree with your wife? Do you think that Paul Oliver was responsible in some way for Lucy's disappearance?"

There are now drops of sweat hanging precariously off the end of his chin and he turns away from me and looks towards Joanna. He is shaking so badly that I think he might be about to collapse, and I reach forward and tap him on the shoulder.

"Mr. Wells, listen to me please. I need to know what you think. Do you agree with your wife? Do you think that Paul Oliver was responsible in some way for Lucy's disappearance?"

Joanna hands him her handkerchief to wipe his face with and then takes one of his hands and gently squeezes it.

"Answer the sergeant, Edward. There is nothing to worry about."

Her reassuring words seem to calm him, and he turns back around to face me.

"Yes, that's what happened, Sergeant."

His response is not exactly what I asked, so I ask him to clarify what he means. "That's what happened, or that's what you think happened?"

"He means, that is what he thinks happened, Sergeant McMillan. You agree with me, don't you, dear?"

Edward once more turns to face his wife and nods.

"Yes, I agree with my wife. I agree with my wife, Officer."

Joanna smiles at her husband and squeezes his hand again. If it wasn't obvious before, it is now completely clear to Cath and me who is pulling the strings in this family. Sir David is a frail old man and Edward Wells is either a doormat or perhaps possibly not the sharpest tool in the box. I know already that I will be wasting my time asking either of them any more questions. Whatever answers I do get will either come from Joanna or will be her opinion, so I might as well just direct them all to her.

"Thank you for your opinion, Ms. Partington-Brown. The O'Hanlon brothers and Paul Oliver are certainly of interest to us and in due course we will be looking into anything that might connect them to the disappearance of your sister. May I also ask about Father James Beale? What can you tell us about your sister's relationship with him?"

"There was no relationship!" Joanna snaps. "Whatever anyone else has said is not true. He was an idealistic Catholic priest trying to boost his congregation in a predominantly Church of England parish. There is nothing more to it than that."

Her comment about what others might have said opens the door for my next question.

"What do you mean about everyone else saying things that were not true. What were other people saying?"

Sir David is looking embarrassed again and I can't help but feel sorry for him. The image and memory of his daughter is unfortunately far from the reality that he has had to face since her disappearance, and the passage of time doesn't make it any easier.

"Please don't play games, Sergeant. You know very well what people were saying about my sister. That she was sleeping with the priest. That she was the village bike. That she was the posh girl from the manor house that got her rocks off with commoners, gypsies, and priests.

Sorry, Father, but it's true and there is no sugar-coating it. That's what people thought – but it's simply not true, Sergeant."

Sir David looks completely crestfallen, but Joanna also now looks visibly upset. Catherine puts down her notepad and suggests that we call an end to the questions for now. Joanna reaches for a box of tissues and dabs the corners of her eyes.

"I think that might be for the best, Sergeant McMillan. My father needs to rest and this whole thing is very stressful for Edward and me."

Catherine is probably right, but I still have a few questions to ask before I am ready to leave.

"Just a few minutes more, if that is okay, and then we will leave you all in peace for today. Ms. Partington-Brown, did you know that Father Beale is now back living and working in another Lincolnshire parish?"

"Yes, we knew about that," she replies. "Beckhampton is not that far from Tyevale and that kind of news doesn't stay secret for very long."

"Did the news bother you? When you found out that he was so close I mean? How did you feel?"

She is clearly annoyed now at my line of questioning and makes no attempt to hide it when she answers.

"I didn't feel anything at all, Sergeant! He means nothing to me and as long as he stays away from me and my family, then it will continue to remain that way."

"So, you never considered the possibility that he might have been responsible for Lucy's disappearance?"

"No, never, there was never anything going on between them. My only gripe with Father James Beale, if any, was that his attempts to convert her to Catholicism led to the completely unfounded and disgusting rumors that you were referring to earlier."

"Okay, thank you. I'm sure that Father Beale will be able to confirm that when we speak with him."

That last statement was a deliberate attempt to elicit a reaction from Joanna. When I get none, I move on to my final question.

"May I ask about your mother and the circumstances of her death?"

If looks could kill, by rights I should be dropping down dead right now. The death of her mother is clearly a taboo subject and Joanna once again makes no attempt to hide her contempt for my line of questioning.

"I fail to see what relevance my mother's death has to this investigation, Sergeant McMillan."

"I'm sorry if it upsets you, but in police business sometimes it's the things that appear to be the most irrelevant that have the most relevance. According to our case notes, she passed away in January of 1974. That was less than two years after Lucy went missing and she was only forty-five-years-old. Had there been any history of illness prior to her death?"

"I really don't see that this is any of your business," she replies. "But if you insist, my mother was bedridden for almost twelve months before her death. The doctors were unable to find anything wrong with her. If you want my opinion, she died of a broken heart. She never got over the loss of my sister."

"And was there an inquest into her death?"

"Yes, there was an inquest! What are you suggesting, Sergeant? I really don't like or appreciate these questions and, quite frankly, the inference that my mother's death might have some connection to what happened to Lucy is preposterous. If that is everything, then I would like you both to leave now."

Her defensive attitude earlier was a surprise, but her unwillingness to talk about the death of her mother now has me wondering about her own possible involvement in the disappearance of her sister and maybe even the death of her mother.

I know already what we need to focus on for the rest of the day, but I need her to answer one final question.

"Yes, of course, we are just about done here for today anyway. Just one final thing, what was the outc …"

"It was an open verdict. Cause of death was heart failure, but what triggered the heart failure was unknown. That is what you were going to ask me, isn't it, Sergeant?"

This latest interruption should not be a surprise to me. The fact that she is predicting my questions suggests again, though, that the death of her mother is a completely taboo subject.

Joanna Partington-Brown is an extremely intelligent woman and I am convinced that she knows far more then she is letting on about both the death of her mother and the disappearance of her sister – and she is not the only one. I want to speak to Eddie Wells again, but without Joanna around.

"It was, thank you, Ms. Partington-Brown. That is what I was going to ask."

I get up to leave and Joanna noticeably relaxes again and escorts us to the door. On the way she assures us of her and her family's full support.

"I'm sorry if I came across a little aggressive, Sergeant McMillan. As I am sure you can appreciate, the loss of my sister is an extremely emotive subject even after so long."

"That's quite alright and perfectly understandable. You have all been very helpful. We will be in touch if there is anything else we need."

The door closes behind us, but my instinct tells me that Joanna will be looking through the spyhole to make sure that we have left. Catherine looks like she is itching to ask me a question, but I stop her.

"Not yet, Cath. Let's get out of here first."

As soon as we are through the gates, I pull into a layby out of sight of the house.

"Go on then, Cath, get it off your chest, was it my completely random questions, or her ladyship's obvious dislike for you?"

Cath pulls a face and then smirks at me.

"Don't flatter yourself, Sean, she wasn't exactly falling over herself with admiration for you either. But, by God, what a complete an utter bitch! The way she looked at me on the steps, I was half expecting her to ask me to use the backdoor with the rest of the servants."

"I shouldn't worry about it too much. She was probably just worried that you were going to make a move on her husband."

This makes Cath laugh and she playfully punches me in the shoulder.

"Oooh, that's disgusting, Sean. And besides, I doubt if Dribbling Eddie has so much as looked at another woman in the last fifty years. The ice queen would have his balls on a silver platter. Don't you think it's a bit of an odd match up, Sean? Joanna and Eddie, I mean. They clearly have absolutely nothing in common."

Cath is right, and I was thinking the same thing myself.

"It is an odd match, Cath. But there must be some reason that she married him. What did you think of her attitude?"

"Defensive and evasive, but in fairness your questions were all over the place. I assume that there was some logic to them and that no doubt you are about to enlighten me?"

Her question is a leading one and a less-than-subtle reference to my withholding of all the facts on our last case. I am thinking over my response when Cath speaks again.

"Listen, Sean. Given what has happened previously, I didn't want to bring this up again and I want you to know that I trust you one hundred percent – but please be straight with me on this one. You owe me that."

I can feel my face beginning to flush with embarrassment and I do my best to answer without giving anything away.

"You saved my life, Cath. I won't ever forget that, and you have my word that you know as much as I do about this case. My questions were just a fishing expedition. That is a huge house. It must cost a lot to keep it running. Could that be the reason for the marriage?

"I don't see Sir David or Joanna having the kind of money needed. Maybe in the past, but the glory days of the aristocracy are long gone. Now, Eddie, on the other hand, he was a farmer and according to the case file he had a considerable amount of land. It's certainly worth looking into, don't you think?"

Cath nods her agreement.

"Yes, it is. It would make sense, I guess. I sure can't see any other reason why they would have married. Whatever the reason, they almost certainly haven't told us everything they know about Lucy and you certainly hit a nerve with Joanna when you were talking about the death of her mother."

"I agree, but could we be reading too much into it?" I reply. "If it was Sir David's idea to reopen the case, maybe she really does believe we are wasting our time. And let's face it, who wouldn't get upset when talking about the death of a loved one?"

Cath shakes her head. "No, there was more to it and you know it as well as I do. Joanna was deliberately trying to mislead us, and her constant interruptions make me think that she was frightened of what Sir David or Eddie might say."

"I agree. If it was me, even after so long, I would want to know what had happened to a family member. Even if there was only the very slightest chance, you would take it, wouldn't you, Cath?"

She nods her agreement and then flips open her pocketbook. "Do you think that Joanna could have killed her sister, Sean?"

"Until this morning, no, I hadn't, but now, yes. We need to consider that as a possibility – and not just Joanna. If Joanna was responsible for Lucy's death or disappearance, then you can bet that Dribbling Eddie was also involved. What are you thinking, Cath?"

Cath refers to her notes again and points to a quote that she has underlined.

"When you were asking her about the night of Lucy's disappearance she said. 'She went off with the O'Hanlons and that was the last time that I saw her alive.' Don't you think that is strange, Sean? Wouldn't you say, that was the last time I saw her, instead of that was the last time that I saw her alive? It almost implies that she saw her when she was dead, or that she knows for sure that Lucy is dead. It makes absolutely no sense in the context of her theory that maybe Lucy skipped town with Paul Oliver – or am I overthinking it?"

"That's a good pickup, Cath, and no, I don't think you are overthinking it. I think you might have been right when you talked about that big bloody ticking hand grenade. Only now I think it might well be the Partington-Browns that are holding the pin."

Obviously pleased to have picked up on something that I had missed, Cath gives me one of her smuggest looks of self-satisfaction.

"Thanks, boss. Who would have thought it? Brains and beauty. So, what next?"

"Drop me back to the hotel, Cath. Then I want you to head into Spalding and pull in a favor with the local constabulary. Get into a station and log onto a computer. Start by looking into Sir David's estate. Look for anything unusual with the title deeds and then have a dig into the finances of all three of them."

Cath gives me one of those knowing looks again.

"Are you onto something, or just fishing again?" she asks.

"Just something nagging at me again about the connection between Eddie Wells and the PBs."

"The PBs?" Cath says, raising her eyebrows. "Is that what we are calling them now? I take it you mean the Partington-Browns and not the posh bastards?"

We both laugh at the unintentional but very appropriate connection.

"You're on form today, Cath. Yes, the first one. I keep tripping over my tongue with the full name. Once you are done with the estate and finances, see if you can get hold of a copy of the inquest and autopsy report for the mother. It's a long shot, but worth a look."

"Okay, anything else?"

"Just one other thing for now – find a number for our mysterious priest. Try and set up a meeting for tomorrow, if possible."

We swap seats and Cath starts the engine.

"What's your plan while I'm gone, Sean?"

"I'm going to do some digging around locally. There must be a good few people still around that knew the family. It would be interesting to know what the locals have to say about them."

For once, I am not lying to Cath, well not entirely. I am going to do some digging with the locals, but it is one specific local that I have in mind and she runs the local Oxfam shop.

Ten minutes later, Catherine drops me outside our hotel and heads off to Spalding. It's likely that she will be gone until at least the early evening, so I should have plenty of time to do what I need to do. I head to my room and drop the case file on my bed and then I head back out onto the high street.

Yesterday I had been wearing jeans and a t-shirt, but today I am in one of my work suits. Abigail spots me as soon as I enter the store and is quick to comment on my attire.

"That's funny, I was just about to call you. I got that suit you were looking for, but I don't think you need it. That one fits you very well."

The insinuation is obvious, but I ignore it and thank her.

"That's great, thank you very much, though I am actually here on official business today."

Her smile changes first to a look of concern and then she looks me up and down with suspicion over the top of her glasses.

"Whatever you are selling young man, we don't need it."

I hold out my badge for her inspection and she shrugs and pushes her glasses back into position. Then she holds out her hands and offers me her wrists.

"I admit it, officer, you've got me. Guilty as charged for selling outrageously outdated fashions that are a crime against humanity. Lock me up and throw away the key."

"That won't be necessary, Ms. Whitchurch," I reply with a smile, "the last time I checked, it was perfectly legal to sell bell-bottoms and platform shoes. Actually, I was hoping to ask you about the Partington-Brown family. They have an estate just outside of town and Sir David Partington-Brown used to be the Member of Parliament for Spalding. Do you know of them?"

Her face goes white and for a second I am concerned that she might faint, but my cougar friend is made of stronger stuff and quickly composes herself.

"Everyone knows that family, Detective. Um ..."

"It's Detective Sergeant McMillan, but feel free to call me Sean. This is purely an off-the-record discussion, Ms. Whitchurch."

My assurance of an off-the-record discussion is less than convincing, but she nods anyway and invites me into her office.

"I was wondering when the police might show up. There has been a rumor going around the village for a few weeks that the case was going to be reopened. Am I correct in assuming that this is connected to the disappearance of the youngest daughter, Lucy? That was nearly fifty years ago. Has some new information come to light?"

"It's partly about Lucy," I confirm. "But also, the death of her mother and the later disappearance of a young man called Paul Oliver. Does that name mean anything to you?"

I can see I have hit a raw nerve and she nervously bites the bottom of her lip before replying.

"Actually, Paul was a friend of mine. Not a particularly close friend, but a friend all the same. In my early twenties, I was good friends with Lucy and Joanna, and we used to hang around with Paul and his mates."

I know this already, of course, but I feign mild surprise at this supposed revelation.

"Oh really? That is very interesting, Ms. Whitchurch. Were you interviewed by the police or asked to give a statement after Lucy disappeared?"

"No, no I wasn't. I had been due to go with them to the carnival that night, but in the end I was unwell and stayed at home. I did take part in the search for her, but I was never spoken to by the police. Oh, and please call me Abigail. Ms. Whitchurch makes me sound like somebody's grandmother."

"Yes, of course, thank you, Abigail. Was Paul just a friend to you all, or was there something more to it?"

She looks puzzled and asks me to explain what I mean.

"I mean, was Paul in a relationship with any of you?"

The look on her face tells me that she knows that I know the answer already and her response confirms it.

"I'm sure that you didn't get to be a detective sergeant without doing your homework before starting an investigation, Sean. I'm sure it is mentioned a few times in whatever statements you have seen. Paul was in an on-and-off relationship with Lucy. It was never very serious. He was more into her than she was into him, but it was never going to go anywhere."

"And do you know if the relationship was on or off on the day that Lucy disappeared?"

My question elicits a small laugh and Abigail shrugs her shoulders.

"You would think as her friend I would know the answer to that question, but you really never could be sure with Lucy. She went to the carnival with Joanna and, Eddie Wells. Apparently Paul went along later with his mates and we all heard about the fight when the carnival guys were flirting with Lucy. You would think then that maybe Lucy and Paul were back on again, but I don't know for sure. I don't want to speak ill of the dead, but let's just say that Lucy was a little loose when it came to her relationships."

I have no doubt at all that I am being told the truth. Earlier today Joanna painted a completely different picture of her sister, but Abigail's description of Lucy's attitude to relationships seems to be much closer to the way in which she was portrayed in the original statements from 1972. Not quite the village bike, but not far off it.

"Why do you think Paul Oliver skipped town, Abigail? Do you think he had anything to do with Lucy going missing?"

"After Paul went missing, the police turned their attention in his direction, but I never believed it. I honestly have no idea why he left town, but I really don't believe that he had any connection to what happened to Lucy. He was a bit of a lad, but he wasn't into anything heavy and was always a gentleman when it came to the ladies."

So, may I ask what you think happened to her?"

She closes her eyes for a few seconds, and I can imagine that she is taking herself back to 1972.

"Lucy didn't have a single enemy in Tyevale that I knew of. So, if you are asking me, I'm sure that it wasn't a local. This was such a close-knit community that it would have been impossible to keep it secret. No, it wasn't a local. The carnival was in town and those kinds of people would have had every opportunity to kill and get away with it."

I nod my head. "You're talking about the O'Hanlon brothers?"

"Yes, I am, Sergeant. I never liked them, and I never trusted them. I think the police didn't push hard enough for the truth back then and it was just way too convenient to leave the shadow hanging over Paul."

I do tend to agree with her. Paul's unexplained absence from Tyevale is a big reason to suspect his motives, but without months of planning and some considerable funds behind you, it is virtually impossible to disappear without a trace. The same would have applied even in the seventies, but since 1972, there hasn't been a single sighting of Paul, real or imagined. This explanation simply doesn't add up.

"Thank you, Abigail. I just have one more question and then I can let you get back to work. You said earlier that you were good friends with Lucy and Joanna in your early twenties. Do you have any contact with Joanna now? Are you still friends?"

She shakes her head and adjusts her glasses.

"I have no idea why, but Joanna dropped me like a hot stone within days of Lucy going missing. I tried reaching out to her for months afterwards, but in the end, I just gave up."

"But that makes no sense," I reply. "Surely at that time she would have needed the support of her friends more than ever."

"I couldn't agree more, Sergeant. But It wasn't just me. She dropped everyone apart from Eddie and her parents. She stopped coming into town and almost completely shut herself away for two or three years in that estate. In the last forty or so years, I can honestly say that I have only seen her come into Tyevale on maybe half a dozen occasions. It doesn't make sense, but I guess people react differently to these things."

This new piece of information adds to my suspicions that Joanna might be involved in some way in this case, but everything I have found out so far is purely circumstantial. Tonight can't come quickly enough. I'm keen to travel back to 1972 again, but there is something I need first. I stand up to leave and I thank Abigail for her time.

"You really have been extremely helpful, Abigail, and I hope that I haven't taken up too much of your time. When I came in, you mentioned something about the suit I was looking for?"

"Oh, yes, of course. I thought perhaps that you might not be wanting it now and perhaps needing the suit was just a cover story. It's hanging outside on one of the racks."

I follow her out of the office, and she leads me towards a rack next to the cash desk.

"Well, what do you think? It's magnificent, isn't it?"

She has found me a blue three-piece suit with a light pinstripe, and I must admit that it looks pretty cool.

"Wow! That's a sharp suit and it's in great condition."

My compliment meets with her satisfaction. She reaches behind the desk and hands me a white shirt, a trilby hat, and the widest tie I have ever seen. The pattern is paisley on a maroon background. I wouldn't normally be seen dead in such a hideous tie, but Abigail is convinced that it will complete my outfit.

"So, when is your fancy-dress party, Sean?"

"Excuse me?" I reply.

"I was just wondering. I mean it must be a very important party for you to take time out of your investigation to look for a suit in Tyevale. Don't they have charity shops in London?"

She has me at a disadvantage, but I laugh it off and smile whilst she takes payment and bags up my outfit. As she passes me the bag, I deliberately brush my hand against hers and look her directly in the eye.

"Oh, there are plenty of charity shops, Abigail. Just none with such amazing and personal service, or indeed such an attractive manager. Thank you for everything."

My compliment and obvious flirting leave her looking flustered and more than a little embarrassed. With a final wink, I turn to leave, happy to have turned the tables on her.


On the walk back to the hotel, I check my phone. There is a message from Detective Chief Inspector Morgan asking me to call him and there are three missed calls from Ben. Obviously, the persistent little shit has changed his mind about waiting to hear from me. I need to find a way to buy more time with him, but for now I push the thought to the back of my mind. I need to plan my next moves before Catherine gets back from Spalding and I also need to call Kevin Morgan before he gets impatient and calls me.

It's just after 1:30 pm and the lobby of the hotel is deserted, apart from the young woman on reception, who politely nods as I pass her, and a pair of stereotypical Japanese tourists heavily laden down with all manner of camera equipment and a moth-eaten guidebook to Lincolnshire.

I can hear the television in my room as soon as I step out of the lift. At first I assume that the cleaner must have turned it on for some background noise. My door is slightly ajar, but strangely I can't see a cleaning cart outside, nor indeed is there one anywhere to be seen in the corridor.

It can't be Catherine. There is no way that she could have got to Spalding and back so quickly and unless Lincolnshire burglars like to watch TV while they work, this only leaves one possibility. If my hunch is right, I am going to stick my shoe so far up Ben's ass that he will be tasting leather in his mouth for a week.

Just in case it's not Ben, I carefully push open the door and cautiously step into the room.

He is so engrossed in watching Jerry Springer tearing into a couple of pug-ugly hillbillies that it takes him a few seconds to notice me standing by the door. When he does finally see me, it is obvious that I am in no mood for a pleasant chat and he sheepishly turns off the TV and stands up.

"Um, Sean, listen, I tried to call you. I, um ..."

"Shut it, Ben. I'm not interested. I bloody well told you yesterday that I would get in touch as soon as I got back into London. Sit the fuck down and keep your mouth shut."

I doubt whether he has ever been spoken to like this and picking wisely he sits down without question as I close the door and position myself in front of the TV.

"Right then, you can start by telling me how the hell you knew where to find me and then you can tell me how you got into my room. By rights, I could have you for breaking and entering."

"The door was open, Sean," he replies. A bit of the previous cockiness that I saw when we met in 1994 is back, but not entirely and I can see he is thinking carefully about his words.

"What do you mean the door was open? I know for a fact that I closed it when I left this morning."

"When I got here this morning, I asked for you at reception, but there was no answer from your room. I tried calling you myself and when I didn't get any reply, I just waited for the cleaner to open your room. I just walked in and she didn't ask who I was. She probably thought I was you. You told me something before about acting as if you belong when you dream travel. I took your advice and just plonked myself down on the sofa in front of the television. It worked like a charm. So, in a way it's your fault, Sean."

The cheeky little shit is mocking me, and I can feel my temperature rising.

"Just because I'm your father and you think you have something over me, don't think I won't kick you around this room. How did you know where to find me?"

There is a short but noticeable pause, and then he smiles and raises his eyebrows.

"I phoned Grandma McMillan. I told her that I was meant to be meeting up with you but that I had lost your phone number."

Now I am absolutely livid. "You, rang my mother! How the hell did you get her number?"

"Your mother, but technically my grandmother, Sean! And don't get your knickers in a twist. We met her at your commendation ceremony. She swapped numbers with my mum. We had a lovely old chat about how proud she was of you and how you were working a special case in Tyevale."

If he wasn't my son and it wasn't against the law, I could quite happily throttle Ben right now, but Catherine could be back from Spalding at any time and I am more concerned about getting him out of here.

"Well, Detective Ben, ten out of ten for ingenuity, but now you need to detect your way back to the train station and piss off back to London and wait like I asked you to."

"Nah, that's not gonna happen," he cockily replies. "This case looks like an interesting one and I want in."

I hadn't noticed before, but the second copy of the case file is not on the bed where I had left it earlier and I look back to Ben.

"Where the hell is it, Ben? You had no right to go through a classified police case file. I've a good mind to have you locked up until this case is over."

The file is pushed down the back of the sofa and Ben lifts it out and places it onto the coffee table.

"The file is perfectly safe, Sean. You left in on the bed and I was worried that the cleaner might throw it away or look inside. I was doing you a favor. It's not my fault that it fell on the floor and all the statements fell out. What was I supposed to do?"

"You were supposed to wait in London, that's what you were bloody well supposed to do," I reply. "There is no way that I am going to let you interfere in my case, Ben. You need to get the hell out of here before Catherine gets back."

"Yeh, that would be interesting, Sean. How would you explain my being here to her? Do you think she would see the family resemblance if I pointed it out?"

The cocky little bastard knows that he has me in a corner, but before I can answer again my phone rings and my argument becomes irrelevant. Catherine is fifteen minutes away and is checking where I am. I hang up the call and turn back towards Ben. He knows that he has won this time, but I don't have any choice.

"Try not to look so smug, Ben. You can travel with me tonight, but there are conditions. This is not a game and you need to understand that what we do in the past can have a major impact on the future. You stick with me and you say nothing, and you do nothing unless I tell you to. Is that understood?"

He nods his agreement and then asks where and when we should meet.

"I haven't figured that out yet. I'll call you later with the details. Now get up and make yourself scarce. I don't want Catherine seeing you. Come on, get the hell out of here!"

"But where should I go?" he splutters. "What am I meant to do with myself until this evening?"

I shrug my shoulders. "Not my problem, Ben. You're the genius. I'm sure you will work something out. Now get a move on before I change my mind."

He stands up to leave and is just about to open the door when I call him back. "Hold on, Ben, you can't travel like that. Wait there a minute. We're both about the same size. I have just the thing for you."

I gather up my outfit from last night and stuff the jacket, the bellbottoms, and the wooly turtleneck into a plastic bag.

I hand over the bag and the platform boots to Ben and his chin drops to the floor. "What the hell! You're not serious are you, Sean?"

"Do you see me laughing, Ben? This is what you are wearing, and it's not open for negotiation. Now make yourself scarce and keep out of sight until I call you later. Close the door behind you."


While I had been arguing with Ben, another message had come in from DCI Morgan, 'I need to speak to you, Sean. Call me as soon as you can'. I tuck the case files under one of my pillows and sit down on the bed to call him. The call connects and after three rings, Kevin Morgan's familiar voice comes onto the line.

"Sean, thanks for calling me."

"It's my pleasure, sir. There's really not much to report, though, at this stage. We met the surviving family members early this morning, but so far we have ..."

"Sean, hold on please," Morgan interrupts. "I'm not looking for a case update. I need you to get yourself back here tomorrow morning for a couple of hours. The boys from Anti-corruption have a question in relation to the Network case that they want to ask you about. I'm sure it's something and nothing but come into the office at 10 tomorrow morning so that we can clear it up and let you get back to work."

When Anti-corruption is involved there is no such thing as something and nothing, but policy will have dictated that Morgan can't tell me very much prior to the meeting.

"Should I be worried, sir?" I ask him.

"Not at all, Sean. Just a storm in a teacup, I should imagine. Ten tomorrow morning, lad. Don't keep AC waiting. I will meet you when you get here."

This is Morgan's way of telling me that the conversation is over. A second later, the call drops, and I am left to guess what the hell I am going to be asked about tomorrow. I am weighing up the pros and cons of calling him back when the decision is taken out of my hands by a knock on the door.

Without waiting for an invitation, Catherine walks into my room and sits down where Ben had been sitting just a few minutes ago.

"Wow! This cushion is nice and warm, Sean. I hope you haven't been shining it with your ass and watching daytime TV all day while I've been working?"

"Nope, I just got back here myself, Cath. How did you get on in Spalding? Any problems with the local plod?"

"All good, boss," she replies. "A flash of my badge and a flick of the hair was enough to have those boys eating out of my hand."

"So, go on then, what did you find out?"

"Well, you were right about the finances – or should I say lack of finances. Joanna doesn't appear ever to have worked

71

and has no discernible income and Sir David stopped drawing his parliamentary salary in 1976. Since then the only regular payments either of them seem to have received are the basic state pension."

"So pretty much penniless then?" I ask her.

"No, far from it actually. Both of their bank accounts are extremely healthy. Your hunch about Eddie Wells was spot on. I made a few calls and had a search done on the land registry. On March 20th, 1972, less than a week after Lucy went missing, Eddie sold his farm and all his land apart from a few hectares. Two days later on March 22nd, he made two large cash deposits into ... yep, you've guessed it … into Joanna and Sir David's bank accounts."

"How large, Cath?"

"Two hundred thousand pounds into Sir David's account and five hundred and forty thousand pounds into Joanna's account."

"Bloody hell, that must have been a fortune in 1972!"

Cath smiles at me and checks her notes. "I checked up on the current value using an online inflation calculator. If it's right, then we are talking about the equivalent of nearly seven million quid today, Sean."

"Bloody hell! Of course, this doesn't necessarily mean that they killed Lucy, but it does almost certainly answer the question of why Joanna ended up marrying a dribbling halfwit."

It also almost certainly gives me the answer to how Sir David managed to get the loan sharks off his back.

"That's not everything, Sean," Cath says. "You remember how Joanna reacted to your question about the house?"

"Yes, of course. How could I forget?"

"Well, it turns out that it was more than just family pride. Joanna has more reason than most to be protective of the property. On August 23rd, 1972, Sir David transferred the title deeds for the house and all his land at Colevale into Joanna's name. She owns the entire estate, one-hundred percent."

"This just doesn't add up, Cath. Why would he do that? He was still a relatively young man and a serving member of parliament in 1972. It doesn't make any sense."

"I was trying to make sense of it myself on the way back here, boss, but the only things that seem to make any sense are that Sir David was in debt and Joanna persuaded Eddie to help, or that Eddie was being blackmailed by Joanna over something. Both scenarios are full of holes, though. Why blackmail Eddie and then marry him? Joanna already had the money before the wedding and why did Sir David transfer everything to Joanna? Was it him that was being blackmailed?"

Cath doesn't know how close she might be to the truth, but I can't tell her what I know just yet. I nod and tell her that I'm as confused as she is and then I ask about the inquest and autopsy reports.

"There is a 24-hour turnaround time on those, boss. I've asked the coroner's office to courier them up to us. Hopefully they should be with us sometime tomorrow."

Cath has had a good day and the delay in getting the reports from the coroner is not a big issue. Cath is also keen to hear my news and I take her through my meeting with the Oxfam cougar. For the most part, my news is unsurprising and concurs with what we know already from the case files. Like me, though, she is surprised when I mention how Joanna dropped her friends just a few days after Lucy's disappearance.

"Wow! That's not normal behavior, Sean. We need to get back up there and turn the thumbscrews on that bitch!"

"Yes, well, let's not jump the gun, Cath. I'm sure you would like nothing more than to get medieval on the lady of the manor, but we still have other leads to explore. They are not going anywhere anytime soon.

Let's get something concrete before we go charging in with all guns blazing. Any luck with contact details for Father Beale?"

"Yes, sorry, I nearly forgot. We are meeting him tomorrow morning at 11 o'clock at Beckhampton Church. He has a christening at twelve-thirty, but we should have enough time to ask him our questions."

I tell Catherine about my call to DCI Morgan and ask her to change the meeting with Father Beale to the following day.

"Sorry, Cath. Morgan was insistent that it needs to be tomorrow morning. Obviously, he doesn't want Anti-corruption hanging around the office for longer than is required."

"Bloody hell, Sean, I hope it's nothing serious. You don't want to get on the wrong side of the Anti-corruption boys. Do you think it might be something to do with Clive Douglas? That slippery bastard would say anything to save his own neck."

To be perfectly honest, I have no idea what it could be about. I took down a whole network of extremely powerful people. It could be to do with any one of them. The fact, though, that it involves the Anti-corruption team suggests that there might have been an allegation made specifically against me, but I don't want to worry Cath unnecessarily.

"I'm sure it's just a routine follow-up. Morgan didn't sound too concerned when I spoke to him."

"Well, whatever it is, I'll drive you there tomorrow. There's probably not much I can do here without you anyway. While you're in with Morgan, I can drop into the Coroner's Office and chase up our reports."

"Thanks, Cath, I appreciate it. Why don't you take a break now for the rest of the day? It's after three now anyway and you must be tired from the driving. I'm going to hit the gym for an hour. Let's meet up around seven for dinner."

Cath looks pleased at my suggestion and nods her approval. "Sounds perfect, my back is absolutely killing me. I'm going to grab a long soak in a hot bath. Thanks, boss."

By 6 pm, I have finished my work out and have spent another couple of hours going through the case file again to see if I might have missed something. Everything is exactly as I would expect, and nothing jumps out at me until I read through the original investigating officer's case summary again. It's not the contents, though, that get my attention; it's the name and the signature at the bottom of the summary: 'Detective Inspector Alan Cuttler'.

The surname is quite unusual, but at the same time is vaguely familiar. I mull it over for a few seconds and then it comes to me. I flip through my pocketbook for the notes I made after my first trip back to 1972. Staring back at me are the names, Donald Cuttler, Landlord, the Tyevale Arms, and Henry Cuttler, Police Sergeant. This must be more than just mere coincidence and whilst it is not unusual to have family members serving in the same force, and nor does it necessarily imply anything suspicious – it does make me think about something else. Who was it that attacked me when I confronted the loan sharks? What was it he said to me? I close my eyes to picture the scene and to concentrate on his voice.

"I think that's good advice, son. Walk away and keep your nose out of what doesn't concern you. Be a good lad and move along."

"Be a good lad and move along."

This sounds a lot like something a cop would say, and the realization hits me like a ton of bricks.

Jesus Christ, it was Sergeant Cuttler, I'm sure of it. But why on earth would he be protecting a pair of loan sharks? Just when I think I might be on the right track, something like this comes along to make me think again. Tonight, I am planning to go back to March 14th,1972, the night of Lucy's disappearance, and it should have been relatively straightforward for me to observe unnoticed. Now I need to avoid the local copper or face having to explain why I don't have a broken nose and black eyes.

I add DI Alan Cuttler's name to my notes and then I add all three names to the list of possible suspects or persons of interest.

Next, I call Ben. He picks up within two rings and is keen to find out what is happening.

"Go on then, what's the plan, Sean?"

"All in good time, Ben. Where are you now?" I reply.

"I found a cheap bed and breakfast place at the end of town. It's a bit grotty, but it will do for now. So, come on, what's the plan?"

"Sunday, March 12th, 1972 – that's two days before the main event. I want you to meet me at the entrance to the O'Hanlon Brothers Carnival at 4 pm and I want you there on time. Do you understand me, Ben? I can't have any screw-ups on this."

"I promise, Sean. I will be there on time. You can trust me." His voice is eager and keen to please.

"Good, now get onto Google and look up some pictures of Tyevale and the O'Hanlon Carnival from 1972 to use as your dream stimulus. The carnival is right on the edge of town. You can't miss it. Don't mess this up, Ben. I'm only going to give you one chance."

"Sean, stop stressing, mate. I've got it. O'Hanlon Carnival, 4 pm on March 12th,1972. I will be there."

I'm enjoying winding him up and am smiling to myself, knowing that I am sending him to the wrong day entirely. It's just too dangerous, though, to have Ben tagging along with me on such an important day.

"Okay, one last thing, do something with your hair and make sure you wear the outfit I gave you. I don't want you sticking out like a bull-dog's bollocks. Good luck, Ben. I'll see you in 1972."

He tries to ask me another question, but I deliberately hang up and head down to the bar to wait for Catherine. She will be keen to ask me about our next steps, but that really all depends on what I find out tonight. While I wait for her, I order myself a double Jameson whiskey and idly leaf through a copy of the Tyevale Evening News at the bar. The main headline is about the former US first lady, Barbara Bush, who has passed away at the age of ninety-two. I am so engrossed in the story that I don't notice that Catherine has joined me.

"Are you sure that's a good idea, Sean?"

"Oh, hi, Cath. Sorry, what was that?"

She points to my whiskey and frowns. "You have a meeting with DCI Morgan and Anti-corruption in the morning. Probably best to have a clear head, don't you think?"

Cath is undoubtedly right, but without a few drinks or some other stimulus, I will struggle to sleep tonight. I pushed myself hard in the gym, but I don't feel tired in the slightest. I'm going to need a few more drinks and whatever I do drink tonight, I should have more than enough time for it wear off before my meeting at 10 tomorrow morning.

"Thanks for your concern, Cath. I'm just going to have one more, then straight after dinner I'm going to get an early night. How was your bath?"

"Well, not that you're really interested, but it was fine. Thanks for asking."

I really should know by now that Cath is far too smart to be so easily deflected and asking about her bath was a lame attempt at doing just that.

"Are you worried about tomorrow, boss? Any idea yet what it might be about?"

"I really have no idea, Cath. There are so many suspects in the Network case that it could involve any one of them. No doubt I will find out in the morning. Come on, let's eat. I'm bloody starving."

We take a table in the restaurant and for the next ninety minutes discuss our theories about the case and each of the suspects. My mind, though, is elsewhere throughout most of the conversation. Thankfully, Cath puts it down to the uncertainty of my morning meeting and doesn't make a big thing of it. She does, however, show her annoyance when I order a third double whiskey.

"Boss, you need to make that your last one. Those boys from AC are no joke. I know you, Sean. You're putting on a brave face for me, but I know that you're worried. Finish that one, then get that early night you mentioned. If we set off around six-thirty, we should be there easily before nine. The traffic should be light enough early on, but better to be safe than sorry."

"What would I do without you, Cath? You're like my sister, my mum, my gran, and my partner all rolled into one. Come on, I'm done, now."

She feigns taking offence at my comment, but she also appears to be happy that I am heading to bed and doesn't comment when I knock my whisky back in one. We confirm to meet at 6:30 am at reception and then we wish each other a good night.

Unlike last night, I have no intention of waiting around until I am sure Catherine is asleep. I have a lot to do and unless the hotel catches on fire, I am confident that Cath won't be bothering me tonight.

I take a quick shower and then I take the new outfit from the bag given to me by Abigail. The suit and shoes are a great fit and to finish off the look, I put on the paisley tie and slick my hair back with slightly less Brylcreem than last night and then I top it off with the trilby. I'm tempted to have another drink from the minibar, but at the last second and conscious of tomorrow's meeting, I return the bottle to its place and close the door.

At about ten-fifteen, I retrieve the same photo of Jed and Tighe O'Hanlon from the case file that I used last night. I also stuff my can of CS gas spray into one of the jacket pockets. I'm hoping not to need it – but, like Cath said, it's better to be safe than sorry.

# The Past – Tuesday, 14th March, 1972

I lay down on my bed but have barely even begun my chant when the light takes me. This time it is noticeably warmer than it was on my last visit and it's also much later in the day.

It's still cold, but the street lights are on and most of the snow and the shitty brown slush that was evident on my last visit is gone. The time is just after 9 pm, so most of the shops, including the newsagent are already closed. But the pubs will be open and there will almost certainly be a copy of one of today's newspapers at the bar or on one of the tables.

Two young guys are chatting outside the Tyevale Arms, but they barely give me a second look as I pass them and make my way inside.

The bar area is slightly busier than it was on my last trip, and whilst the domino-playing pensioners are at the same table next to the fire, this time there are no comments about my appearance. My suit has obviously met with their approval and the landlord is smiling as he greets me.

"Good evening, sir. What can I get you?"

I'm pleased that he hasn't recognized me from my last visit, which was just a week ago in 1972. If he doesn't recognize me, then perhaps his truncheon-wielding brother, Sergeant Cuttler, might also be less likely to recognize me if we bump into each other.

"A pint of John Smiths please, landlord. Oh, and a read of your newspaper, if that's okay?"

"Help yourself," he replies, pushing across a copy of the Daily Mirror. "I wouldn't bother though. There's no good news in there. It's all bloody strikes, unemployment, and the hunt for those paddies that blew up the barracks."

I'm less interested in the news than I am in the date, which thankfully confirms that it is March 14th.

Donald places my pint down on a beermat and I thank him and turn back to face the rest of the bar. Unlike my last visit, tonight the pub is completely empty of anyone under the age of twenty-five. I have a good idea why, but I ask Donald anyway.

"Is it always this quiet? Where are all the youngsters?"

"It's half price at the carnival tonight. They always do a half-price Tuesday on the last week in town. Most of the young'uns were in earlier for a drink, but then they headed over there. They're all bloody mad, if you ask me, riding around on those death-trap rides in this weather."

I nod my thanks and take a large gulp from my beer, "Yep, that's kids for you. Did you say that this was the last week for the carnival?"

"That's right, the last day is this Saturday and bloody good riddance to them. Every year they turn up and they leave a right bleeding mess when they leave."

Clearly, Donald is not a great fan of the carny folk, but I don't have time to stand around and debate the rights and wrongs of the carnival with him. I swallow the remainder of my pint and turn to leave, with Donald still moaning to anyone that will listen to him.

Outside the pub, I check my watch. It is now nearly 10 o'clock and according to the witness statements, the scuffle between the O'Hanlons and Paul Oliver took place at around 10:50 pm. I reach into my pocket to check that I still have my CS gas spray and then I set off towards the O'Hanlon Carnival.

I've barely covered more than twenty yards when my copper's instinct kicks in and I turn around to see who is following me.

"I suppose you think that was bloody funny, don't you, Sean? Well, the joke's on you, mate. I knew when you didn't show up on Sunday that you would be here today, so I waited."

He looks so miserable and deflated that I am tempted for a second to be nice. That thought quickly passes when I see his footwear.

"You look like shit, Ben. And seriously, you turn up in 1972 wearing a pair of Nike Jordan's. What did I say about a bull-dog's bollocks? What happened to the boots, I gave you?"

"Don't even bloody start about those boots, Sean," he replies, clearly extremely pissed off with me. "I could hardly stand in them, let alone walk. And yes, I do look like shit, but so would you if you'd been sleeping rough for the last two nights. You're lucky that I didn't bloody freeze to death."

"Don't be so dramatic, Ben. Remember, you're immortal in your dreams. If you had frozen to death, you would have woken up in your nice warm bed."

"Fuck you, Sean! That was a shit's trick and you know it. Seriously, it's no fun sleeping rough in the middle of March, and I'm bloody starving. There's a hot-dog stand at the carnival. Buy me one and I might think about forgiving you for being an asshole."

He now looks so pathetic, that I am almost beginning to feel sorry for him. I'm also feeling quite impressed that he had the balls to wait around for me so long. The kid might actually have some potential.

"Fine – but, like I said before, you say and do nothing unless I tell you to. Is that understood?"

"Yes, it's understood. Now can we get going? My stomach feels like my throat has been cut."

As we get closer to the carnival, the smell of greasy food and cotton candy fills the air. Tormented by the tempting aromas, Ben quickens his pace and arrives at the entrance at least thirty seconds before me. When I do get there, he looks at me expectantly and after an unnecessary pause to make the point that I am in charge – I take out my wallet and hand him a five-pound note.

"Get your food and then come straight back and find me. I'm going to see if I can find the girls."

Without even waiting for me to finish speaking, he snatches the note from my hand and disappears in search of food, and I move inside to start my search.

The carnival is one of the biggest I have seen. It is busy with families and groups of young people, but the lights from the rides mean it is well lit. I still have nearly forty minutes before the fight is due to kick off and after ten minutes of searching, I spot the back of two blonde-haired young women standing next to a shooting gallery. I'm sure it's them, and as I move closer, Eddie Wells comes into view and confirms it.

I move within three or four feet of them, close enough to hear the girls encouraging Eddie to have a go with one of the rifles. Joanna asks him to win a giant teddy bear for her, but he appears to be reluctant and even a little bit shy of making a fool of himself. When he declines a second time, Joanna speaks to him again, but in a much more surprising way.

"What's wrong, Edward? Are you worried about making a fool of yourself? You shouldn't worry. It won't make any difference – you're already the village idiot!"

Eddie is red with embarrassment and looks like he is about to burst into tears, but his obvious discomfort doesn't stop Joanna from carrying on and taunting him further.

Just when I think that he might walk away, Lucy picks up one of the rifles and hands it to him.

"Don't be frightened, Eddie. They're only tin cans. They don't bite."

This comment and the laughter of the onlookers seems to do the trick and Eddie loads a pellet into the rifle. As he aims, he is shaking so badly that the outcome is a foregone conclusion.

By the time he has finished his five shots, all the cans remain standing and Joanna wastes no time in berating him again.

"You really are a bloody waste of space, Eddie Wells. I bet the pheasants on your farm love you, don't they? I don't know what the hell I see in you, you bloody useless lump."

Joanna's behavior towards Eddie makes absolutely no sense. Eddie is her boyfriend and now that I know that his money seems to have been the main attraction in their relationship, why would she risk losing him?

In less than a week he will be selling his farm and most of his land. Surely by now, they must have already discussed this. Why risk him breaking off the relationship, or changing his mind about selling up and giving Joanna and Sir David his money?

I'm thinking this over, when Lucy grabs Joanna's arm and pulls her away.

"Come on, I'm bored of this. Let's head over to the Ferris wheel. Paul and the lads usually hang around over there."

The girls walk away together, but Eddie seems unsure whether he should follow. Realizing he is not with them, Joanna stops Lucy and nudges her in the arm.

"Hey, sis, watch this."

Joanna stops a young girl and hands her some money in return for her ice cream. Then she scoops the ice cream off the top of the cone and launches it at Eddie's head.

Unlike Eddie's poor attempt with the air rifle, Joanna is deadly accurate, and the ice cream hits him square in the face. Lucy laughs hysterically, but Joanna remains steely faced and throws out another insult to Eddie before both girls turn away towards the Ferris wheel. "Get yourself bloody cleaned up, you spastic."

If I had thought before that Joanna was a bitch, her behavior now confirms it. Lucy is only slightly better. She's not directly taunting Eddie, but neither is she doing anything to stop it. I have met spiteful people before, but It almost seems that Joanna is deliberately trying to wind Eddie up. Whatever it is, they are both being disgusting human beings right now.

Eddie takes a handkerchief from his pocket and wipes his face before obediently following behind the girls. I follow at a safe distance behind Eddie and watch as the three take a seat on a bench in front of the Ferris wheel. Paul and his friends are nowhere to be seen, but I knew that already. I'm not expecting them to turn up until after the O'Hanlons arrive. The girls chat for a few minutes and then, right on time, the brothers arrive with two other scruffy-looking carnies.

Tighe is the older brother, but it is Jed that has the looks in the family. He is nearly fifteen years older than Lucy, but it is easy to see how she would be attracted to him. The posh girl going for a bit of rough is a story as old as the hills and whilst I can't hear everything that is being said, the body language between them is obvious. He hasn't wasted any time with laying on the Irish charm and I carefully move closer along the Ferris wheel railing to try to hear what is being said.

I am so intent on listening in that I don't notice Ben approaching me until it is too late, and his less-than-discrete arrival brings us some unwanted attention.

"Hey, Sean. That hit the spot. I'm ready to get started now. What's going on? Are they the girls?"

I pull Ben towards me and tell him to be quiet, but we have already been spotted and Tighe O'Hanlon walks towards us.

"What was that you said? Are you spying on us, ya pair of bloody perves?"

I push Ben aside and step forward to try to placate Tighe, but we are quickly forgotten when he hears raised voices behind him. Paul Oliver has arrived with his gang and is unhappy at the sight of Lucy holding Jed's hand.

"Lucy, what the hell is this? You asked me to come here tonight. Is this some kind of sick game?"

Joanna stands up and is about to speak, but Lucy holds out her hand to stop her.

"Don't worry, sis. I've got this."

Then letting go of Jed's hand, she pokes Paul in the chest and pushes him backwards.

"Nobody asked you to come here, Paul. Go home and take the rest of these little boys with you. Jed is going to take me for a ride, isn't that right, Jed?"

Tighe has rejoined the group and he slaps his brother on the back. "Too bloody right he is, Lucy. My brother likes a good ride, don't you, Jed? Now why don't you ladies do one, before you all get a bloody nose."

Paul is the first to swing a punch, and his boys are close behind, but the carnies are ready for them and quickly respond. Neither side seem to be making much progress and almost as soon as the fight has started, it ends when a bellowing voice calls a halt.

"What the hell is this! Break this shit up right now, you bunch of miserable bastards!"

His truncheon is out and, based on my own experience, I have no doubt that he would be happy to crack a few skulls given half the chance. The two groups separate and Sergeant Cuttler steps in between them. His voice is calm, but at the same time has that air of authority and confidence born of long experience in the job.

"Paul, get yourself home, lad, and take your boys with you. Go on, get along now."

I can see that Paul is reluctant to leave and, just as Joanna said during our meeting at Colevale, he asks Lucy to go home as well.

"Please, Lucy. This isn't what you want. The carnival will be gone in a few days, and then you will be knocking on my door again."

Lucy is not even listening. Despite Joanna also asking her not to go with the O'Hanlons, she ignores everyone and walks away holding Jed's hand. The rest of the carnies also leave and Cuttler puts away his truncheon and nods to Paul.

"Off you go, lad. I won't ask you again."

Paul leaves with his gang and Sergeant Cuttler next turns his attention in our direction. For a moment it seems like he is staring right at me trying to remember where he knows me from, but then to my great relief he turns away again and tells the rest of the gathered crowd to move along.

"Nothing to see here, folks. Go on, get back to whatever you were doing."


With the crowd dispersed, and Cuttler gone, I turn my attention back to following Lucy and the O'Hanlon brothers, but they have already disappeared into the crowd. Joanna and Eddie are also leaving and will also soon be out of sight.

"Ben, I need you to follow those two, but for God's sake don't let them see you. If nothing suspicious happens in an hour, then make your way back here. I'm going to try to find Lucy."

Searching for Lucy and the O'Hanlons amongst the crowd will be a waste of time and I already know where they are likely to be anyway. At the far edge of the carnival and set far enough away for privacy, are a cluster of crappy-looking caravans that the carnies must call home. Almost certainly they will be heading there.

Ben heads off in pursuit of Joanna and Eddie and I push my way through the crowd and head towards the caravans to find Lucy.

The caravans are arranged in a semi-circle around the burnt-out remains of a bonfire and my arrival is met by the barking of a mangy-looking Irish Wolfhound chained to a steel post.

Only one of the caravans has any lights on. At the sound of the dog barking, I push myself into the shadows of the adjacent caravan just as the door opens and Tighe looks out to investigate.

"Who's out there? Come on, show yourselves, ya fuckers!"

From inside, I can hear Jed shout to his brother.

"Get yourself back in, ya eejit, it's nothing. That bloody dog is afraid of its own shadow."

Satisfied that the dog just has the jitters, he calls the dog an idiot, then goes back inside and slams the door behind him. Barely ten seconds have passed, and I am just about to leave my hiding place when the door opens again and Lucy comes out, followed by Jed.

"Lucy, come on, there's no need to leave. Come back inside. Just stay and have a drink. I thought you were up for it tonight?"

She is already level with the bonfire, and it is obvious that she is intent on leaving when she answers the question but carries on walking. "Sorry, I've changed my mind, maybe tomorrow … if you're lucky!"

Tighe has appeared at the door and he stops Jed from following her.

"Leave it, Jed. Plenty more posh crumpet where she came from. Let's get a drink."

Jed's pride is obviously hurt and as Lucy carries on walking, he hurls an empty beer bottle at her. It doesn't even get close. Whether she can hear or not, he finishes off with an insult before rejoining his brother back inside. "Go on then, piss off, ya stuck-up, cock-teasing cow!"

So, I guess this rules out the O'Hanlon brothers – for now anyway. I doubt very much that she will change her mind and come back here tonight. Not after that little episode. So, where the hell could she be going? I leave my hiding place and run back towards the main carnival area. The hound is barking again, but I am already in amongst the carnival goers before anyone is likely to come out to investigate.

I spot Lucy just as she reaches the exit and I slow down my pace and hold back. She seems unsure at first in which direction to go and seems to be either looking for someone or possibly waiting for someone. Another five minutes pass and just when it looks like she is about to give up and leave, a smartly dressed young man calls out to her from the other side of the road. I can't see the dog collar, but the road is well lit, and Father Beale is easily recognizable.

After a brief exchange of words, they link arms and turn left out of the exit onto the road that would eventually take them to Colevale if they kept on walking. I can't imagine that is where they are going, though. At a normal walking pace, it would take them at least an hour in good conditions. In the middle of March on an unlit country road in the middle of the night, it would take much longer.

I cross to the darker side of the road to follow them, but my progress is stopped immediately by Ben who surprises me when he steps out from behind a tree and pulls me towards him.

"Sean, get in here. Joanna and Eddie are just up ahead. They must be waiting for her. Who is that with her?"

I hadn't noticed before, but Ben points out two figures silhouetted in the moonlight standing next to a wall. Lucy and Father Beale join them and the four of them start talking.

"It's the priest, Father Beale. How long have those two been waiting there?"

"Since they left the carnival," he replies. "They stopped for a smoke and I thought they might carry on walking, but they haven't moved."

I pull Ben back out into the road. "Come on, let's try and get a bit closer. It's less conspicuous with both of us and I need to hear what they are saying."

We move to within fifty yards of them and I tell Ben to face me.

"Make it look like we are chatting, Ben. Keep looking the other way in case they spot us."

At this distance I can hear them, but only barely. Eddie is angry and appears to be venting at both girls, which is hardly surprising, and Father Beale seems to be trying to calm things down, but without much success.

At the carnival, Eddie was being tormented mercilessly by both girls, but his manner now indicates something more. He is growing increasingly frustrated and lets his feelings be known to both girls. I can't make out who it is, but one of the girls is giving back as good as she gets and as tempers rise, so too does the volume.

"Why would you do this to me? Her I can understand, but you, what have I ever done to hurt you?"

"Oh, stop being so bloody pathetic, Eddie Wells. We all know that you're not a real man. Why do you think that we go and get our fun elsewhere?"

Even through his anger, I can hear the pain in his voice, and I can't help feeling sorry for him.

"That's not true, take that back. Tell her it's not true, go on, tell her."

"It is true, you moron. Look at me, you're so stupid that you can't even see the truth when it's staring you in the face. Well, the party's over Eddie. You should just piss off back to that bloody farm of yours."

The darkness is making it difficult to see which of the girls is speaking each time, but to get any closer would almost certainly give us away. There is no doubt who swings the punch though. Eddie is much taller and much broader than the girls and even with the sounds of the carnival still in full swing behind us, the sound of his fist striking Lucy in the face is unmistakable and she falls backwards. Ben has heard it as well and turns to face them.

As always, my first instinct is to call out and run to help, but I know I can't intervene. I pull Ben away back into the shadows and push him against the wall. His whole body is shaking, and he can hardly speak.

"Jesus Christ, Sean. Is she dead?"

"I don't know, Ben. We need to keep watching. Just try and keep quiet."

Joanna and the priest rush to help Lucy to her feet. After a few seconds she is able to stand unaided. She then launches her own verbal tirade against Eddie.

"You stupid bastard, you don't even realize what you have done, do you?"

Eddie doesn't reply and is almost certainly in shock. Lucy leans in towards him and whispers in his ear. Whatever she has said seems to upset him even more.

"Why, why would you do that? I didn't mean it. It was an accident. I just lost my temper. I would never have hurt you on purpose."

Father Beale tries to intervene again and is stopped by both sisters. Joanna now turns her aggression towards him.

"You stay out of this. You're as bad as he is. But you're a witness to this. You had better both do exactly as we say, or we will be going to the police and the bishop to let them know exactly what has been going on."

I now have no idea at all what is going on.

This whole thing seems to be a premeditated set up by the sisters, but I am still no closer to finding out why or what happened to Lucy. The O'Hanlons and Paul Oliver seem to be out of the frame tonight, and the way Lucy and Joanna are now talking to Eddie and the priest, I wouldn't blame either one of them for killing her.

But a single punch and raised voices are not enough. I need to stay with them to see for myself.

The voices now are much lower, and it is a strain to hear anything clearly, but I can see that it is one of the girls talking. When she finishes, Eddie walks towards a car parked ten feet further along the road and a few seconds later the engine roars to life.

The car reverses to let the sisters and the priest get in and then it heads off on the road out of town. Realizing that I am going to lose them, I pull Ben back out into the road.

"Shit, come on, we need to find a car and quick."

Just opposite the entrance to the carnival, three of four cars are parked up and a group of young guys are leaning against the wall, smoking and drinking from cans of beer. Music is playing from the radio of a Ford Cortina and the keys are hanging in the ignition, which means that the doors must be unlocked.

I nod to Ben and tell him to follow my lead.

"You need to move at the same time as me, Ben. As soon as you are in, lock the door. On the count of three, okay?"

He nods and after a last check to make sure that we are not being watched, I start the count.

"Okay, one, two, thre..."

"Oy, you, stop right there!"

My heart drops when I recognize the voice of Sergeant Cuttler. I must have been wrong earlier when I thought that he hadn't recognized me. I turn to face him, but it is not me he is looking at; it is Ben. Cuttler has two other men with him. Both are in their late fifties or early sixties. One of them is wearing a tweed three-piece suit and the other is wearing a white apron and a white cap.

Cuttler moves forward and takes Ben firmly by the arm.

"You've been a busy boy, haven't you, son? Is this him, gents?"

Both nod and the guy in the suit steps closer to get a better look at Ben.

"Yes, that's him, Sergeant. The thieving little sod came into the supermarket twice and helped himself to chocolate and soft drinks."

And this is why I didn't want him tagging along with me. Way to screw things up, Ben.

Cuttler turns back to Ben and asks him what he has to say for himself. Until now Cuttler doesn't appear to have noticed me, but as Ben replies, it is obvious that he is looking at me.

"Sorry, Sergeant. I put it down to my upbringing. No father figure in my family to keep me on the straight and narrow."

Cuttler is less than impressed at Ben's flimsy attempt at courting sympathy and he now turns his attention in my direction.

"And who might you be, sir? Have we met before?"

Wearing a suit changes you into a completely different person and that's just as well. This situation is complicated enough already, without him remembering where we met before.

"No, this is my first time in town. I just came for the carnival, but I do know this guy. What has he done?"

"Shoplifting from the local supermarket this morning and yesterday evening."

"And running off without paying for his cod and chips," interjects the guy in the apron.

"Yes, quite," replies Sergeant Cuttler. "And the theft of one large portion of cod and chips."

I look towards Ben with disbelief and he shrugs his shoulders.

"What? I didn't have any cash and I was hungry."

The chance of catching up with the sisters is already long gone and even if I can get Ben out of this, I have no idea where they are going. I'm resigned to the fact that I have lost them for now and I reach into my pocket for my wallet.

"Listen, Sergeant. Let me pay these gentlemen for their losses and I will make sure that you never see this idiot in Tyevale again. There's no need to waste your valuable time on unnecessary paperwork. What do you say, Sergeant?"

He looks me up and down for a few seconds and then points to my wallet.

"What I say, sir, is that unless you want to be joining your friend in the cells, you need to put that wallet back away in your pocket."

There is no point pushing the point any further and I nod towards Ben and shrug my shoulders.

"Sorry, mate. Don't worry, though – you'll be fine."

As Ben is pulled away back towards the town, he shouts over his shoulder, "Sean! Sean! what should I do?"

"Oh, I don't know, Ben. I'm sure you'll figure something out."

I never wanted Ben to travel with me in the first place, but if nothing else, this will have taught him a few valuable lessons. I'm sure that after a night in the cells, he will be kicked back out on the streets and will find his way home from there. There is no way that Cuttler is going to waste too much time over some fish and chips and a few groceries. It's more hassle than it's worth. Ben is not my problem now anyway. Getting home is. The time now is nearly midnight and I need to be as fresh as possible for my meeting with Anti-corruption in the morning.

The crowd at the carnival has started to thin out and some of the rides and stalls have already started to pack away, but the Ferris wheel is still operating.

There are only a handful of people waiting to board the ride. After a few minutes, I pay for my ticket at the booth and climb aboard an empty gondola.

At the highest point of its rotation I estimate that I am more than sixty feet above the ground and the volume of steel and machinery below will almost certainly guarantee me an instant death. I allow the wheel to complete two more full rotations and then I release the safety bar and stand up. I don't even need to jump. As the gondola reaches and crosses over the high point, I fall forward, and my body flips out and hurtles towards the ground. On the way down, I collide with two of the other gondolas and briefly see the looks of horror and hear the screams of the occupants, before my head smashes against the steel casing on the motor housing.

# Present Day – Thursday, 19th April, 2018

The alarm on my phone is set to go off at 6 am but, worried that I might oversleep, I am woken by the sound of a text message from Catherine ten minutes before.

Hey, Sean. Just checking you are awake?

Bleary eyed and slightly disoriented, I send a short reply and then spend fifteen minutes jotting down my observations from last night's travel. With everything I can remember captured in my notebook, I finish with a short summary. Not for the first time after a dream episode, I am left with almost as many questions as I have answers.

The O'Hanlon brothers appear to have been telling the truth in their original statements – Lucy did leave them just after 11 pm – but is it possible that she went back later? I think that this is unlikely given the way that she left them and the fact that I last saw her driving away with her sister, Eddie Wells, and the priest.

Paul Oliver also seems to be in the clear, but whilst it's improbable that he met or went looking for Lucy later, it's not completely beyond the realms of possibility. Abigail Whitchurch more or less told me that he was infatuated with Lucy. He was very upset when she left with the O'Hanlons and love does make you do some crazy things.

Then there is Father James Beale. I can't say yet if he is a murderer or a kidnapper, but he is most certainly a liar. He stated quite clearly in his interview notes that he was at home and that he never saw or spoke to Lucy on the night of her disappearance.

It also appears that he lied about his relationship with Lucy. Joanna's aggressive attitude towards him seemed to indicate strongly that there was something he would rather the bishop did not know about and it's not too difficult to guess what that might be. I can't think of any other reason why he would lie about seeing her or indeed of knowing about Eddie assaulting her, yet he never mentioned this in his statement to the police.

Lastly, we have the sisters themselves and Joanna's boyfriend, 'Bumbling Eddie Wells'. The assault on Lucy by Eddie was a shock, but almost understandable given the level of provocation he was subjected to. Lucy appeared to be relatively unhurt, but it wouldn't be the first time that someone who initially seems to be okay after an assault subsequently dies through a slow internal bleed or some kind of hemorrhage. It's a possibility, albeit a slim one. But if that is what happened, did Joanna cover it up by blackmailing both Eddie and Father Beale?

Was she blackmailing Eddie in return for his cash to clear her father's debts? Marrying him then would have been the next logical step to keeping him close and within her control. And did she buy Father Beale's silence by agreeing to keep silent about his affair with Lucy?

Even in 2018, something like that would be frowned upon. In 1972 he would most likely have been defrocked and excommunicated by the Catholic Church. Reason enough then to want to keep it secret.

Nothing is clear yet, but my next move is obvious. I need to return to 1972, to follow them when they drive away. This time I already know where they will be, and I already know where to find a car. I think I might even take Ben along with me for the ride. He was right last night; it was a bit of a shit's trick sending him to the wrong day. In the cold light of day, I'm actually feeling a little bit proud of his resilience in waiting around for me for two days.

I'm less proud of course that the dipshit got collared for pilfering groceries and take-away food, but I suppose I can't really blame him given the circumstances.

I'm sitting on the edge of the bed wondering how Ben has managed to get home when I am interrupted by a new text message from Catherine.

Heading down now, will meet you at the car.

I have been so engrossed in trying to make sense of things that the time has flown past. It's almost six-twenty and Cath was hoping to be on the road by half-past the hour. I put my notebook away in my jacket pocket and then quickly type a reply to her message.

No worries, nearly ready. Will be down in 10 mins. See if you can rustle up some takeaway tea or coffee ☺

I had been hoping to arrive for my meeting in London looking refreshed, but my shave and shower will have to wait. With DCI Morgan and investigators from the Anti-corruption unit involved, it is better to arrive looking a bit rough than to arrive late. My morning routine today is restricted to a cold face cloth, a bottle of mouthwash, and a can of Lynx. At six-thirty exactly I climb into the car smelling like an industrial accident at a deodorant factory.

"Jesus Christ, Sean! You're going to meet Anti-corruption, not going to a scratch and sniff convention. What happened? Did the top come off your bottle of Old Spice?"

"Yeh, good one, Cath. A bit less of the jibber-jabber please, Detective Constable, and a bit more of passing me one of those cups, if you don't mind. What is it?"

Cath can see that I am less than with it right now and has the good sense not to comment on my stubble.

But she can't resist a knowing smirk as she hands me one of the takeaway cups.

"It's coffee, that's all that was ready. Regretting that last double whiskey, are we, boss?"

"I regret a lot of things, Cath. But whiskey is not one of them. Come on, let's make a move. We don't want to keep Morgan waiting."

Cath puts her own coffee cup into the holder between the front seats and we head out of the village and south on the motorway towards London. She was right to be overly cautious with the time it would take us this morning. Twelve miles outside of London, there is a jack-knifed lorry blocking two of the four lanes and by the time we pull into the car park of Blackwell Station it is already nearly 9:45 am. Catherine wishes me luck before turning the car around and heading off to the coroner's office.

Inside the station, Detective Sergeant Sarah Gray is waiting for me at reception, but she doesn't waste time with pleasantries. She ushers me straight into the lift.

"Go straight to Morgan's office, Sean. He wants to speak to you before AC do."

The boys from Anti-corruption are obvious as soon as I step out of the lift. The term 'sticking out like a bull-dog's bollocks' comes to mind again. They are both coppers about my age, but other than that, I seriously doubt whether we have anything in common. Anti-corruption are a necessary part of modern policing, as I know only too well from recent experience, but no copper in their right mind wants to spend time with them. This is probably why Morgan has them sitting outside his office like a couple of naughty schoolboys waiting to see the headmaster.

As I pass, they recognize me immediately and nod politely.

Morgan is waiting at the door and invites me in. He tells them that he won't keep them long. I wait until the boss has sat down and then I take a seat opposite him.

"I'm sorry to put you to all this trouble, sir."

"It's no problem at all, Sean. You were instrumental in putting away some big fish and there were bound to be more questions for you at some stage. Just assure me that there is nothing I should be worried about?"

"One hundred percent, sir. I've been completely transparent with you and in all of my interviews about what I know. I really have no idea what this could be about."

My response seems to satisfy him, and he reaches over the desk and pats my arm.

"Good lad, I never doubted it. Let's get those two in and get on with this, so we can get back to some real police work."

Morgan calls his PA to let her know that we are ready and thirty seconds later the two detectives from anti-corruption come in and we stand up to meet them.

"DS McMillan, good to meet you finally. My name is Detective Inspector Tony Robertson, and this is my colleague, DS Chris Marshall."

I shake both of their hands and then Morgan asks them to sit down.

"I take it, DI Robertson, that there is no objection to me sitting in while you talk to DS McMillan?" Morgan asks.

"Not at all, sir. Out of respect to DS McMillan, this is not currently a formal matter and neither do we expect it to be. There has been an allegation made about his conduct during his time in Meerholt Prison, but we don't believe it to be credible. I'm not expecting this to take long, sir."

Morgan looks pleased with the explanation from DI Robertson and indicates for him to carry on.

"That's good. DS McMillan is a fine police officer and I won't stand by and let any of those crooked bastards tarnish his hard-earned reputation. Let's get on with it please, so we can all get back to work."

Robertson thanks him and then turns to his colleague.

"Chris, when you are ready."

DS Marshall removes two case files from his briefcase and lays out the contents of both on DCI Morgan's desk. Next, he pushes the mugshots of Senior Officer Phillip Cartwright and Prison Officer Brendan Taylor towards me and asks if I recognize them.

"Yes, of course I do," I reply. "They were running a smuggling racket into Meerholt Prison. They were on DS Douglas' payroll and it was these two that handed me over to Bellmarsh and Huntley."

Both Robertson and Marshall nod their agreement and then Marshall puts away the mugshots and replaces them with two handwritten statements.

"Yes, that was a nasty business, DS McMillan. You opened a real can of worms when you took that case on. It's great to see that you are on the mend though and back at work. I'm almost a bit embarrassed to be asking you this, but an allegation has been made, and we need to follow up on it."

DCI Morgan is looking impatient and nods to DS Marshall to continue.

"We're all adults here, DS Marshall. No need to be shy."

"Yes, sir, of course."

He clears his throat and then turns the two statements towards me.

"Both Senior Officer Cartwright and Officer Taylor have alleged that whilst you were being held in Meerholt Prison you smuggled in and supplied four ounces of marijuana to the prisoner Frank Butler."

He has barely finished speaking when Morgan leaps to my defense.

"Are you seriously wasting our time with something so preposterous, gentlemen? Sean was only in Meerholt for around a week. When was he supposed to have had the time or the opportunity to do such a thing? And more to the point, why on earth would he want to? Frank Butler is the cousin of Paul Donovan. What utter crap!"

Out of respect for his rank, DI Robertson allows Morgan to finish venting and then he apologizes.

"Sir, we couldn't agree more. But please, if you could allow us to finish and refrain from interrupting. We need to hear from DS McMillan so that we can close this."

Morgan looks annoyed at the rebuke from Robertson, but he keeps quiet and allows him to continue.

"DS McMillan, I need to ask you if there is any truth in this allegation. Did you smuggle marijuana into Meerholt Prison and give it to Frank Butler in return for his protection?"

The allegation is of course one hundred percent true, but it's interesting to see that they only have statements from Cartwright and Taylor and not one from Frank Butler. To implicate me in the supply of drugs would be to implicate himself, so it would make sense that he wouldn't say anything against me. Add to that the fact that I gave him the evidence to prove that DS Douglas murdered his cousin, I'm confident that the word of the two crooked screws is all they have.

"No, I did not smuggle marijuana into Meerholt Prison. May I ask when I was meant to have supplied these drugs to Frank Butler?"

DS Marshall double checks his notes and then tells me it was on Friday, February 16th, 2018.

Morgan laughs to himself and unable to keep quiet, he goes on another rant.

"This is ridiculous. Sean was remanded into Meerholt on 15th February. Prior to that he was strip searched at least three times and I assume again when he was processed on arrival at the prison. Are these jokers seriously expecting anyone to believe that less than twenty-four hours after his arrival into prison he was able to arrange for four ounces of marijuana to be smuggled into him? What complete and utter rubbish!"

Robertson wisely chooses not to rebuke DCI Morgan again and turns to me.

"Listen, Sean. We know that it's far-fetched, but both statements were taken separately, and they do seem to corroborate each other. Why do you think that they would both try to implicate you in the supply of drugs?"

"To save their own skins," I reply. "They are both looking at significant sentences for the Meerholt racketeering operation and for the collusion with Clive Douglas. If I were to guess, I would say that they are clutching at straws in the hope of a reduced sentence. Did Frank Butler corroborate their story?"

Robertson shakes his head. "No, he didn't. He denies any knowledge of any involvement in drugs or of any agreement to protect you."

"Well, there you have it," Morgan exclaims. "This is nothing more than a last-ditch attempt by a couple of bent screws to deflect attention from themselves and to dent DS McMillan's credibility. Are we done here, gentlemen?"

DI Robertson closes the two case files and stands up.

"Yes, I think that's enough. I apologize for wasting your time, sir. And for dragging you off your current case, DS McMillan."

Both officers shake my hand again and then Morgan escorts them out. I can hear them talking with Morgan for another thirty seconds before he comes back in and sits down.

"Is there something more to that, Sean?"

DCI Morgan is no fool and he knows as well as the AC boys did that the allegation from Cartwright and Taylor is so far-fetched as to almost be true. I have no intention of giving anything away though.

During my stay in hospital and after my discharge we spent many hours discussing the Network Case and there was nothing ever mentioned about my involvement in the supply of drugs. I have no intention of revealing anything now.

"Nothing, sir. It's all complete rubbish. Like I said to DI Robertson, they are both just clutching at straws. Thanks for your support. May I get back to work now, sir?"

Morgan stands up and shakes my hand.

"Think nothing of it, Sean. It's nothing I wouldn't do for any of my officers. Check in with me tomorrow and give me an update on the Partington-Brown case."

I thank him and walk towards the door, but Morgan calls me to hold on. As I turn, he is looking at his computer screen. He is typing something, but he stops and looks in my direction.

"One of these days, I'm going to get the full story from you, DS McMillan. I don't know when, but I will get it."

"Sorry, sir. I'm not following you?" I reply.

"The full story of how you managed to get in and out of Meerholt Prison on the night that the CCTV picked you up at Assistant Chief Constable Butterfield's house. You never did fully explain that and a few other things to me. Carry on, Sean."


As soon as I am in the lift, I breathe a sigh of relief. I know full well that Morgan is not entirely convinced with my explanation for the drugs allegation, but whether he believes it or not, there is no evidence to support the claims of Cartwright and Taylor and I am confident that neither Morgan nor Anti-corruption will have the appetite to pursue the claims further. To do so could seriously damage my credibility, which might put at risk the chance to successfully convict some of the big fish scooped up in the aftermath of the Network case. There is no way that they would allow that to happen.

The time is approaching 10:45 am and I'm keen to get back up to Tyevale. I message Cath to let her know that I am done with AC and then head to the canteen for a late breakfast while I wait for her. Twenty minutes later she replies to say that she is back, and I head down to the carpark to meet her.

On the passenger seat there is a beige A4-sized envelope bearing the coat of arms of the Coroner's Society of England and Wales. The envelope is still sealed, and I ask Cath if she was able to discuss the reports with anyone.

"Hang on a second," she says. "How did your meeting go with DCI Morgan and AC?"

"It was fine, Cath," I reply. "AC wanted to ask me about some bullshit allegation that the two bent screws had made against me."

Cath raises her eyebrows. "And?"

"And nothing. Statements were made alleging that I had brought drugs into Meerholt with me and that I had used those drugs to buy the protection of Frank Butler. It was nothing more than a feeble attempt to discredit me and to possibly wangle a reduction in sentence. I explained to AC that it was bullshit and the meeting finished. But for the fact that it took me away from this case, it would have been laughable."

"Wow! Did they really think that anyone would believe such utter nonsense?" Cath says. "Even Anti-corruption are not that gullible. I bet Morgan was fuming that they were even entertaining the idea."

"Morgan was great, Cath, and at the end of the day, AC was just doing its job."

I'm keen to end this conversation and so I ask her again about the sealed envelope on the seat.

"It's just the inquest report, boss, and, no, there was nobody around to discuss it with.

The report was ready to collect, but the coroner's not based in the same office. I haven't read it yet. I figured you would be keen to get back on the road."

"Yes, I am," I reply. "Come on, let's get going. I can read it on the way up. What about the autopsy report? Did they say when that would be ready?"

"I think the answer to that is, never. There was no autopsy done," Cath replies.

"Seriously!" I exclaim. "A woman in her mid-forties with no significant prior history of illness is bedridden for twelve months, then dies suddenly in her sleep and there is no autopsy? That doesn't add up, Cath. I'm starting to think that we might be investigating more than just the disappearance of Lucy. Surely this mystery illness would have been reason enough for the coroner to call for an autopsy?"

Cath nods and then starts the car. "Yep, you're right. It doesn't make any sense. Open the envelope and take a look at the report. I'm intrigued now to see what the coroner's verdict was."

Cath pulls out of the station and sets course back towards the motorway. I break the seal on the envelope and take out the contents, skimming the main headings in the coroner's report. If I had been expecting to find a detailed report on the death of Beatrice Partington-Brown, then I would have been sorely disappointed. The report is made up of just two typed A4 pages, comprising mainly of the deceased's personal details, date of death, and the inquest verdict, which states the cause of death as 'heart failure following a prolonged bout of unexplained illness.'

Accompanying the coroner's report there is also a copy of Beatrice's medical records, a copy of her death certificate, and a statement from the Partington-Brown's family doctor. Interestingly, the death certificate and the statement from Dr.

Clarke both use the same wording as the inquest report when describing the cause of death. This could mean nothing, of course, but it does make me wonder if the coroner could have been unduly influenced in reaching his verdict.

I slide the other items back into the envelope and focus my attention back on the inquest report. This time I read it word for word. As before there is nothing startling in the main body of the report, but there is a small handwritten note at the bottom of the second page that I hadn't noticed during my first review. It's only two words and the handwriting is difficult to decipher, but when I finally get it, it's unmistakable.

"Autopsy required. It says autopsy required."

My comment is to myself, but it gets Cath's attention.

"Sorry, what was that you said, boss?"

"Autopsy required, Cath. The coroner wanted an autopsy. He's made a note at the bottom of the report. So why was there no autopsy? Jesus Christ, Cath! She was killed, and someone stopped the autopsy going ahead."

My outburst causes Cath to take her eyes off the road for a second before she quickly turns back.

"What do you mean, she was killed? Killed by whom and why? You think she might have known something about Lucy's disappearance?"

"I really don't know, Cath, but the only person with the kind of influence and connections to stop an autopsy would have been ..."

Cath interrupts and finishes my sentence, "Sir David Partington-Brown."

"Exactly, Cath. I think we need to pay the PBs another visit. But this time, let's not tell them we are coming. Put the blue light on, Cath. We have work to do."

We arrive back at the Winchester Hotel at just past one in the afternoon. Before heading upstairs to freshen up, I ask Catherine to do some more research into Beatrice Partington-Brown.

"See if you can find out the date of her burial. If you have no luck on the phone, St. Benedict's Church is at the end of the high street. Have a walk down and check the births, deaths, and marriages register. I'll bet my next month's salary that the PBs will have a family plot in there. I'm going to head up and get my thoughts together. Back here for two-fifteen, yeh?"

"Sounds good, boss."

Cath checks the time on her watch and then sits down in reception to make some calls while I head up to my room. The door is locked but the TV is on again and when I get inside, Ben has his feet up on the coffee table watching daytime TV and is tucking into a huge slice of pizza.

"Feel free to make yourself comfortable and to abuse my room service account, Ben. Why don't you order yourself a bottle of champagne while you're at it? I assume the cleaner let you in again?"

Ben takes his feet off the table and puts down the remains of the pizza slice.

"I'm good, Sean. Thanks for asking. And I think buying me a pizza is the least you could do after leaving me to rot in jail."

With everything that has happened so far today, Ben had completely slipped my mind and I'm now feeling slightly guilty. Bizarre as the situation might sound, at the end of the day he is still my son.

"Yep, sorry. I guess I deserved that. How are you after last night's shenanigans? How did you get away?"

"Well, all things considered, I'm fine, thank you. That copper was determined to keep me in, and he arranged for some detectives to come from Spalding to speak to me."

"For stealing fish and chips and a few groceries?"

"No, of course not," Ben replies. "I didn't have any ID on me, and he wasn't able to verify the name and address I gave him. Then he started asking me what I knew about the IRA and if I had ever been to Aldershot."

At the mention of the IRA my face drops and I sit down on the sofa next to him.

"Ben, what name did you give to Sergeant Cuttler?"

The accusing tone in my voice gives away my concern and Ben hesitates to answer.

"Ben, this is serious, I need to know what name you gave him?"

"What does it matter? I'm back now, no harm done."

"Ben! Tell me the name," I snap at him.

"Paddy, I told him my name was Paddy."

"Just Paddy?" I ask him.

Ben starts to snigger slightly, "No of course not, he wanted my full name, so I told him it was Paddy O'Doors. You know, as in patio doors, like in the joke, 'What do you call an Irishman with a pane of glass either side of his head?'"

"I know the bloody joke, Ben, but do you see me laughing? You absolute bloody tit – this could completely screw everything up for us."

Ben has stopped laughing and is now looking completely bewildered.

"It was just a joke, Sean. What's the big deal?"

I have to hold myself back from throttling him and after taking a few seconds to calm myself down, I explain to him what the big deal is.

"The big deal, Benjamin, is that less than a month after one of the most audacious bombings by the Irish Republican Army on the British mainland since the start of the troubles, you get yourself banged up in jail and pretend to be an Irishman. That's what the big deal is. Please tell me that you managed to get away before the detectives from London arrived?"

My question puts the smile back on his face and he is clearly pleased with himself.

"Yes, of course I did. Cuttler was finished with me within an hour. After that, he locked me up in one of the interview rooms and I put that bloody turtleneck to good use."

I have a bad feeling about this, but I ask anyway.

"Good use? What did you do, Ben?"

"I looped one end over the ceiling fan and put the other end around my neck. The label said it was a hundred percent wool, but the friction burns on my neck told a different story. If strangulation hadn't got me first, the burns from the polyester would have got me eventually."

I put my right hand to Ben's mouth and lift my left index finger to my own.

"Stop talking right now, before I strangle you myself. You do realize that this could change the course of this case and investigation entirely? It was probably special branch that were on the way up from London to speak to you. Don't be surprised if the army and special branch are crawling all over Tyevale 1972 in their hunt for the Aldershot Barracks bombers. I need to sort this out and fast."

"So, we're going back tonight?" Ben asks.

"Not you, Ben. I want you on the next train back down to London. I should never have let you get involved in this. I knew that it was a mistake."

"But I can still help you," Ben protests. "Just tell me what you want me to do."

"I want you on that train, Ben, and if I have to, I will put you on it myself. Do I make myself clear?"

Reluctantly, Ben nods. He knows that he won't be able to change my mind and he stands up to leave.

"I'm sorry, Sean. I really didn't mean to screw things up. I'll message you when I get home. If there is anything I can do from there, just let me know."

In reality, I am more annoyed with myself than I am with Ben. I should have been more insistent in sending him home when he first showed up yesterday, or I should have ended our travel when he found me in 1972. Now, I have no idea what might be waiting for me when I go back there. My only consolation, if there is one, is that with Ben out of the way, at least he won't be able to do anymore damage and I already know where the girls and Eddie are going to be. I just need to get to a car without running into Sergeant Cuttler.

I quickly shower and shave and then head downstairs to meet Catherine. Coincidentally, as I step out of the lift, she has just got back, and we bump into each other near the reception.

"That's good timing, Sean. I was just about to call you. You were right about the Partington-Brown family plot at St. Benedict's. It's a bit run down and overgrown, but thankfully I didn't need to get down and dirty to clear the weeds away. The church verger was kind enough to dig out the records for me. Beatrice died on January 12th, 1974 and she was buried less than a week later on January 16th."

"The inquest was the day before, on January 15th," I tell Catherine. "This all seems way too fast to me – sudden and unexplained death, an inquest, and a burial in less than a week. Come on, let's go and wake Sir David up."

On the way to Colevale, Catherine smiles and comments on my appearance.

"Good move getting cleaned up, boss. There is no way that Lady Muck, would allow you in looking like a down-and-out. You might even get a few extra smiles out of her today."

"Somehow I doubt that, Cath. I don't think she is going to be particularly pleased with us turning up unannounced. Let me lead again but keep an eye on them for any unusual reactions."

Cath does her usual eyebrow raising at my comment, then turns back to face the road.

"Is this going to be another one of your pushing the boundaries informal chats? If it is, please just be careful how far you push it. Particularly with Sir David. Let's not forget the man is in his nineties, Sean. What's your plan?"

I briefly refer to my notes and then I tuck my notebook away in my jacket pocket.

"I'm thinking a two-pronged attack today, Cath. I want to start with Sir David and find out why he was so keen to get his wife in the ground so fast. Then I want to have a go at Eddie. Your job, Cath, is to keep control of the Rottweiler."

"Thanks, boss. That sounds almost as fun as nosing around in an overgrown family burial plot. You're giving me all the good jobs today. It's not my birthday, you know."

"It's just as well it's not," I reply. "I doubt very much that Joanna will be wheeling out any cake today. Right, we're here – get your game face on, DC Swain."

As soon as we pull up onto the graveled driveway opposite the house, the curtains in one of the upper bedroom windows starts twitching and I tell Cath that we have been spotted.

"Well, there goes the element of surprise. What's the betting that the lady of the house will be at the door before we get halfway up the steps?"

Cath turns off the engine and opens her door. "That's not great odds, Sean, but let's go and find out, shall we?"

Surprisingly, by the time we reach the top of the stairs, the door is still closed and after waiting for another few seconds, I reach forward to ring the bell. With no response after another thirty seconds, I ring the bell for a second time and then I nudge Cath.

"Maybe you should have taken that bet after all, Cath. You could have been on a nice little earner."

"Yeh, because of course you would have paid me ... not! What are they playing at? Someone is definitely at home. Try again and if they don't answer, let's check around the back."

I ring the bell once again and for added measure Cath also taps on the door with her car keys.

"Ms. Partington-Brown, this is Detective Constable Swain and Detective Sergeant McMillan. We were here yesterday. Open the door please. We have a few more questions for you."

Behind the door, there is the sound of glass or ceramic breaking and I tell Cath to be quiet. When the door still doesn't open, I knock on it again.

"Open the door please. There are a few questions that we need to ask that could really help us in the search for Lucy."

After another short pause, there is a faint but nervous reply, followed by the sound of a security chain sliding into place.

"My wife is not at home, come back tomorrow please."

Cath touches my hand and suggests that it might be better to come back when Joanna is at home.

"I'm not sure we should be talking to Eddie Wells on his own, boss. Remember what happened when we tried that with Terry Fletcher?"

I remember it only too well, but I also remember how the case turned out in the end. We may not get another chance to speak to Eddie without Joanna or a lawyer present and I am not prepared to let this chance slip through my fingers.

Despite her look of concern, I tell Cath to keep Eddie talking and then I make my way to the back of the house.

Traditionally, the rear doors, or the tradesman's entrance, in these big country houses were always kept unlocked during the day to allow the servants and tradesmen to come and go freely. Even without servants, these traditions die hard and, in his panic or nervousness at our arrival, Eddie has forgotten to lock the door and I quietly let myself in and make my way to the front of the house.

Shards of ceramic from a broken vase litter the hallway floor and Eddie has his faced pushed up against the front door. I can hear Catherine trying to reassure him that there is nothing to worry about, but he has his hands pressed firmly across his ears to block out her words.

In 1972, it looked like Eddie might have some kind of learning or behavioral problem, but with the onset of old age, this current behavior could be an indicator of some kind of dementia or other mentally debilitating condition. With this in mind, I decide to take Cath's advice. Unfortunately, when I turn to leave, my shoe presses down on a large piece of the broken vase.

As the shard breaks in two, the cracking of the ceramic on the tiled floor is enough to startle Eddie and he launches himself in my direction.

"Get out, get out! You shouldn't be in here. I can't speak to you."

I brace myself for his body to slam into mine, but at the last second, he stops just inches away from me. His face is red and contorted with anger and both his fists are clenched tight by his side, but I know already that any immediate threat has subsided.

"Just calm down, Eddie. Nobody is here to hurt you. I just wanted to make sure that you were okay. I'm going to leave now. Is that okay?"

Outside, Catherine would have clearly heard the commotion and she is now banging on the front door and calling to me to find out what is going on. This new commotion startles Eddie again and he rushes back to the front door to check that it is still locked.

"Eddie, listen to me. She's not going to come in. You have my word." Then I call out to Catherine, "Everything is okay, Cath. Give me five minutes please and I will be coming back out."

Reassured, Eddie turns back to face me, and I ask him if everything is okay.

He nods and then unlocks the front door, "You need to go now. I'm not supposed to be talking to you."

I know I need to leave, but I take a chance and ask him if there is something that he wants to tell me about Lucy's disappearance.

"Anything you tell us will be completely confidential, Eddie. We can arrange to take you into a police station if you would feel more comfortable. Would you feel safer if we could do that for you?"

His face goes red again and he is now visibly sweating.

"I can't talk to you. I'm not allowed. You have to go."

"But you want to talk to us? Is that what you mean, Eddie? Do you know what happened to Lucy?"

From behind the door, Catherine shouts that I need to get out, but the warning is too late and just a few seconds later the door opens a few inches until it is stopped by the security chain.

Joanna is furious and shouts to Eddie to remove the chain. Once inside she wastes no time in expressing her displeasure and orders me to leave.

"This is highly irregular, Sergeant McMillan. I will be calling your senior officer to express my displeasure. You had absolutely no right to enter our property without any warning or invitation."

"My apologies, Ms. Partington-Brown, we had been hoping that you would all be home, and I only entered the house to check on the well-being of Mr. Wells. He sounded a bit distressed when we arrived."

Until now her focus had been completely on me, but now she focuses on her husband.

"What have you been saying?"

He looks absolutely terrified of her and is unable to answer before she tells him to wait upstairs and then asks me to leave again.

"If you wish to speak with us again, I would appreciate some prior notification, Sergeant. Now, if you don't mind, my father is waiting for me to help him from the car."

She watches us all the way to the car and only goes to help her father when she is sure that we are not coming back.


Nearly a minute passes before either of us speaks and then it is Cath that breaks the silence.

"Well, that didn't quite go to plan, boss. What the hell happened in there?"

"We need to speak to him alone, Cath," I reply. "He knows what happened to Lucy. I'm sure of it."

"So, let's get him into a station with a solicitor present. I can get onto it right away."

I shrug my shoulders and tell Cath not to do anything yet.

"I think he might have dementia or Alzheimer's. There is definitely something going on in his head. He was completely trying to block you out and when I scared him, he rushed at me like a madman. I thought he was going to flatten me. We need to tread carefully with him."

"So, what then?" Catherine asks me. "You want to make an appointment to come back to speak with them all together?"

"Yes, do that Cath. What time are we meeting Father Beale tomorrow?"

Cath checks her notes and confirms that the meeting is at 11 am.

"We can head straight to the PBs after that meeting. How about I set it up for 2 pm? That should give us enough time."

"Yep, sounds perfect, Cath. Let's get back to the hotel. It's been a long day already. I need to gather my thoughts and unwind in the gym."


The rest of the day follows the same pattern as yesterday. I spend an hour in the gym followed by a review of my notes and planning for my next trip back to 1972, and then I meet Cath for dinner at eight-thirty.

We discuss our theories and tactics for tomorrow over a bottle of red wine. Cath quite rightly is still concerned about pushing Eddie, Joanna, and Sir David too hard without having legal representation present, but I'm not ready to take things to a more formal level yet. To do so, would alert them to the fact that my suspicions are turning in their direction and I think that this would close the door on cooperation completely.

Despite her concerns, she agrees to play it my way and after a gin and tonic, Cath wishes me a good night and heads upstairs to her room.

Two minutes later and satisfied that she is not coming back downstairs, I stand up and order myself a double Jameson at the bar. The guy at the other end of the bar with his hoodie pulled low down over his face has been nursing his pint and watching us for the last hour. Cath might not have noticed him, but I certainly did, and I have been waiting for Cath to leave so that I can speak to him.

"I thought I bloody told you to get the train back to London."

Ben drops his hoodie and gives me half a smile.

"Would you believe me if I told you that I missed the train?"

I lower my voice so that we can't be overheard by the barman and I pull Ben's barstool closer towards me.

"You need to go back to that B&B that you're staying in and you need to let me get on with my job, Ben. This is not a game. I want you on the first train back to London in the morning. Do you understand me?"

"You can't tell me what to do, Sean. It makes no difference anyway. I can follow you back to 1972 from my bed in London as easily as I can follow you from here. I just want to help."

I push his stool back and take a drink from my glass.

"You can help me by listening to what I am saying. What we do, what I do I mean, is dangerous, not just in the past, but right here and now, Ben. This is not some TV show or a video game where you can get extra lives when you die. These are real criminals and when you get hurt in real life, you stay hurt.

"Go home and I promise, once this case is over, we can meet and talk properly about how you can help me in the future."

He drinks the last few sips of his pint and then stands up.

"I hope you're not bullshitting me again, Sean. I trusted you before and then you did your best to avoid me. I'll message you in the morning to let you know I have left."

Ben leaves and I turn my stool back to face the barman, pushing my empty glass across the counter.

"You'd better give me another one of these. I think I'm going to need it.

Back in my room, my outfit is hanging neatly on the back of the door. The shoes, though, have dried mud on them from the carnival field, so I wash them off in the bathroom sink and then leave them to dry whilst I get ready. Ten minutes later and content that my look is identical to last night, I put on the shoes and lie down on my bed. Tonight, the image of the O'Hanlon brothers and the carnival is clear in my head and, with my head spinning from the whisky and wine, travel comes easily.

# The Past – Tuesday, 14th March, 1972

I get my bearings and am shocked to realize that I have arrived outside the carnival just in time to see Lucy walking away with Father Beale. It's already past 11 pm and if my recollection of my last trip is correct, this means I have less than ten minutes to steal the car and to get myself in position before they disappear with Eddie and Joanna.

Opposite the entrance, 'I'm Gonna Run Away from You' by Tammy Lynn is playing on the stereo of the Ford Cortina. The guys leaning against the wall are too busy wolf-whistling and calling out to any girls passing by to notice me as I edge closer to the car. It is only when I pull open the driver's side door that one of them objects and walks towards me.

"Oy! I think you've got the wrong car, pal."

By this time, I am already in the driver's seat and fumbling with the gears trying to find reverse.

Alerted by their friend, the whole group of guys and some other onlookers are now rushing towards me and just as I find reverse gear and speed backwards onto the road, a full can of beer flies through the open passenger side window and painfully catches me in the side of my head. The force of the can leaves me momentarily stunned and for a second the car stops in the middle of the road. Conscious that I am going to get caught and lynched by an angry mob if I don't do something quickly, I find first gear and floor the accelerator. The sudden burst of forward acceleration causes my pursuers to scatter left and right to avoid being knocked down. As I pass them, a few of the braver individuals continue to chase me and hurl missiles, but within fifty or sixty yards they also give up when they realize that I am not going to stop.

Clear of the crowd, I touch the side of my head. There is a small gash and some minor swelling, but the injury is superficial, and my main concern now is to find Lucy and the gang. I turn onto the road out of Tyevale and speed up when I see the tail lights of what must be Eddie's car fading into the distance. I pass the tree where I had hidden with Ben last night, and my heart sinks when I see him standing behind it.

He runs out onto the road behind me and starts waving in an attempt to get my attention. I can't stop. If I stop now I will surely lose them for a second time. I watch in my rear-view mirror and eventually he gives up and I see him turn and start walking back into Tyevale. I feel guilty for not stopping, but at the same time I am annoyed that he has defied me again.

Then something else occurs to me, something that I have never had to deal with before. By coming here alone tonight, is it possible that I have only changed my own timeline and not Ben's? Could his timeline have played out exactly as before? Usually, I only have myself to consider. If I'm right, then Ben is walking right back into the arms of Sergeant Cuttler, who will now be on the scene responding to the theft of a Ford Cortina.

Common decency is telling me to go back and get Ben, but the tail lights of a car are now in sight up ahead. What's the worst that can happen to him anyway? Death by turtleneck strangulation and waking up again in his warm bed. I can think of a lot of worse things. Despite my earlier desire to put things right, I put Ben out of my mind and concentrate on the lights ahead.

Ten minutes outside of Tyevale we reach the turn-off sign to Colevale, but Eddie's car keeps going and after another five minutes of driving it slows down and takes a right turn onto an unlit dirt track. Reluctantly, I turn off my headlights so that they don't realize I am following them, and I precariously navigate the track using Eddie's tail lights as a guide.

It seems that Eddie is familiar with where he is going and so I assume that we must be going to his farm.

Shortly afterwards, my suspicion is confirmed when I pass a handmade sign for Meadow Farm and the lights of a farmhouse come into view a short distance ahead. I can't risk following them into the farmyard, so I stop the car on the track and move towards the house on foot.

Just in front of the house there is a drystone wall and I crouch down behind it. All four of them are standing next to Eddie's car and once again the girls are berating Eddie and Father Beale.

"What are you afraid of, Eddie? Are you afraid that there might be ghosts or witches? So, what if there are? That's what we have James for. He can throw his holy water at them, isn't that right, Father?"

"I think this has gone too far, Lucy," Father James replies. "Please take me home, Eddie. You have my word that I won't say anything about what happened tonight."

From my hiding place, I can't see, but from Joanna's reaction, Eddie must have agreed with Father James.

"Don't you dare move, Eddie Wells. Both of you are coming with us, or I swear to God, we are going to the police and the bishop. Don't think we're bluffing either. We will tell them everything. About how you assaulted Lucy, Eddie, and about how you have been sleeping with her, James. Eddie go and get a lantern."

I can hear a key turning in a lock and the creak of a door as it opens. Less than a minute later, the area in front of the house and the top of the wall is bathed in a warm orange glow. The four of them move away from the house and as the light starts to fade I hop over the wall and follow them into a wooded area at the edge of one of the farm fields.

The trees are densely packed, but the lantern is bright, and the girls are laughing as they walk, so it is easy to follow them.

Around two hundred feet further on, the woods open into a clearing and one of the girls tells Eddie to light a fire. Through a gap in the trees I watch as Eddie lights a rolled-up newspaper with a match and pushes it into the bottom of a pile of tree branches and wood that was clearly prepared earlier. Within minutes the fire is burning brightly, and the girls waste no time in taunting Eddie again.

"Go on, Eddie, show us how you raise the dead."

"Yes, go on, Eddie. Is it true that your mother was a witch? Go on, do the dance. Go on, Eddie, dance around the fire for us."

Lucy moves closer to Eddie and raises her hand to poke him in the shoulder, but Father James steps in between them and grabs her wrist.

"That's enough, Lucy. This has gone too far. Why are you behaving like this?"

Joanna leaps to the defense of her sister and pulls at Father James' shoulder. As he lets go of Lucy's wrist his elbow inadvertently strikes Joanna in the chest and she falls to the floor with the wind knocked out of her. Eddie is momentarily torn between his loyalty to Joanna and his confusion with why they are treating him so badly, until Joanna gets back to her feet and pushes him forward.

"What kind of man stands by and lets another man strike his girlfriend? Hit him, you bloody coward."

Eddie is a much bigger man and his fist sends Father Beale careering towards the fire. Lucy pulls him away from the danger, but Joanna is not satisfied and urges Eddie to carry on.

Lucy calls out for Eddie to stop and she also appeals to Joanna to intervene, but to no avail.

To protect him, Lucy steps in between Father Beale and Eddie, but spurred on by Joanna, Eddie is now wild eyed and has picked up a thick branch from the forest floor. Sensing the danger, Father Beale jumps aside, but it is too late for Lucy. The full force of the branch catches her in the throat, and she falls backwards into the fire.

The night air is filled with the agonizing screams of Lucy as she is writhes in the flames and Joanna screams desperately for someone to help her sister.

By now, the heat from the fire is so intense that Eddie and Father Beale are beaten back from each of their attempts to rescue her and they quickly realize the situation is hopeless. When Lucy's screams finally end, Joanna falls to her knees sobbing hysterically.

"This wasn't meant to happen. It wasn't meant to happen."

Father Beale tries to console her and asks what she means, but she stands and pushes him away. Her tears are gone and have been replaced with aggression and defiance.

"This was your fault, both of you. Both of you are going to go to prison if you don't do exactly as I say."

Eddie is completely silent and is probably in shock, but Father Beale has no intention of blindly following orders.

"You can't be serious, Joanna. Your sister is dead. We have to report this."

"You're right, my sister is dead," Joanna replies. "You killed her when she tried to stop seeing you. You lured her here and then you pushed her into the fire when she refused your advances. I saw it and so did Eddie."

The priest turns to Eddie for support, but when Eddie sees the way Joanna is looking at him, he nods and agrees with her.

"That's right, you killed her. We both saw you push her into the fire."

Realizing that it is his word against theirs his shoulders drop and, resigned to his fate, Father James reluctantly nods and asks what he should do.

"Go back to the house with Eddie and get some shovels. We need to get this mess cleaned up and get home before it gets light."

Father Beale turns towards the house and Joanna orders Eddie to follow him.

I am already running back through the woods before Joanna has finished speaking. There is no point in risking getting caught by staying around any longer. I know for sure now that Lucy is dead, I know how she died, and I have a good idea where she is going to be buried. All in all, it's been a good trip.

Out on the track, I retrieve the car and as soon as I am far enough away from the farmhouse, I turn the headlights on and increase my speed. It's getting on for three in the morning and my thoughts once more return to Ben. When I spoke with him earlier today, he told me that Sergeant Cuttler had left him alone in an interview room after around an hour of questioning. Assuming that he didn't wait for too long before hanging himself with the turtleneck, this should mean that he was long gone by now and that there is no need for me to go looking for him.

Pleased with how tonight has gone, I reach the main road and head back towards Tyevale to find a way home. Tomorrow, we are due to meet Father Beale at eleven in the morning, but now that I know the probable location of Lucy's body, Meadow Farm is going to be the first stop of the day.

The night is crisp and clear and with an empty road ahead, I reach the outskirts of Tyevale in less than ten minutes. Unsurprisingly the town and the carnival are both in near complete darkness, with the only light coming from the street lamps on the high street. Feeling guilty about stealing the Cortina earlier I pull up opposite the entrance to the carnival and shut off the engine. In the morning, it will be returned to its owner and he will be none the worse for the experience other than his car having a few extra miles on the clock and a little less gas in the tank.

With one last check of my pockets and a quick check on the seats to make sure that I haven't left anything behind, I turn to reach for the door handle at exactly the same moment as the driver's side door caves in and the window explodes in my face.

The force of the collision with the other car throws me almost fully across to the passenger side and before I have a chance to react, the driver's side door is pulled open and I'm dragged out by my jacket collar by at least two pairs of hands and a familiar voice speaks.

"Steady on, lads, we don't know if he is with the other one yet. He could just be a car thief."

Even though I am probably concussed and there is blood in my eyes, I can recognize the voice of Sergeant Cuttler. It seems like he is referring to Ben, but his words fall on deaf ears. I fall heavily to the ground and the hands on my collar are replaced by a shoe pressing down on my throat.

"I doubt that very much, Sergeant. These bastards always work in twos or threes. How many cars do you have stolen in this town anyway? Not so many I'm guessing. No, my guess is that this lad was coming back to pick his mate up."

Then looking down to me, he added, "Isn't that right, Paddy?"

Unable to answer with the foot on my throat, I am pulled to my feet and a handkerchief or something similar is wiped across my face to clear the blood out of my eyes. Along with Sergeant Cuttler, I am being held by two other men.

Both are stereotypical 1970s special branch and would not have been out of place in an episode of The Sweeney or The Professionals. Both have non-regulation hair and moustaches and even in the dark, the outline of their holsters is clear under their almost matching black leather jackets.

The taller of the two reaches forward to search me while the other keeps a firm hold on my jacket. Other than my watch and my wallet containing some cash, I literally just have the clothes I am wearing, so I am not overly worried until he pulls out my can of CS gas spray.

Immediately both officers draw their weapons and I am forced back down onto my knees with the shorter of the pair screaming in my face.

"What the hell is this? You had better start speaking, boy, or things are gonna go badly for you."

It's written on the side of the can so unless this pair are illiterate, there is no point in lying.

"It's CS gas. It's for self-defense," I reply.

The taller of the two guys slaps me in the face with his free hand and then kicks me in the side.

"Shut it, you lying bastard. This is what the boys in Ireland use against the paddies when they are rioting, Sarge."

When he spoke, he was referring to his colleague and not Sergeant Cuttler. So, now I know who is the more senior of the two.

The special branch sergeant examines the side of the can and then he leans over and holds it near my face.

"Is that where you got it? Did you take it off one of our colleagues in the Ulster Constabulary when you were throwing bricks and petrol bombs? What's your name, fella?"

Unbeknown to him, my interrogator has unintentionally presented me with an opportunity to make my escape. Before he can react and pull it away, I lunge for the can and pull the safety tab away from the trigger. Both special branch officers take a blast of liquid CS straight in the face, but Cuttler moves quicker than I would have expected for an old guy. He swings his baton into the back of my knees and my legs buckle beneath me.

As I fall, I turn and aim the can at Cuttler's face. Liquid CS burns like a bitch and he quickly drops his baton and retreats towards the town. Knowing that I only have seconds before the special branch boys can function again, I struggle to my feet and run towards the carnival entrance.

I don't look back to my pursuers, but I can almost feel the sights of the revolvers trained on my back. When the first bullet hits me in the shoulder, I am stunned but not surprised. The impact slows me down, but I keep running. When the second and third rounds hit me in my lower and upper back, I am already where I need to be.

The wolfhound has signaled my arrival, but by the time my pursuers arrive, or the O'Hanlons wake up to investigate the noise, all they will find is the trail of blood leading up to the gap between the caravans where I will already have died in the shadows.

# Present Day – Friday, 20th April, 2018

It's only just after six in the morning, but I have already been awake for more than an hour. Last night was a real breakthrough and, conscious of how much we need to do today, I call Cath to wake her up. With no reply from her cell phone, I use the handset by my bed to call room to room. The call connects and after two rings a grumpy-sounding Cath picks up.

"This had better be good. Who is this please?"

"Get your ass out of bed, DC Swain, we're going for a walk in the countryside. Jump in the shower and meet me downstairs at seven."

"What? Sorry, hang on, Sean. What are you talking about and what's the time now?"

"It's six-twenty," I reply. "I'll explain everything when I see you but bring the land registry documents for Eddie Well's farm. You do have them, don't you?"

There is a short pause and then she confirms that she does.

"Um, yes, I do. I downloaded copies when I was in Spalding."

"Great, I'll see you at seven."

Before she has a chance to say anything else, I end the call and finish getting dressed. My plan today is to scout out possible locations for Lucy's burial site and then to call DCI Morgan to ask for permission to initiate a search with ground-penetrating radar. I'm certain that she will be buried somewhere near to the woods where she died, and I won't be at all surprised if it's within the piece of land that Eddie kept hold of when he sold the rest of the farm.

Morgan will want more than just a hunch, though, before he approves an expensive search. My dream travel is not going to cut it, but if I can get Father Beale to talk, then that might just be enough.

This might be the leverage we need to bring Eddie and Joanna in for questioning. And if we find Joanna's remains on Eddie's land, it should in theory be game over.

Something about this case is still nagging away at me, though, and it has been since my first trip back to the night of Lucy's disappearance. On both trips, the behavior of Lucy and Joanna towards Eddie and then to Father James was both shocking and surprising.

But more than anything else, it has felt completely premeditated and almost as if the girls were play-acting. The behavior of both girls has been disgraceful, but it's also been inconsistent. At the carnival the sisters were almost as bad as each other. In the forest, however, it was Joanna that was encouraging Eddie to attack Father Beale and Lucy who tried to intervene to stop the fight. Without a doubt this whole thing stinks of premeditation, but not as far as the death of Lucy is concerned.

Lucy is dead, of course, but it did look genuinely to be an accident. Joanna said it herself 'This wasn't meant to happen', so the question remains, what was meant to happen? For me, this was a blackmail and extortion attempt that went too far in the wrong direction. It makes no difference, though; a young girl has been killed and it is my job to find the answers and to close the case. One way or another, today is going to be interesting.

Cath is waiting for me next to the car and even at such an early hour, I can't resist a sly smirk and a dig at what she is wearing.

"Nikes and a suit, Cath. Did I forget to tell you to bring your wellies?"

"It's either these, or you sign off an expense claim for a pair of Jimmy Choo's, boss. Somehow, I don't think Morgan will approve that though. How about you let me in on what we are doing?"

I point to the car.

"Like I said on the phone, we're going for a walk in the country. Come on, I'll explain on the way. Head out towards Colevale and I'll direct you from there."

Cath hands me the land registry documents and then sets a course towards Colevale.

"So, what's the big hurry, boss? Have you found something out?"

It's time to lie to my partner again. With a twinge of guilt, I reply with my prepared answer. "Just a working theory to be honest. I was looking through my notes last night and it was bugging me why Eddie would sell his farm and land so quickly, apart from just a small parcel. I'm interested to see where exactly it is and what it's being used for now."

"You think that's where she is buried, boss?" Catherine asks.

"Yes," I reply. "That thought had occurred to me. I can't think of any other logical reason why he might want to hold onto the land."

"So, you must also believe that he was involved in her disappearance or death in some way?"

"Don't you?" I ask her.

"You could be right, boss. There's no doubt that Eddie and the PBs are hiding something."

Catherine points to the documents on my lap. "Take a look on the second sheet – the area that he kept hold of is highlighted in red on the plans. It looks like it's close to where the farmhouse was, but it seems to be mostly woodland or forest. I can't see it being used for crops or livestock."

I turn over the second sheet of paper and my heart starts to race. The outlined area includes exactly the spot where I saw Lucy die in the fire. The entire area covers almost three hectares, but almost the entirety of what I saw last night was densely wooded. The burial site must be somewhere in the clearing. It was nearly three in the morning when Lucy died, and Joanna was panicking about getting home before daylight. The clearing is the only logical place where she could be. We pass Colevale and I fold up the registry documents and tuck them into my jacket pocket.

"Just slow down a bit, Cath. There should be a turn, just up here on the right."

Cath looks at me with a questioning look on her face and I tell her that the turn is marked on the plans.

"I didn't see that, but I'll take your word for it, Sean. I never was very good with maps and plans, but then why would I be? I'm only a woman after all. Now if it was a knitting pattern, well don't even get me started on those."

I ignore the obvious sarcasm and point out the turn, but Cath has already seen it. It is clearly marked with a freshly painted sign pointing the way to 'Meadow Farm Guest House'.

When we reach the farmhouse, we could almost be in a different place to the Meadow Farm I remember from 1972.

The new owners have clearly spent a lot of money in extending and renovating the original building and it is now almost three times the size and has a small parking area and a well laid-out garden and patio to the front of the property. Three cars are parked up and there is a middle-aged guy smoking on the patio, but otherwise there is nobody else around.

We park the car next to the others and, instantly regretting my words, I point out the edge of the woods, which are clearly visible from the farmhouse.

"That must be it over there, Cath."

Her mock look of surprise means that coffee or no coffee, she is now wide awake and is about to punish me for stating the obvious.

"Really, boss? Are you sure about that? I mean, it does look like a wooded area, but what if it's just an overgrown field?"

"Yeh, I guess I deserved that, Cath. Sorry for being a patronizing dick sometimes."

"That's alright, Sean," she replies, before adding, "I would worry if you weren't being a dick at least once a day. I'll forgive you, though, if you tell me that you brought bolt-cutters."

"Bolt-cutters?" I ask. "What for?"

Cath points out the edge of the tree line and the fence that wasn't there in 1972. The chain link is so badly rusted that it is almost camouflaged against the backdrop of thickly clustered trees.

"So, what do you think that's for? To keep something in or to keep nosey coppers out?"

"Whatever it's for, boss, there had better be a gate or a hole in the fence somewhere. This suit is not bloody cheap and there is no way I am going to rip a hole in it climbing over a rusty fence."

I make a sarcastic show of checking my pockets for a set of bolt-cutters before shrugging my shoulders and frowning.

"Looks like you're shit out of luck, Cath. Don't worry, though, I'll give you a boost over. Come on, we have work to do."

We set off towards the woods and the guy smoking on the patio politely nods and then goes inside after smiling at Cath's odd pairing of a suit and running shoes. A minute later, we reach the fence. If there is a gate, then it's certainly not on this side of the woods. I send Catherine to check left for the gate or an opening and I tell her that I will be checking on the right.

As soon as she is out of sight, I move close in against the fence at the point where I think we entered the woods last night. Behind, it is heavily overgrown, but I can make out the faint outline of a path. More than forty years of rain and snow have left the chain link heavily corroded and with the help of my extendable baton, I am easily able to break away a large enough section for us to get through. I call out to Cath to come back to me and a couple of minutes later she reappears, and I point out the hole and gesture for her to go through first.

"I decided to make my own gate, Cath. It looks like there was once a path here. Let's see where it takes us."

Cath climbs through the hole and I follow behind her. Although it is almost fully daylight, the density of the trees means that the further we progress the darker it gets, and I curse myself for not bringing a flashlight. Cath offers to go back to the car to get one, but it will be lighter in the clearing and I tell her to keep going.

"Let's just go a bit further. It seems to be a bit lighter up ahead."

A minute later we are just about to step out into the clearing when we are both startled by a huge flock of birds that had been nesting in the trees above us.

As they take to the sky, we both jump back and then laugh together when we realize how foolish we both look.

"Bloody hell, Cath! That scared the fuck out of me. Not a word back at the office. I have a reputation to keep."

"That's fine by me," she replies. "I think I might have peed my pants just a bit. This place is creepy as fuck. It's no wonder they put a fence around it. Mind you, nobody in their right mind would come in here willingly."

We step out into the clearing and I ask her what she thinks.

"This looks as likely a place as any to hide a body, boss. It's surrounded by trees on all sides and with that fence around the perimeter, I doubt anyone has been here in years. She must be here. Why else would he keep this piece of land and do nothing with it?"

This is definitely the place where Lucy died. Any sign of the fire has long gone and like everywhere else it is heavily overgrown, but this is the only reasonably open space on this side of the forest. I tell Cath to look for any obvious signs of a disturbance in the ground or anything else that doesn't look right.

"Even after more than forty years, if there is a body buried here, then the ground might not be quite the same as the area around it. If we can find something that's not quite right, then we might be able to convince Morgan to authorize a detailed search."

We have been searching for around five minutes, when Catherine calls me to join her. She has scraped back a patch of brambles to expose the ground below and I can see instantly that it is different from the area around it. The ground here has subsided slightly, which is a classic indication of a chamber or a disturbance deeper below. I kneel down for a closer look but am startled again by the same flock of birds taking off again from the treetops.

By the time I am back on my feet, Catherine has already extended her baton and is pointing towards the trees.

"There's somebody in their boss. I only saw them briefly as I turned, but there's definitely somebody there."

I ask Catherine to stay where she is and then I move towards the trees. As I get closer, the outline of a body becomes clearer in the shadows and I shout for the person to show themselves. When I get no response, I move to within ten feet of the watcher. They are holding something in both hands. By the time I realize what it is, it is already too late and what happens next takes me completely by surprise.

From my left, a voice shouts a warning and a figure appears in my peripheral vision and pushes me away from the danger. At the same time there is a blinding flash of light and a deafening explosion as the firing pin strikes the percussion cap in the shotgun cartridge.

As the muzzle smoke clears, I can hear my attacker retreating through the forest at speed, but Cath pulls me back when I try to follow.

"Sean, no. That was only one barrel and you're not armed." Then pointing towards the ground. "Come on, help me with him."

My guardian angel is lying face down in the thick grass. His shoulder has taken the full force of the shotgun blast. Reassuringly, though, he is making enough noise to let us know he is still alive. Catherine reaches down to turn him over, but his hoodie is easily recognizable to me. Ben's face is ashen, and his breathing is coming in short gasps.

Catherine also recognizes him and doesn't hold back her feelings.

"You've got some bloody explaining to do, Sean. I hope to God that you haven't got this boy involved in one of our investigations. What in God's name were you thinking?"

Seeing Ben like this has badly shaken me and Cath takes charge. She places Ben into the recovery position and then orders me to take his hand.

"Get some pressure on that wound and talk to him, Sean. Don't let him close his eyes or go into shock. Keep him talking while I call this in and get help."

Catherine turns away and runs back through the forest to raise the alarm. Ben is still conscious but has lost a lot of blood and is struggling to stay awake. My mind is racing with a million thoughts. About who just tried to kill me, about how to explain why Ben is here to Cath and Morgan, and about what I would say to Maria if Ben died. The last thought is unimaginable, and I focus my attention back on Ben.

"Hang in there, mate. It won't be much longer. I promise you, son, help is on the way."

His breathing now is heavily labored, but he squeezes my hand to indicate that he can hear me and then he tries to speak.

His voice is low, and I tell him to keep quiet and save his energy, but he is determined to tell me something and pulls me closer.

"What is it, Ben? I can't hear you properly. Did you see who it was?"

He squeezes my hand again and then takes a deep breath.

"A priest, it looked like a priest. He was wearing a hat, but I could see the white of the dog collar."

In the distance, I can hear approaching sirens and Cath returns with the middle-aged man we had seen smoking earlier.

"Boss, this is Mr. Peter Jackson. He's the owner of Manor Farm Guest House. He thinks he might have seen the shooter."

I nod my acknowledgment to Cath and then turn back to Ben again.

"Ben, this is really important. Are you sure it was a priest? Did you actually see him?"

He is now barely conscious, but with the last of his energy he nods his head. I am about to ask where the help is when my question is answered. Two teams of paramedics accompanied by an armed response team enter the clearing. I leave Catherine to brief our colleagues while I follow the paramedics and watch as they load Ben into an ambulance. Shortly after, Catherine rejoins me and introduces me again to Peter Jackson.

"Mr. Jackson, would you please tell my colleague what you just told me?"

He looks a little nervous, but Cath reassures him.

"Just tell us what you saw, Mr. Jackson."

"Well, I was inside when I heard the noise. I knew it was a shotgun – you get used to that sound in the countryside. I came outside for a look and the first thing I saw was a fella climbing through the hole in the fence."

"Did you get a good look at him?" I ask.

"Not really, no. It's a good distance and I didn't have my glasses on. I'm sorry about that."

"That's okay, Mr. Jackson. Did you see where he went?"

"He ran off towards the north side of the woods and then I heard the sound of an engine. Not a car, though, more like a motorbike or a quadbike."

I look at Cath, but she is way ahead of me and confirms that she has already given this information to the armed response team.

"They are also trying to get a chopper up to see if they can locate our suspect."

I thank Mr. Jackson for his help and then tell him to go back and wait in his guest house.

"Please wait there until our colleagues get to you for a full statement. Thanks again – you've been very helpful."

Once he is out of earshot, Cath asks me if I am okay.

"You look like you've seen a ghost, Sean."

"I'm fine, Cath. We need to get moving," I reply. "If it was the priest, we need to get to Beckhampton before he can cover his tracks."

I turn to leave, but Cath stops me.

"Hang on, boss, we can't just leave. The uniform boys will need to speak to us, and you need to call Morgan to explain what has just happened. Before you call it in, though, how about you tell me what has just happened? What was Ben Pinto doing here, Sean?"

"I really don't know, Cath. That's the truth. While I was in hospital, he came to see me a few times and told me that he was interested in joining the force. He asked whether I might give him some advice from time to time, but that's as far as it went. I have no idea what he was doing here or how he knew where we would be."

Normally, Cath can read me like a book, but now she looks unsure of herself.

"If I find out that you're lying to me again, Sean, then this is the end for us as partners. You had better just hope Ben pulls through and that he backs up your story. You need to call DCI Morgan now to let him know what has happened. And what about Ben's mother? I can call her while you speak with Morgan. This news is surely better coming from me, than from a total stranger."

I agree to her suggestion and then I call DCI Morgan. It's only just after eight in the morning, but Kevin Morgan is an early starter and will already be in the office. After two rings, the call is picked up and Morgan's radar is immediately alerted to something urgent.

"DS McMillan, I take it by the early hour, that this isn't a social call, or the case update I asked you for yesterday?"

Over the next ten minutes I take him through everything that has happened since our arrival in Tyevale. He doesn't interrupt, even when I tell him about Ben, but I know that he will be writing everything down. When I finish, he is unusually calm. He first asks about Ben's condition and then he asks me what I want to do next.

"We will talk more about Benjamin Pinto when you are back in London, Sean. But for now, and from what you have just told me, it does certainly appear that the Partington-Brown family and Father Beale are our main suspects in the disappearance of Lucy and in this morning's incident. How do you want to play this? My advice would be to get the priest into custody as soon as possible and apply the pressure. Your witness is more than enough to justify reasonable cause and if he cracks, then you can go after the others. Until then, you need to tread lightly with the Partington-Browns, or we will have the Home Secretary all over us."

I thank him for his support and then I ask for a search team with ground-penetrating radar to search the clearing.

"If you could give approval for that, sir. I'm convinced that this is where we will find her body. In parallel, my plan is to move to pick up Father Beale before he can disappear or dispose of any potential evidence."

Morgan agrees to both of my suggestions, but only on the basis that we have armed back up.

"We nearly lost both of you once before, son. Don't go playing the hero – that's what those lads get the extra allowance for. Call me as soon as you have him in custody."

I thank him again and the call ends. Catherine has been listening in and nods towards the woods.

"Local plod has taken over the crime scene and the scene of crimes officer is on the way. Shall I let the senior officer know what is happening and brief the firearms team?"

Cath looks to me for my approval and I nod. She walks towards the forest, but I call her back.

"Did you speak to her? Did you speak to Maria? How did she take it?"

"She took it like any parent would. She was distraught. I did my best to reassure her, but how would you react if it was your son that had just been blasted with a shotgun?"

I would react exactly as I had when I saw his face. I froze, which is totally out of character. Catherine must surely be wondering what the connection is. She doesn't ask, though. The question will come sooner or later.

"And how was it left?" I ask.

"It wasn't left any way, boss," Cath replies. "But I would imagine that she is probably already on her way to Spalding, so I suggest you think carefully about what you are going to tell her. She is going to want answers and she is not the only one."

Without another word Catherine walks away and leaves me alone with my thoughts. I walk to the car and it is only when I get in to start the engine that I realize how badly my hands are shaking. There is no way that I can drive like this, so I get out and climb into the passenger side.

Shortly after, Cath emerges from the forest with four armed-response officers. Two of them join us in our car and the other two, climb into an unmarked saloon. I am introduced to the team leader, Sergeant David Manners. As Cath drives, I give him a potted version of the case and what we know about Father Beale.

The information is relayed to his colleagues in the vehicle behind and at just after nine-thirty in the morning we pull up and park about fifty feet from the entrance to Beckhampton Church.

"Okay, DS McMillan, DC Swain, my colleagues and I will lead. You both need to remain at least twenty feet behind us at all times and if I ask you to stay put, you stay put. Is that clear?"

I confirm it is and Sergeant Manners smiles.

"Great, let's go and catch a bad guy. Follow me."

The armed response guys separate into pairs either side of the road. Catherine and I tuck in behind Manners and his partner and after a suitable interval we follow them towards the entrance to the churchyard. Apart from a bus at the far end of the street, it is completely deserted. I watch as an elderly woman gets on and the bus drives away. When we are within twenty feet of the churchyard gate, the front door of a house on our side of the road opens and a young woman pushing a Baby Buggy steps outside. The shock of seeing four heavily armed police officers in this quiet residential street startles her and Catherine gently ushers her back inside.

We continue on and, once inside the churchyard, Sergeant Manners directs Cath and me to take up position behind an elaborate granite mausoleum.

"I need you both to wait here. Turn your radios to channel twelve so that you can listen in to our throat mics."

We confirm the radios are working and a few seconds later, Manners orders his men towards the church. Soon they disappear out of sight, but the running commentary from Manners is clear.

"Armed police! Show yourself! You have ten seconds to comply or we are coming in."

There is a brief pause and then the instruction is repeated. When there is still no response the team prepare to move in.

"Team one, prepare to move. Team two, hold and cover."

We can hear clearly as Manners and his partner move into the church and call out to Father Beale to show himself. The search of the church goes on for more than five minutes, before Manners finally gives the all clear.

"Church is clear, moving to the vicarage. Team two lead. Team one will cover."

The vicarage is within sight of our hiding place and we watch as the two teams move into position. Sergeant Manners' orders the second team forward and after they get no response to the mandatory challenges, the door of the vicarage is forced open and they move in.

Seconds later, the radio bursts into life and the leader of team two comes online.

"Suspect located, I repeat, suspect located. Urgent medical response requested. Sarge, you need to get yourself in here."

Manners and his partner are already up and running. We also break cover and run towards the vicarage door but are waved back by Manners' partner.

"Stand down, DS McMillan, you need to wait for the boss to give the all clear."

Reluctantly, we are forced to wait outside while the armed response teams work inside. After an uncomfortable few seconds of silence, Catherine is the first to speak.

"I bloody hope you are right about Lucy's body, Sean. The pin is now well and truly pulled on that grenade we were talking about a couple of days ago and I have an awful feeling that we're not going to be getting any answers from Father Beale. We need to find that body."

Before I can respond, Sergeant Manners appears in the shattered doorway and calls us forward.

"I'll warn you now, it's not pretty. It's definitely our man, though. There is a shotgun on the floor and there is an off-road motorbike at the back of the church. The engine is still warm. A few minutes earlier and we could have probably intercepted him."

Manners ushers us into the study and my nostrils are instantly filled with the smell of fresh blood. The body is slumped backwards over a chair and there is a shotgun lying at its feet. But for the fact that I can see the blood-soaked dog collar, it would not be immediately obvious who I was looking at. The blast of a shotgun at such close range is devastating and the top and back of his head is almost entirely missing.

Catherine has her hand over her mouth and looks like she might throw up. I pull her away and Manners follows us outside. While we have been inside, back up has arrived and have started to cordon off the church.

Word has quickly got around about the police presence and a small crowd has gathered at the gate.

I ask Sergeant Manners about the motorbike and he points towards its location.

"We haven't secured that area yet, so please maintain forensic discipline. There is another team on the way to fully secure the location and the body."

The color has returned to Cath's cheeks and we move away to find the bike, which is lying on its side at the back of the church. The wheels are covered in fresh mud and as I lean in for a closer look, I can feel the heat still emanating from the engine and the exhaust.

"This has been ridden hard, Cath. He probably had around thirty minutes start on us, but even so, that is a hard ride across country. This is total bullshit!"

"That's why we're the detectives, boss. Manners and his guys just see what's in front of them. Is anyone seriously expecting us to believe that a seventy-five-year-old priest tracked us to those woods, took a pop at you with a shotgun and then hopped onto his dirt-bike for a cross country ride, before calmly sitting down and blasting his own brains out? This must be Joanna and Eddie. They are the only ones left alive that stand to gain from his death. We have to pull them in before this goes any further, Sean."

Cath's theory mirrors my own exactly, but we still don't have anywhere near enough to pull them in or hold them.

"You might be right, Cath, but any half-decent brief would have them out within hours. Your point about the motorbike would apply equally to Joanna and Eddie. There has to be somebody else involved."

"So, what then? We just wait around until someone else gets killed? We have one person dead and one seriously injured and it's still only ten in the morning, Sean. We have to do something."

Catherine is visibly upset, and I let her finish ranting before I speak.

"We are going to do something, Cath. We are going to find out who did this, and we are going to put them away. That's what we do, Cath. We put away the bad guys that think they have gotten away with their crimes. It's been a bad day so far and it's only going to get worse if we let it. Are you with me?"

She wipes her eyes and composes herself.

"Sorry, boss, seeing him like that was just a bit of a shock. What's our next move?"

"Don't apologize, Cath. That's not something that you can ever get used to seeing and I was hardly the model of composure myself when I saw Ben. The important thing is to focus now on the job at hand. Whether this is the PBs or someone else entirely, we have spooked them, and this is when they will be at their most dangerous. I'm going to call this in to Kevin Morgan. I need you to pull the footage from any traffic cameras in the area and find out who owns the bike. We need to know who was riding it."

Pleased to have something to focus on again, Cath regains her usual composure and leaves me to deliver the bad news to DCI Morgan.

After two unsuccessful attempts to call him, I send a message asking him to call me back urgently. Two minutes later my phone rings and his number appears on the screen.

"Sorry, Sean, I was on the other line to the Chief Constable of Lincolnshire. I was explaining to him why a young boy was shot in the back on his patch this morning. He's calm enough for now, but please tell me you have the shooter in custody."

"Actually, sir, things just got a whole lot worse. The priest is dead."

There is a short but noticeable pause before Morgan replies.

"Christ almighty, son! Please tell me it wasn't our boys that killed him? What the hell is going on up there?"

"He was already dead when we got here, sir," I reply. "The armed response boys have assumed that it was a suicide after this morning's attack. That's rubbish, though."

Morgan listens as I explain about the dirt-bike, the assumed cross-country ride and the shotgun.

"It just doesn't stack up, sir. We were due to meet with Father Beale today, but other than DC Swain arranging the meeting, he had no other information on the case or our likely whereabouts today."

"You're right, Sean, this completely stinks and your theory about Edward Wells and Joanna being the only ones that could possibly benefit from his death makes sense. Are they the only remaining original suspects?"

"Just Eddie, Joanna and Sir David himself – but wasn't it him that requested the case to be reopened?"

"Yes, you're right. What about the other boy, the one that went missing? Paul something. What was his name?"

"You mean Paul Oliver, sir. There has been no trace of him for more than forty years. Unlikely that he would have reason to show up to cover his tracks after all this time."

I of course know already who killed Lucy and it wasn't Paul Oliver. I still need to play the game, though, with Catherine and DCI Morgan. I need the body if I am to have any hope of turning Eddie.

"I think Paul Oliver is a dead-end, sir. If we can find Lucy's body or find out who killed the priest, we might have a fighting chance of closing this case. DC Swain is checking the traffic cams to see what they have picked up. Is there any update on the search team?"

Morgan asks me to wait and I can hear him talking on his office phone. Less than thirty seconds later he confirms that the team has been approved.

"They should be on location by 2 pm today. I hope to God that you are right about the body being there. The Home Secretary has been chasing me for some good news. After this morning, we need a major victory. Do you need any more bodies on the ground? I can spare DC Walker for a few days if you need him, just say the word."

The last thing I need is for another copper to babysit, so I politely decline and after promising to call him back as soon as there are any new developments, I hang up and make my way back to the car to meet Catherine.

Her notebook is resting on the roof of the car and she is listening to her phone and making notes. The dirt-bike registration is written at the top of the open page and the word 'stolen' has been underlined. When Cath finishes her call I already know what is coming.

"It's a dead end on the bike, unfortunately. The owner reported it missing from an address in Spalding yesterday evening. Local PD have confirmed that the owner was at work when it was taken."

"What about the traffic cameras?" I ask her. "Did they pick up the bike leaving or coming back to the church?"

"The server for Beckhampton is in Spalding, boss. I've already put in a call, but it might be worth us heading there to shake them up a bit."

I check my watch, which is showing just after ten-thirty and then I ask Catherine if she would mind driving again.

"Spalding, boss?"

"Yep, you can drop me off at Spalding General Hospital. I need to check on Ben and speak to Maria, if she is already there. While I'm there you can check out those traffic cameras."

As we drive, I update Cath on my last call to DCI Morgan.

"You were right about the urgency of finding Lucy's body, Cath. In addition to the Home Secretary, Morgan also now has the Chief Constable of Lincolnshire on his case. We need a result and fast."

Cath nods her agreement and then outlines her own theory to me.

"While I was waiting for the information on the dirt-bike, I was giving some thought to everything that has happened today and your comment about Eddie and Joanna being the only ones with anything to gain from the death of the priest. We both know that he didn't kill himself and it is unlikely that it was him that took a potshot at you in the forest."

"Okay, go on, Cath. Where are you going with this?" I ask her.

"It has to be Eddie and Joanna. Despite her age, Joanna is as smart as they come and, apart from them, Father Beale was the only other living original suspect, if we exclude Paul Oliver that is. The first time we met Joanna, she made it very clear that she was unhappy with her father's decision to re-open the case. They might both be pensioners, but I wouldn't be at all surprised if they setup the whole scenario to make it look like Father Beale was trying to cover his own tracks. It was never going to work, and we were never going to believe it, but people do desperate things when they think that they are cornered."

"So, let's call their bluff, Cath."

"What do you mean?" she asks me.

"We were meant to be visiting them at two this afternoon. After you drop me off, give them a call. Tell them that there has been a significant development in the case and that we won't be needing to speak to them after all. Let them relax a bit."

Cath smiles at my suggestion and for the rest of the journey we discuss the possibility of the search team locating Lucy's body. I'm certain that they will find it in the clearing, but I dampen my enthusiasm to stop Cath getting too suspicious.

"If Eddie and Joanna are involved, then it's the logical place to search. We won't know, though, until the team start the search.

"Okay, Cath, it looks like the hospital entrance is just up here on the right. You can drop me here. I'll walk the rest of the way. I need to get some fresh air before I face Maria."

Cath wishes me luck and as she drives away, I take a deep breath before walking the last fifty feet to the car-park entrance. Spalding General Hospital is a grand-looking four-story granite building dating back to the late Victorian period. After another pause to gather my thoughts, I cross the car park and head into the main reception.

A young nurse with a tattoo of a dolphin visible on her neck directs me towards the Intensive Care Unit located on the second floor. If Maria left home as soon as Cath spoke to her this morning, then it is feasible that she will be here already and, as I step out of the lift, I am more nervous of seeing Maria than I was about seeing the Anti-corruption boys.

Like all hospitals, the smell of antiseptic is heavy in the air, but in the ICU corridor the smell is almost overpowering. Maria is at the end of the corridor with two uniformed police officers looking through a window into one of the isolation rooms.

When she sees me approaching, she immediately bursts into tears and I instinctively pull her close and try to reassure her.

"He's going to be fine, Maria. The wound looked a lot worse than it was. He's a tough young man."

At my mention of the wound, one of the police officers asks me to identify myself.

"And who would you be, sir?"

I show him my badge and then I ask him to give me some time alone with Maria.

"We'll just be at the end of the corridor," he replies. "Let us know if you need anything, Sergeant."

They both move away, and I take Maria towards the window. Ben is sedated and there is a nurse monitoring a blood transfusion drip in his arm. I ask Maria if a doctor has spoken with her yet.

"He just left, Sean. He spoke to me just before you got here. They managed to get most of the pellets out of his shoulder and back. He came out of surgery around an hour ago, but they want to keep him under for a while longer and get some more blood into him."

"But he is going to be okay?" I ask her.

"Yes, the doctor is confident that he will make a full recovery."

As she says this, Maria breaks down again and then asks me what Ben was doing in Lincolnshire.

"I don't understand, Sean. What was he doing here and how did he know where you and Catherine were going to be?"

I tell her exactly what I told Catherine, but she is not convinced and presses the issue.

"He worships you, Sean. It's all I can do to shut him up about you. Did you know that he is thinking about dropping out of university and joining the police?"

I had no idea about that, and my look answers the question.

"Well he is. He's been talking about that since you helped us. Please tell me that you had nothing to do with him being here and that you haven't been encouraging him to drop out of his journalism course?"

Seeing my son in an intensive care bed and seeing his mother pleading for the truth sends my guilt levels racing towards maximum. I had tried to stop Ben following me, but I should have tried harder. The situation could have been a lot worse and we could be standing in a mortuary now instead of a hospital. But mortuary or not, it is my fault. I swear to her that I had nothing to do with Ben being here and I also promise to convince him to stick with journalism.

"I have to go now, Maria. But please call if you need anything. I promise, as soon as this is over I will come and see you both."

"Okay, thank you, Sean. When Ben wakes up, I will let him know that you were here. It will mean a lot to him."

I can't leave the hospital quickly enough and as soon as I am outside I take off my jacket and suck in the fresh air. My shirt is soaked in perspiration, and I feel a cold shudder run through my body when I picture my son lying on the ground bleeding.

A few days ago, this case was purely professional, but now it is most definitely personal. Eddie Wells and Joanna Partington-Brown are firmly in my sights, but we need to find the body if we are going to have any hope of getting them to talk. I call Cath and ask her to pick me up as soon as she is done with the traffic cams.

When she does finally arrive, and I join her in the car, her face is giving nothing away and quite rightly she asks me about Ben and Maria before telling me what she has found out.

I quickly take her through my update and assure her that Ben will be fine and then I press her for her own news.

"Do you want the good news or the bad news first, boss?"

"Go on, start with the bad news," I reply.

"Okay, well there are eight traffic cameras that cover the roads around the church. The guys in the control center checked them all. They went back as far as five in the morning and right up to when we arrived on the scene. That motorbike never went in or out of the church during that time."

I had been banking on getting something from the cameras and with this disappointment I struggle to contain my frustration.

"Shit! So, we have nothing. That bike didn't just get in and out on a bloody magic carpet, Cath. Call the center and get them to check again. Tell them to widen the search if necessary. We need to know who was riding that bike."

Just like I did with her this morning, Cath wisely lets me finish my rant before speaking again.

"I think we are going to be wasting our time, boss. I got a call from one of the forensics boys on my way back here. This was the good news I was referring to. Well, not so much good news, but news that backs up our own thoughts that it wasn't a suicide."

"What are you talking about, Cath?"

"I'm saying, we were right that he didn't kill himself. It wasn't the shotgun that killed him either. Forensics have a theory that he was already dead before the gun went in his mouth. As we know, most of the back of his head was taken off by the force of the blast, but they have identified an area of bruising at the base of his skull that is consistent with a blunt force trauma sufficient to kill. They think possibly that it could have come from a shovel or a steel pipe."

"So, someone bashed his head in and then staged the suicide. What about the bike, though? The engine was still warm. It had to have come from somewhere."

Cath refers to her notebook and then gives me another shocker.

"Yep, that I haven't figured out yet. It's particularly puzzling when you consider that our priest had been dead for at least six hours by the time we got to him. The bike had to have been here all the time."

"What?" I exclaim. "That would put the time of death at around 3:30 am. We hadn't even got to the forest at that stage. Christ, Cath, are you as confused as I am?"

She nods her head and laughs.

"Yes, the only thing I am sure of now is that the priest was murdered and that our posh friends were somehow involved. After that I have no idea. Where do we go from here, boss?"

"Back to Tyevale," I reply. "I need you to get back out to Meadow Farm and meet the search team.

See if you can get a room in the guest house for the night so that you can freshen up and get something to eat. It might be a long search."

"And what about you, boss?"

"Me, Cath? I'm going to have a bit of a poke around at Colevale to see what I can turn up. I want to see if I can find out anything more about the death of Joanna's mother."

Cath looks concerned and asks me if it's wise to go back to Colevale before we have some concrete evidence.

"I called them to let them know that we wouldn't need to see them today and Joanna seemed to be genuinely relieved. Why risk alerting her to the fact that we are on to them again?"

She is right to be concerned, but I have no intention of going to Colevale 2018. I promise to be careful and because she has been doing all the driving so far, I offer to drive, and she gladly swaps seats with me.

We separate in the hotel reception and while Cath heads to her room to pick up some fresh clothes for an overnight stay in the guest house, I head out to the high street to find an off-licence. Ten minutes later, I return to the hotel with a liter of Jameson Whisky and I'm pleased to see that Cath's car has already gone.


Back in my room, I pour myself a large whisky and then I search online for pictures of Colevale Manor in the 1970s. Travelling in the afternoon with Catherine less than fifteen minutes away is high risk, but after everything that has happened today, it is clear that Joanna and Eddie will do whatever it takes to keep us off their scent.

I know with one hundred percent certainty that they were involved in the death of Lucy and that in all probability they killed

Father Beale, but we still don't have any evidence that would justify pulling them in for questioning.

I'm confident that the search team will locate Lucy's body on Eddie's land. If so, this will give us enough grounds to bring Eddie in for questioning. But I am also determined to find out what happened to Beatrice Partington-Brown. Her unexplained illness just doesn't fly with me and with Cath busy at the search site, this is the ideal opportunity for me to have a dig around.

At just after four, I change into my seventies suit and shoes and with over a quarter of the whisky gone, I take a last look at the pictures of Colevale Manor on my phone and then lie down on my bed to chant my way back to January of 1974.

# The Past – Saturday, 12<sup>th</sup> January, 1974

I'm surrounded by dense woodland and for a few moments I think that I may have made a mistake and taken myself back to Meadow Farm. As I turn, though, I am relieved to see the Manor House standing proud through a gap in the trees. The sun is shining, but the frost underfoot and my icy breath reminds me that this is the middle of winter. With hindsight, an overcoat would have been a good idea and as a gust of icy wind sends a shiver down my spine, I turn up the collar on my jacket to keep out the chill that is already creeping in around my neck.

It's just after eleven in the morning and from the edge of the woods, I patiently watch the comings and goings at the house and look for an opportunity to get inside. There is no sign of Joanna, Sir David, or Eddie, but over the course of twenty minutes, I do count at least seven others entering and leaving by the back door.

Three are middle-aged women and judging by their attire would appear to be domestic staff. Two young men are working in the stables and there is an elderly gentleman tending to the flowerbeds scattered around the property. The last person is dressed in tweeds, walking boots, and a deerstalker hat. If any further clues were needed, the shotgun confirms my suspicion that he is the estate gamekeeper. The last thing I need to be worrying about is a gun-toting gamekeeper, so I am greatly relieved that after collecting something from one of the women at the back door, he drives away in a canvas-covered open-backed Landrover.

Shortly after, another vehicle approaches the house and parks opposite the back door. The legend on the side of the Morris Minor delivery van proudly proclaims William J Tunstall, Purveyor of the Finest Fruit & Veg, Since 1898.

The driver is in his mid to late twenties and is wearing a flat cap and a light brown knee-length smock typical of greengrocers and removals men of the time.

His arrival at the back door is met with an unexpected level of enthusiasm by a young girl smartly dressed in a traditional maid's uniform. After checking behind her to confirm that they are alone, it soon becomes apparent that fruit and veg is the last thing on either of their minds.

After breaking away from a particularly passionate embrace, the young man throws his cap and smock into the back of his van and leads the girl quickly away in the direction of the stables.

Seizing the opportunity, I sprint across the lawn to retrieve the cap and smock from the van and with two boxes of assorted veg under my arms I brazenly stroll through the back door and ask the cook where I should put them. She is busy preparing a goose for the oven, but when she sees that I am not who she was expecting, she stops and wipes her hands on her apron.

"Where's Derek today?" she asks. "The last time he took a day off, they messed up the order."

I shrug my shoulders and tell her that Derek has the flu, but she is already distracted in checking the contents of the boxes.

"Okay, it looks like everything is there. Put them in the pantry at the back of the kitchen. Oh, and keep your sticky fingers to yourself, young man. I know exactly how many pies are on the tray in there. Don't think I don't know how you boys like to help yourself."

I push open the pantry door with my shoulder and place the boxes of veg onto a shelf next to a tray of freshly baked pies. Despite the delicious aroma filling the air, I resist temptation and leave without stuffing one in my pocket.

The cook has resumed plucking the fat goose and when I ask if she would mind me using the bathroom, she points towards the end of the hallway.

"The servants lavvy is at the end of the corridor on the right. Don't make a mess and don't touch anything."

The corridor barely looks any different now to how it does in 2018. Close to the front door, my eyes are drawn to a ceramic vase filled with fresh flowers sitting on a mahogany side table. For a second I picture this same vase smashing on the tiled floor as Eddie bumps into the table in his panic to hide from me and Catherine. Then, sure that I am not being watched, I turn left and silently make my way past the main living room towards the study.

The door to the study is open and another middle-aged woman has her back to me dusting the top of the fireplace. The rest of the ground floor of the house seems to be deserted, so I turn back towards the stairs to check the upper levels. As I reach the top stair, the peace and quiet is shattered by the raised voice of a woman. Just in time, I duck behind a grandfather clock as the door to one of the bedrooms flies open and Joanna storms out followed by Eddie.

"This is not bloody working, you stupid great lump. It's been nearly a year already. Why do I ever listen to you, Edward Wells?"

Joanna pauses until Eddie gets ahead of her and then shoves him in the back, nearly sending him tumbling headfirst down the stairs.

"Well, what are you waiting for? Get outside and get some more. I want this over with today. This has gone on long enough."

Eddie turns back to face Joanna and conscious that he might be able to see me, I squeeze myself further behind the clock. It's not me he is worried about, though. Whatever Joanna is referring to, he tells her that it's the wrong time of the year and that they don't have anymore. Joanna is having none of it and pokes him hard in the chest.

"Do I have to do everything myself around here? Jenkins is outside tending to the shrubs. I should have married him instead of a useless bloody farmer."

She grabs Eddie by his arm and pulls him down the stairs. Presumably they have gone to look for the gardener. Realizing that I probably only have a matter of minutes before they return and assuming I might find some answers in this bedroom, I step inside. The curtains are partially closed, but there is a lightly scented candle burning next to the bed.

Not for light, but in a miserable attempt to mask the scent of the dying woman lying in the bed.

I'm no doctor, but even I can see that she should be in hospital. Her face is gaunt and pale, her breathing is heavily labored, and her forehead is covered in a fine coating of perspiration. Even though I am standing right over her, and her eyes are slightly open, there is not even the slightest hint that she knows I am there.

On the side table, there are half a dozen pill bottles. The labels indicate that they are for the treatment, amongst other things, of depression, headaches, lethargy, and loss of appetite. These are hardly scientific diagnoses but what worries me the most is that despite carrying dates from as early as March 1973, the bottles appear to be almost completely full. If I am right and have arrived on the day of Beatrice's death it would seem that she has not been receiving her prescribed medication.

Next to the pill bottles, there is a water jug and a glass. The glass appears to be empty, but on closer inspection there is a small amount of residue at the bottom. I lift the glass to my nose and breathe in. There is a faint, but slightly unpleasant odor that I don't recognize. It crosses my mind, that Joanna might have been trying to treat her mother's condition with a plant-based remedy.

This would make perfect sense in the context of trying to find the gardener. Unfortunately, though, and knowing what I know about Joanna already, my suspicion is that far from treating her with a plant-based concoction, that same concoction has more likely been used to create the condition.

I move to the other side of the room to see what else I can find, but my search is interrupted by the sound of Eddie and Joanna returning. I conceal myself in a wardrobe, leaving one of the thick oak doors slightly ajar so that I can see the bed and hear what is being said. As soon as the bedroom door is closed Joanna verbally attacks Eddie once again, but with even more venom than before.

"You were meant to be keeping an eye on how much we had, you bloody idiot! I told you yesterday to check, or to pick some fresh leaves and seeds. What the hell are we supposed to do now?"

"I did tell you before that foxglove is a summer plant, dear. I told you tha ..."

Joanna strikes Eddie across the face and then pulls him towards her by the collar on his jacket.

"Don't you ever back chat me again, Edward. I asked you a question, what the hell are we supposed to do now?"

"Um, I could go to one of the garden centers tomorrow," Eddie nervously replies. "They might have a few plants still."

"Is that it, is that the best idea you have?" Joanna hisses. "Do you want her to wake up and tell the world what we have done? It's your fault that she's not dead yet. You told me that it would only take a few weeks for it to work. You have to do it now. We can't risk her talking."

Eddie looks both confused and terrified and when he doesn't respond, Joanna picks up a cushion and throws it at him.

"Do it now, Edward. Do it now, or you are going to spend the rest of your life in prison."

He is shaking like a leaf, but I can't tell whether it is fear of Joanna or fear of spending the rest of his life in prison. Either way he bends over and picks up the cushion from where it has landed next to his feet and walks towards the bed.

This is clearly a scenario that they have discussed before and after a final nod from Joanna, he leans over the bed and forces the cushion down onto Beatrice's face.

The prolonged administration of small doses of foxglove has left Beatrice so weak and disorientated that she barely has the strength to struggle and in less than a minute she is dead. My heart is beating so fast and so hard that I am convinced Eddie and Joanna must be able to hear it. It's a completely irrational thought and with Beatrice Partington-Brown lying dead in her bed there is absolutely no reason for either of them to even look in my direction.

Joanna leans over the body of her mother and lifts her wrist to check for a pulse to confirm that she is gone. Satisfied that she is dead, Joanna takes the cushion from Eddie's hand and calmly places it back on the chair where it came from and then claps her hands to get his attention.

"Edward, you need to concentrate. Doctor Clarke is going to come, and you need to tell him that you found her like this. Have you got that? You need to tell him that she was dead when you came to give her, her medicine."

He nods and tells her that he understands. Joanna tells him to hold out his hands and then she pours out half of the pills from each bottle.

"Get rid of these and then meet me downstairs in the study. Don't speak to anyone until I tell you to."

Eddie leaves to go downstairs and through the gap in the door, I watch as Joanna moves carefully around the room tidying up. She picks up a dressing gown from the floor and my heart sinks when she arranges it on a wooden coat hanger and walks towards the wardrobe. Noticing that one of the doors is not fully closed, she momentarily pauses as if she is considering whether she had closed it earlier. There is no possible way for me to hide completely, so rather than waiting for her to open the door, I leap from the wardrobe, push Joanna to one side, and run for the stairs.

My surprise appearance causes Joanna to scream with fright, but she quickly composes herself and as I reach the bottom of the stairs she is out onto the landing calling for Eddie to help. Her screams have also got the attention of the rest of the household and I am met in the corridor by the gardener, an angry-looking cook, and an even more angry-looking delivery driver.

"That's the fella," the cook shouts. "He told me he needed to use the bathroom."

The delivery guy pushes past the cook and the gardener and squares up to me with a rolling pin that he has taken from the kitchen.

"Oy! That's my coat and hat. What's your bleeding game, pal?"

Behind me, Eddie has appeared and when I see him loading a shotgun, the choice of which way to go is obvious. I jab my clenched fingers into the veg man's windpipe and he goes down on the floor like a sack of spuds clutching his neck and gasping for breath. Not wishing to get in my way, the gardener and the cook obligingly step aside to let me pass.

Joanna and Eddie have no intention of letting me get away so easily and why would they? I have just witnessed them smothering Joanna's mother after overhearing them more or less discussing slow poisoning her with the leaves and seeds from the foxglove plant. They have too much to lose and Joanna urges Eddie to get after me.

He might be an old man now, but in 1974 Eddie is still in his twenties and years of working the farm have left him trim and athletic. As I reach the tree line, he is less than twenty feet behind me when he lets loose with both barrels. A hail of lead pellets whistle past my head but miraculously none hit me. Seemingly safe for a second, I momentarily turn to face my pursuer who is busy fumbling in his jacket pocket for replacement cartridges. Not wishing to wait around to give him a second chance to shoot me, I turn again and run through the woodland towards the road.

Eddie is still following behind, but I am puzzled when I realize that he isn't running. I slow down my own pace and look back over my shoulder. Eddie is still there and still coming towards me, but he is walking and is almost being cautious about where he steps.

The answer to this puzzle should have been obvious, but I find out the answer too late when my foot presses down on the steel pressure plate. In a split second the tension releases the springs of the man-trap allowing the steel jaws to slam shut on my leg. The pain is instant and excruciating and as I drop to the ground, I can feel my ankle and my shin bones splintering.

Eddie continues to walk towards me in the same careful fashion as I desperately try to free myself. When he reaches me, he doesn't say anything. Instead, he props his shotgun up against a tree and then calmly lights a cigarette. He takes three long puffs before stamping it out on the ground and retrieving his gun.

"The wife doesn't approve of smoking, so I have to do it in secret. It's a bit pathetic really, but you saw how she is."

Then pointing to my leg, he adds.

"Bloody horrible those things, but they do the job. They were used for catching poachers, but they were banned years ago. I knew they would come in handy eventually, though. Poacher or not, you're not going anywhere anytime soon, pal."

I'm struggling to think through the pain, but I'm determined not to pass out and disappear in front of him. Picking up on the comment about Joanna, I try to appeal to his better nature.

"It is pathetic how she treats you. No man should have to put up with that. Help me out of this and I'll tell the police what I saw. I will tell them that it was her that killed the woman in the bed."

Eddie smiles at my comment and then moves closer and holds a hand across my mouth. He presses the butt of his shotgun down on my shattered ankle.

The pain is even worse than before, and it is all he can do to muffle my screams. After a few seconds he releases his hand from my mouth and stands up.

"I wish it were as simple as that, fella, but I think that you know perfectly well who that woman was. The wife said that she thinks she recognizes you. You just hold tight there. She will know what to do with you."

Eddie turns and walks back through the woods towards the manor leaving me in exactly the kind of position that I never want to be in. I am badly injured, unable to move, and if I don't find a way out of this quickly, I will be totally at the mercy of the main suspects in my case.

I desperately try to release the steel jaws from my leg, but the pain and loss of blood has left me weak. Each time I manage to open them more than a few inches, they inevitably snap back again causing me even more pain. After trying unsuccessfully for five minutes, I give up. I lie back and close my eyes to try to block out the pain.

A few more minutes pass and when I finally hear the voices of Joanna and Eddie in the distance, I am surprised when just a second later, a shadow blocks out the sun that has been flickering through the top of the trees and a familiar voice tells me not to worry.

"This is for the best, Dad. I'm not strong enough to open the trap and they will be here in less than a minute. We don't have any other option."

Ben is looking down at me and I am shocked to see him struggling to lift a large rock above his head wearing nothing but his hospital gown. His feet are bare, and his shoulder is bleeding heavily from the exertion of lifting the rock. I know exactly what he is planning to do and before I can stop him, he tells me again that there is no time for him to release me from the trap.

"You can thank me next time you see me, Dad. Now, shut your eyes."

I don't shut my eyes and I swear to God, he is actually smiling as he releases the rock. As it slams down onto my head, my last memory is of him sprinting towards the road with his white ass cheeks flashing through the open back of his hospital gown.

# Present Day – Friday, 20ᵗʰ April, 2018

My head is banging like crazy and it takes me a few seconds to realize that someone is also banging on my door and trying to get into the room. I struggle to get off the bed and stumble towards the door, but I am too late. The door is opened with a keycard from the outside and an extremely pissed-off-looking Catherine marches in and demands to know why the hell my phone is switched off. When she sees the Jameson bottle at the side of the bed and the clothes I am wearing she loses it completely.

"Do not tell me that you have been bloody partying, while I've been freezing my tits off in a forest for the last five hours, Sean? For God's sake, boss, it's not even 10 pm yet and I can smell the booze on you from here. You had better have a bloody good explanation for this."

Having any kind of reasonable explanation for this is beyond even my own capability to bullshit my way out of things. I am drunk, hungover, and dressed like a cross between Leo Sayer and Gilbert O'Sullivan. There is no explaining this and I don't even try.

"Cath, I'm so sorry. I poured myself a drink whilst I was working, and things just got a bit out of hand. Has something happened?"

"Really? That's all that I am going to get?" she replies. "There is getting out of hand and then there is getting off your face. You were meant to be looking into the death of Beatrice and instead I find you looking like an extra from Saturday Night Fever. I've been trying to call you for the last hour. Your cell phone is switched off and your room phone has been set to 'do not disturb'. After everything that has happened today, I was going out of my mind thinking that something might have happened to you."

My embarrassment at being caught out quickly turns to shame and I apologize once again for being unreachable and for causing her to worry. The second apology and my pitiful appearance calms the situation slightly and Catherine tells me to go and get changed.

"Just save it for now, Sean. While you've been doing whatever it was you were doing, the search team have struck gold."

"They found the body?" I ask.

"Yes, they have. The duty pathologist is on site examining the remains now. We need to get straight back there before Lincolnshire PD get their noses too far in the trough."

Cath switches on the kettle to make herself a coffee while I get changed and from inside the bathroom I hear her call out to say that she is making one for me also.

"I think you could do with one to clear your head, boss. Oh, and bring some mouthwash with you. You're breath smells like ass and not a cute one either."


Thirty minutes later, we arrive back at Meadow Farm and Cath leads me towards the search site. The clearing is lit up like a Christmas tree by portable floodlights. A dozen uniformed officers are performing a detailed search of the area surrounding the burial site and the location pointed out by Catherine earlier today has been covered with a white canvas tent to protect against unauthorized access or contamination of evidence.

A young constable checks our warrant cards and then hands us forensics suits, shoe covers, gloves, and masks before allowing us to enter the tent. Inside, Catherine introduces me to the pathologist and to a detective inspector from Lincolnshire CID.

"Boss, this is Dr. Carl Mason and let me also introduce DI Patrick Miller from Lincolnshire CID. As soon as we are done here, DI Miller and his team will be taking over and will clear the site."

I shake both their hands and thank them for their support and then I move closer to the area that has been excavated. A skeleton is clearly visible, but it is still partially covered in places by soil. I can see enough, though, to see that the bones are charred and blackened. The image of Lucy falling into the fire nearly fifty years ago replays in my head in graphic detail. The combination of this and a quarter bottle of Jameson just a few hours ago leaves me nauseous and for a second I think that I might throw up.

Sensing that something is wrong, Cath hands me a bottle of water and then diverts the attention away from me by asking Dr. Mason if he has managed to establish a cause of death yet.

Although he probably doesn't need to, Monroe refers to his notepad before shaking his head.

"It's a little too early to say, DC Swain. I need to get the body back to the lab. Until then I wouldn't like to speculate if the body was burnt pre- or post-mortem. Based on my experience, though, and the condition of the remains, I'm reasonably confident that we are looking at a burial sometime between forty and fifty years ago."

Catherine and I both look at each other at the same time and we have clearly read each other's mind.

"This is it, boss," Catherine says. "Finding her body on Eddie's land is more than enough reason to bring him in for questioning. Will I …"

"Sorry to interrupt you, DC Swain. But did you say, 'her body'?" Monroe asks. "I'm sorry to disappoint you, but whilst I'm unable to comment yet on the cause of death I can say with absolute certainty that we are looking at the skeleton of a young adult male, not a female."

To emphasize his point, he leans over the skeleton and points towards the pelvic area.

"The most obvious difference between male and female skeletal make up is the pelvic bone. In females it has a much more rounded appearance. There are a few other less obvious differences such as the shape of the jawline and the thickness of the bones, but in this case, the pelvic bone is most definitely male."

"Paul Oliver," I say to nobody in particular.

"Sorry, boss. What was that you said?" Cath asks me.

"It has to be Paul Oliver. That's the only explanation that makes sense."

My comment has got the attention of DI Miller and he asks me to explain myself.

"Yes, sir. Paul Oliver was one of the original suspects in the case that we are working on. It was assumed that he had skipped town shortly after the disappearance of Lucy Partington-Brown. Nothing has been seen or heard of him since 1972, but if I was a betting man, I would say that we have just found him."

Miller is busy scribbling in his pocketbook, and I suggest to him to pull Paul Oliver's medical and dental records.

"Start on the assumption that this is Paul Oliver, sir. You might save yourself a lot of time."

"Thank you, DS McMillan, that's very helpful," Miller replies.

We swap numbers and then DI Miller leaves to brief his men on the latest developments. I ask Catherine to go outside to call DCI Morgan to give him the news and to ask his permission to bring Eddie Wells in for questioning tomorrow.

"Don't you think it would be better coming from you, boss?"

"You're probably right, Cath. But I'm not feeling particularly great at the moment. If he asks, just tell him that I'm busy with the pathologist. Go on, I need to ask Dr. Mason a few things anyway."

As soon as Cath has left the tent, I tell Monroe that the search team need to continue and excavate deeper.

"I don't understand, DS McMillan. We have found a body where we were asked to search. Is there something else that we need to know?"

"You've found 'a body', doctor, not 'the body.' We were hoping to find the body of our missing person, Ms. Lucy Partington-Brown. Our investigations led us to believe that this is where we would find her, and I still believe that to be the case. Look closer at the excavation site, Dr. Mason."

I take him back to the edge of the site and we both stare into the hole. Mason puts his glasses on for a better look, then tucks them back in his jacket pocket and looks at me with a puzzled look on his face.

"Okay, so I'm looking at this body with the eyes and brain of a pathologist and I assume that you are looking with the eyes and brain of a detective. What am I meant to be looking at, DS McMillan?"

"How far down did you have to dig before you found the body? Two feet or perhaps two and a half?"

"Twenty-three inches to be precise," Mason replies.

"Twenty-three inches, doctor. Look around you. Even now, this area is totally secluded. Forty or fifty years ago, I doubt if this area saw more than a few passing visitors in a year. Why would somebody be so lazy as to only bury the body just two feet below the surface? They would have had all the time in the world to go deeper and why take the risk of the body being dug up by wild animals or being exposed by the weather?"

Mason is still looking none the wiser and before he can attempt to answer my question, I interrupt and answer it for him.

"Because, doctor, there was already a recently dug hole containing another body and it was too easy just to dig up the same patch of freshly dug earth and throw this one in on the top. Once you have finished the excavation of this body, you need to dig down further. I suggest that you prepare your team for a long night."

I can see that he is skeptical about my theory, but out of concern for his professional reputation, I know that he won't refuse my request. If he was to refuse and a second body was discovered later by another team, his reputation would be in tatters. Reluctantly, he agrees to my request and leaves to instruct the search team to be prepared to resume the search. Outside the tent, I hand back the forensic suit and other items to the young constable and make my way back through the woods to find Catherine.

The lights from the guest house are all on and outside on the patio, the owner, Peter Jackson, is handing out plates of sandwiches and mugs of steaming tea to some of the search team and police officers. I ask him if he has seen Catherine and he points at the kitchen window.

"She was inside a few minutes ago making a call."

I make my way inside and find Catherine standing next to the sink looking absolutely exhausted.

"Tough day, Cath?" I ask her.

"A tough day and a bloody crazy one," she replies. "One attempted murder, one actual murder, and one body buried in a forest. I knew this case was going to be a can of worms, but this is just crazy. A few days ago, this was a simple missing person case, now we seem to have a serial killer on the loose."

"A bit dramatic, don't you think, Cath?" I ask her.

"Oh, and did I mention that once again my partner is shutting me out and acting like a complete and utter asshole? Or is that still a bit dramatic for you, John Travolta?"

I laugh at her comment and raise my eyebrows.

"Thanks, I guess I deserved that. I know I'm an asshole, Cath, and I know I keep saying it, but we're a good team and whilst there are things that I can't always share with you we do get there in the end. Today has been a shit day, but we have also made some real progress. We didn't find Lucy's body, but finding this other body has opened the door for us with Eddie Wells. If we can get him alone in a station, we have a real chance at getting to the truth about what happened to Lucy."

Even Catherine can't deny that we have made progress and she is as keen as I am to interview Eddie.

"DI Morgan has given us his full support to bring Eddie in for interview."

"That's brilliant," I reply. "Let's pull him in bright and early tomorrow."

"Yep, a bit of a problem with that, boss. Morgan wants them to have at least twelve-hours' notice before the interview. He is concerned if we drag Eddie in without warning, he will have the Home Secretary jumping all over him if Sir David makes a complaint."

This news is a massive kick in the nuts. With twelve hours, Joanna and any good solicitor will have enough time to fill Eddie's head with all kinds of advice and suggestions. Whilst I can understand Morgan's reasoning, it doesn't make the news any easier to swallow.

"For fuck's sake, Cath, there is an unexplained body buried on a tract of land owned by Eddie Wells. If we wanted to, we would be perfectly within our rights to kick down his door and drag him out of his bed right now. This is total BS, but we don't have a choice. Make the call now. Get them into Spalding station early tomorrow afternoon. I'm gonna head back to the hotel."

"Okay, give me a few minutes to get my stuff from my room," Cath replies, before I stop her from leaving the kitchen.

"No, I want you to stay here, but get some sleep. I need you on form tomorrow."

I explain to Cath about my conversation with Dr. Mason after she had left.

"You really think she is down there, boss?"

"She is, Cath. I'd stake my reputation and my life on it. I need you to be here, just in case anything else turns up tonight. Hit your bed, though. Doc Monroe will call you if they find anything."

"Hmm," Cath murmurs, with the same look of skepticism as Monroe had. "That's fine, but don't forget, it's my reputation as well, Sean."

"Have I ever let you down, Cath?" I ask her.

"You might not like the answer to that one, boss, so I think I will exercise my right to silence. Do you want me to give you a lift back to Tyevale?"

"That's okay, Cath. I'll cadge a lift from one of the boys in blue. Call me if there are any developments or if you need anything."

She raises her eyebrows and then tells me that I can count on it, before sarcastically adding.

"Don't forget to turn your phone back on, boss. It generally makes it easier for me to call you."

I thank my uniformed colleague for the lift back to Tyevale and then I head to the hotel bar just in time to catch last orders. It's almost one in the morning and I need to take the opportunity to travel again, but for the last few hours something has been worrying me and it won't wait until tomorrow.

I take a large gulp of my drink to steady my nerves and then I scroll through my contacts and make a call. Given the time, I'm surprised when Maria answers almost immediately.

"Sean, hi. Is everything okay? Has something else happened?

"Everything is fine," I reassure her. "I'm really sorry to call so late, but it's been a hectic day. I hope that I didn't wake you. I was calling to check on Ben."

"That's okay, Sean. I can't sleep anyway. He seemed to be doing okay, but then this afternoon, the strangest thing happened."

I have a feeling I know what she is about to say, but I feign ignorance and ask her what she means.

"The doctors woke him up a couple of hours after you left. He was very groggy still, but we managed to talk for a few minutes before he went back to sleep again. I stayed with him for another twenty minutes to make sure he was okay. The color was back in his cheeks and he seemed to be sleeping soundly, so I stepped outside to get myself a coffee and a bite to eat. I was only gone ten minutes, Sean. I don't know what happened."

Her voice is breaking up and I can imagine that she is welling up as she speaks.

"What happened, Maria? Please try not to get upset. Tell me what happened."

"It's crazy, I was only gone for ten minutes," she repeats. "When I got back, he was lying face down in the bed tangled up in his IV with blood all over his back from where some of his stitches had burst."

"What did Ben say?" I ask her. "Was he able to tell you what happened?"

"He didn't say anything, Sean. He was still asleep and heavily sedated. After repairing the damage to his stitches, the doctor increased his level of sedation again to ensure he gets a good rest tonight."

I suggest to her that he might possibly have had a nightmare or a flashback to the shooting.

"I know from experience, Maria, that it's not something that you can easily forget. It's getting on for two months since I was shot, and I am still struggling to sleep properly. Even with heavy sedation, it's possible that he might have turned himself over."

"Okay, well that might explain his stitches bursting, but there was something else, Sean. When I touched him, his skin was freezing. I don't just mean cold, I literally mean freezing. Like he had spent the night outside and his feet were filthy. It doesn't make any sense and I feel like I am going mad. I'm his mother and I should be able to protect him."

"You're not responsible for any of this, Maria, so please don't take any of the blame on yourself. Just being there for him is enough and the thing he will want to see most when he wakes up is your smiling face. We are close to finding the person responsible. Just hang in there and in a few days, Ben will be strong enough for you to take him home."

Maria thanks me for calling and promises to keep me informed of any developments before we end the call. I've probably had enough to drink already today, but my mind is working overtime again trying to make sense of everything that has happened since we arrived in Tyevale.

Just before the barman turns off the lights, I order one more drink. I take it to my room and sit down in front of the TV to write up my notes.

Cath was right earlier, in less than a week our case has changed dramatically from an investigation into the disappearance of a young woman, to an investigation involving multiple murder and attempted murder. Tomorrow we are going to question Eddie Wells about the disappearance of Lucy, the death of Father Beale, the attempted murder of myself, the wounding of Ben, and now the discovery of a body on his land. Unbeknown to Cath, and now that I know what happened to her, I am also going to push Eddie on the subject of Beatrice Partington-Brown's death.

Away from the influence of Joanna and with the right amount of pressure, I am certain that he will spill his guts. If he does and if he confirms Joanna's part in the deaths, this will be all the reason we need to bring her in for questioning.

Eddie is guilty of his crimes and needs to be held accountable, but it is Joanna that has set him up as the fall guy through a sustained campaign of bullying and blackmail. Joanna is a cold and calculating bitch who needs to be taken down before she can hurt anyone else.

We are close to breaking this case, but we can't be complacent.

My plan for what's left of the night is to travel back to the last time that Paul Oliver was seen in Tyevale. The approval to bring Eddie in for questioning was partly based on my belief that the body found on his land is that of Paul Oliver. I'm certain that it is Paul in the hole, but it can't do any harm to see what happened for myself.

In my rush to leave the hotel earlier, I had discarded my outfit on the bathroom floor. The suit is wrinkled and slightly damp, but its already very late and I'm in no mood for ironing. I splash some cold water on my face, dress in the suit, and then retrieve a badly creased black-and-white photograph of Paul Oliver from the case file. In the picture he is smartly dressed in a suit and is posing next to a Lambretta scooter. In my mind, I picture him riding the scooter through the streets of Tyevale. It is the beginning of April and although the sun is shining, he is wearing a khaki-colored fishtail parka that is blowing in the wind. As he speeds away down the high street, my eyes close and I am there.

# The Past – Sunday, 2nd April, 1972

In the distance, I can hear shooting from more than one weapon and the sound of dogs barking. It sounds like a shooting party and as I peer through the gap in the trees, my assumption is confirmed. A line of beaters is thrashing away at the waist-high grass to spook the grouse or pheasant to take flight in the direction of the waiting shooters and half a dozen hounds are dashing back and forth to retrieve the birds that have been hit.

I had been hoping to catch up with Paul Oliver somewhere in Tyevale, but I'm disappointed to see Colevale Manor another half mile or so further on from where the group of shooters are standing.

This must then be land owned by Sir David and I must be standing in a part of the same forest where I fell victim to the mantrap on my last trip. If my memory serves me correctly, this land wasn't transferred into Joanna's name until sometime in August of 1972 and Joanna and Eddie didn't marry until 1973. It's unlikely that there are any mantraps lying around now, but regardless, I know that I need to tread carefully. If by chance, there are any here and I get caught again, it will be game over for this trip and, with Ben so heavily sedated, there is only a very slim chance that he will be showing up again to rescue me.

I watch the shooting party for a few minutes whilst I try to work out my next move. My arrival in this spot has left me more than a little confused. My accuracy recently has been extremely good for both location and date. The image of Paul Oliver had been clear in my mind and I had fully expected to open my eyes and be standing in the middle of Tyevale.

There must be a reason for being here. Because I can't see anything obvious amongst the shooting party, I figure the reason must be at the house itself. I follow the tree line for as long as I can and when I am far enough away from the shooting party and am confident that they won't be able to see me, I step out onto the grassland and make my way towards the manor house.

Within fifty feet of the house, my earlier confusion is fully cleared up when I see Paul's Lambretta parked on the graveled driveway next to the same Landrover that I had seen the gamekeeper driving. Joanna and Paul are both standing at the top of the stairs. I can't hear what they are saying, but it is obvious from Joanna's body language that Paul's presence here is not welcome.

I move up closer and duck behind a marble sculpture of a military figure on horseback to the right of the steps. Joanna pushes Paul towards the stairs and demands he leave, but he is having none of it and brushes her hand away.

"I'm bloody going nowhere until I get the truth about what happened. The coppers think that I'm responsible, but we both know different, don't we? Either you go to the cops or I will. It's your choice. What's it to be?"

Paul must know of Joanna's involvement in the disappearance of her sister, and she now looks terrified. She reaches forward and takes Paul's hand. This time, though, she pulls him towards her and pleads with him not to say anything.

"You don't have to do this. If the police really thought that you knew anything or were responsible, they would have arrested you by now. In a few weeks, they will get bored and will close the case. Until then, perhaps we can come to an arrangement."

Joanna reaches down to touch Paul's crotch and he pulls away with a look of disgust on his face.

"You bloody make me sick, you bitch. Your sister is missing and all you can think of is protecting yourself. It would suit you down to the ground if the cops arrested me. Well, guess what? That's not going to happen. If you won't tell them yourself, then I will."

Paul is already halfway down the steps when Joanna calls him back.

"Okay, Paul. I'll do it. I need to speak to Edward first though. Will you come to his farm to speak to him with me?"

"Why the hell do I need to speak to Eddie?" Paul replies.

"Because he is involved in this to. Please, Paul, just do this one last thing for me and then I promise I will tell the police everything."

Paul points to the Landrover. "Do you have the keys for that?"

"I do," Joanna replies. "It's probably better, though, if you take your scooter and meet me there. Father will go berserk if he knows that you have been here. Go now and I'll grab my coat and let Edward know that we are coming. I'll be right behind you."

Paul starts his engine and then warns Joanna that she had better not be messing him around.

"If you're not there five minutes after me, then I'm heading straight back to Tyevale to spill the beans."

Joanna assures him that she will be there, and he guns his engine and speeds off down the driveway. Once he is out of sight, Joanna goes inside the house and closes the front door. My only hope of staying with them is by hiding in the back of the Landrover, so after checking that the coast is clear, I pull back the canvas flaps and climb in over the tailgate.

The window at the back of the driver's cabin is dirty and scratched, but to be safe, and in case Joanna does look back, I press myself as low to the floor as possible. Less than two minutes later, the driver's side door opens and the engine splutters to life. The gear box squeals as she tries to find first gear. When she does find it, the vehicle lurches forward and I can hear the tires crunching on the gravel as we accelerate down the path and onto the main road.

After five minutes, I can hear the tick tock of the indicator and we slow down and take a right turn as Joanna steers the vehicle down the track towards Meadow Farm. Rather than risk being found hiding in the back, I wait until she slows down again before, one hundred yards short of the farm, I roll back over the tailgate and duck into some bushes until I am sure Joanna is far enough away.

As Joanna parks next to Paul's Lambretta, I crouch down and run as fast as I can to the drystone wall. Paul is as angry as before and is demanding to see Eddie.

"Where is he? I've tried the house, but it's deserted. If he is not here in five minutes, I'm leaving."

"He's in the forest," Joanna replies. "Come on, I'll take you to him.

"What do you mean he's in the forest? What's he doing? Did you call him?"

"I tried, but there was no answer. Then I remembered that he told me that he would be chopping firewood today. He usually spends the whole day at it, so unless you want to stand here waiting, let's go and find him."

Joanna starts walking towards the tree line, but Paul is hesitant and doesn't move. Joanna turns back to face him.

"You do want this over, don't you?"

Paul nods and then follows Joanna as she leads him towards the trees. This time and without the benefit of the cover of darkness, I am forced to wait in my hiding place until they enter the woods. Once they are out of sight, I leap over the wall and sprint as fast as I can to catch up with them. Joanna has almost certainly set a trap for Paul and I can't afford to miss the moment that the trap is sprung. Out of breath and sweating heavily, I reach the tree line and cautiously make my way inside.

I pick up the sound of Joanna's and Paul's voices and, I round a bend in the path just in time to see the back of Paul's parka as Joanna leads him into the clearing. Crouching down in the same place as before, I can clearly see them both standing next to a pile of freshly cut branches, arranged in the shape of a bonfire. With no sign of Eddie and with no sign of the firewood he was supposed to have been cutting, Paul grabs Joanna by the arm and demands to know what is going on.

"Enough of your bloody games, where is he? You said he would be here."

Until now, I hadn't seen Eddie either. With his back facing the opposite side of the forest, Paul is completely oblivious to the impending danger as Eddie silently emerges from the edge of the trees clutching a shovel in both hands.

Still caught in Paul's grip, Joanna smiles and gestures towards Eddie.

"He's right there, Paul."

Paul releases his grip on Joanna and swings around to face Eddie. I was expecting Eddie to strike him immediately with the shovel blade, but he hesitates and lowers the shovel.

Realizing that he has been set up, Paul turns his head and calls Joanna a bitch, but Joanna is looking past him scowling at Eddie and this time there is no hesitation.

The shovel slams down on Paul's head with a sickening thump and he drops to the ground like a ragdoll. I can hear his moans and Joanna tells Eddie that he needs to finish the job.

"You know we can't let him go, Edward. He knows too much. Finish him, then hurry up and light the fire. I need to get back to Colevale before the Landrover is missed."

I know that I can't intervene, but no matter how many times I witness a violent crime, it never gets any easier to stomach. By the time Paul finally goes silent, the back of his head has been reduced to a bloody pulp and the blade of Eddie's shovel is slick with bright red blood.

With the fire blazing away, Eddie lifts the deadweight of Paul's body and hurls him into the flames. Joanna tells Eddie to burn his own clothes and to get rid of the shovel and then she leaves him to finish his gruesome task.

I can almost feel some sympathy for Eddie, but I have nothing but scorn for Joanna. When she gets back to Colevale, she will resume her life as easily as if she had just stepped on an ant. She might be a product of the privileged class, but I struggle to believe that any young woman could be so callous and calculating. The death of her sister and one of her friends seems to mean nothing to her and in less than another two years she will instigate the murder of her own mother. And for what? To pay off her father's debts and to keep the estate within the family.

It really takes a special kind of evil to behave in such a ruthless way. I am looking forward to meeting Eddie tomorrow and to bringing this case to a close, but for now I need to find a way home.

Eddie has stripped down to his underwear and is staring into the fire watching his clothes burn. For a second it occurs to me to run past Eddie and to throw myself in. I've never yet burnt to death to get home and it might almost be worth it to see the look on his face. The potential repercussions, however, would not, and I quickly dismiss the thought. I leave Eddie to his thoughts and make my way back towards the farm.

Joanna has already left in the Landrover and I consider stealing Eddie's car. Instead, I turn my attention towards the barn behind the farmhouse. The doors are heavy, and it takes far more effort than I was expecting to pry one of them open far enough for me to get inside.

The effort is worth it. Although it is starting to get dark, there is still enough light coming in to allow me to see the Aladdin's cave of tools, chemicals, and farm machinery laid out on shelves and cluttering the floor. Like a kid in a candy store, I don't know where to start. The options for my demise are endless and with the very real possibility that this case is coming to an end, I want this ending to be something quite spectacular.

My eyes settle on a steel frame full of propane gas tanks. The frame is rusty, but the propane tanks are shiny and new. One of them has a brass valve attached to the top of the tank. There is a pipe leading off from it and out through a small hole in the side of the barn. I'm no expert on the subject of propane gas, but I do know that it is commonly used for heating in rural homes, so more than likely the pipe is leading off to the farmhouse. I also know that propane burns hotter than home-heating oil or diesel fuel due to its high hydrogen content – ideal for an inferno hotter than the sun.

I wrench the pipe away from the valve and the air is immediately filled with the hiss and the smell of escaping gas.

This is not enough, though. With the size of the barn and the barn door open, it is going to take more than just a single leaking propane tank to kill me with any degree of certainty. I hack away with a pickaxe at the sides of the remaining cylinders and as each of them rupture, the air gets thicker and thicker with the smell of leaking liquid propane and escaping gas. I continue to strike the sides of the tanks with the pickaxe, but despite the copious amounts of sparks flying through the air, the gas doesn't ignite.

By now, the effects of the gas have caused my heart to race and I am struggling with fatigue. If I don't do something soon, I will be overcome by the fumes, but I might not die. I struggle towards the barn door and suck in a huge lung full of the crisp evening air.

My head clear's immediately and I am just in time to see Eddie rounding the corner of the farmhouse.

He is still in just his underwear, but he has his shotgun and has obviously been alerted by the sound of the pickaxe striking the gas tanks.

I duck back inside and drop down behind the tanks. Eddie pulls open the barn door further but immediately shuts it again and backs away when he smells the gas. The answer to my problem is right there in his hands and I have no intention of letting him leave.

"Where are you going, Eddie?" I shout.

For a few seconds there is silence and then he responds.

"Who is in there? How do you know my name?"

"I'm your worst bloody nightmare, Eddie Wells. I know what you and Joanna have done."

I start to choke on the gas and in a last-ditch attempt to provoke a reaction, I hurl a hammer against the door.

The door slides open just a few inches and by the light of the moon, I can see the barrel of the shotgun poking through and I launch the pickaxe towards the door. It falls short, but whether through fear or intention, Eddie pulls the trigger and the barn explodes in a white-hot ball of flame. My own cries are lost in the roar of the inferno, but as my skin falls from my bones, I swear that I can hear Eddie screaming and can only imagine that some part of the explosion must have caught him.

# Present Day – Saturday, 21st April, 2018

By 9 am, we are already on the road and heading to Spalding. The meeting with Eddie Wells is not until 1 pm, but Cath has arranged for us to meet with DI Miller this morning at Spalding Central Station to agree on our game plan.

With no further updates from the search site, Cath had rejoined me at the hotel and over breakfast she had calmly informed me that Miller would be joining us in the interview. I was less than pleased to hear this, but the discovery of the body on Eddie's land, the death of Father Beale, and the shotgun attack have shifted jurisdiction for these elements of our case in favor of Lincolnshire Constabulary.

This is a far from ideal situation. Whilst I will still be heading the interview overall, DI Miller will also be playing a leading role. His presence means that I may need to adjust my interview tactics somewhat and I'm annoyed that Cath waited until this morning to tell me about this new development.

"What time did you speak with Miller last night, Cath? I really wish that you had called me. I could at least have prepared myself."

Cath is driving and keeps her focus on the road ahead, but she does raise her eyebrows when she answers.

"Like I said over breakfast, Sean. It was past three in the morning. There was really nothing you could do at that time. What's the big issue anyway? Miller seems to be a good guy."

"That's not the point, Cath. I'm sure Miller is a good guy, I just like to be kept informed."

"Don't we all," Cath mutters under her breath.

"What was that?" I ask.

"Nothing," Cath replies "And sorry – I'll make sure to keep you fully informed from now on."

Before I can say anything else, my phone vibrates in my pocket. It's DCI Morgan and for him to be calling during the slot normally reserved for his morning briefing it must be something urgent.

"Good morning, sir. We are on our way to Spalding Central now. Is everything okay?"

"Yes, everything's fine, Sean. I'm just calling to ensure that it stays that way."

"Sorry, I'm not following you, sir," I reply.

"As we expected, Sir David has been making noises about the planned interview with the Wells chap today. The Home Secretary just called me for an update. Obviously, he was surprised to find out that the investigation has moved so quickly in the direction of the immediate family but, based on recent developments, he is supportive of the decision to bring Eddie Wells in. You can go ahead with your interview, lad, but tread carefully. Don't be at all surprised if they wheel out the big guns to represent Wells."

"Thank you, sir. I fully understand."

"Good," Morgan replies. "Any ID on the body yet or any further developments from the search site?"

"No, nothing yet, sir. I'm hoping to get confirmation on the ID before we start the interview. If it does turn out to be Paul Oliver, it will strengthen our hand due to the connection with the sisters and Eddie Wells himself."

"Well, let's hope you're right, Sean. Call me later please."

With that, Morgan ends the call and I turn to Cath.

"I guess you heard most of that?"

"Yes, I did. It shouldn't change anything, though," Cath replies, before adding, "As long as we play by the book, boss."

I ignore the insinuation and tell Cath to concentrate on the road.

"We're nearly there now. You just keep your eyes on the road and make sure not to miss our exit. I'm going to have a flick through the case file and make some notes for the interview.

I know most of the contents of the file intimately, but with my newly gained knowledge of the deaths of Paul Oliver and Beatrice Partington-Brown, I'm determined to use this to my advantage today. I know how they both died, but I still don't know why with any degree of certainty. Paul seemed to know that something had happened to Lucy and was therefore killed to silence him. It might then be safe to assume that Beatrice also somehow found out, but assumption and theory is not enough. I need Eddie to talk.

I open the file and pull out the sections relating to Paul and Beatrice. Without even having to look at the contents, I realize straightaway that something has changed. Both sections of the file are much heavier than they were before and now contain additional statements and other documents.

I start with the file on Beatrice Partington-Brown and my heart nearly skips a beat when I check the death certificate. Prior to my witnessing her murder, the cause of death had been recorded as 'cardiac arrest following a prolonged bout of unexplained illness.' Now, however, it says 'Unlawful killing by asphyxiation.'

There is still no autopsy report, but with two eye-witness statements and another half-dozen witnesses to the suspect fleeing the scene of the crime, it was most likely deemed unnecessary.

This change to the timeline is no surprise to me of course. I know only two well the risks of dream travel and I smile to myself when I compare the remarkably similar suspect descriptions given by each of the witnesses. It's evident that Joanna has coerced or coached her domestic staff when describing the suspect, but it's the other similarity in the statements that is the real master stroke.

The photo-fit looks remarkably like me, but it also looks remarkably like another well-dressed young man in a suit. Without exception, the witnesses have named Paul Oliver as the man seen fleeing Colevale Manor after the death of Beatrice Partington-Brown. Joanna and Eddie specifically state that they caught him standing over her body with a cushion in his hand and Derek Burgess, the fruit and veg delivery man, states that it was Paul Oliver that attacked him in the ground-floor corridor.

Just in case the statements were not enough to fully implicate Paul in the murder, the all-too-convenient discovery of a set of keys to a Lambretta scooter under Beatrice's bed was the final nail in his coffin. The keys were discovered by one of the first police officers on the scene, but it was Joanna that was able to helpfully suggest a name to go with the stylized P & O on the monogrammed leather key fob. No surprises, of course, that they were the same initials as the suspect's.

Inadvertently then, my trip back to the past has given Joanna and Eddie a convenient scapegoat in the form of Paul Oliver. The new round of investigation notes all now name him as the prime suspect in both the murder of Beatrice and in the murder/disappearance of Lucy. That's a pretty good result for Joanna and Eddie when you consider that Paul had been rotting in the ground for at least eighteen months before the death of Beatrice.

Thinking back to our last case, I assume that Cath must already know all of this. When changes to the past impact the present, it only seems to be me that is unaffected by those changes. For everybody else, there are no changes.

I'm about to ask Cath a question to test out my theory when her phone rings and she answers using the hands-free car speaker.

"Good morning, DC Swain speaking."

"DC Swain, good morning. This is Detective Inspector Miller, are you on your way to Spalding?"

Cath confirms that we are and then asks if there has been any progress in identifying the body found yesterday.

"Yes, there has," Miller replies. "Is DS McMillan with you?"

I answer to confirm that I am, and Miller tells me that I was right.

"It's your boy alright, McMillan. The height, approximate age, and approximate date of burial all point to Paul Oliver, but the dental records confirm it one hundred percent Just to be sure we had two medical examiners on site, and both are ninety-nine percent certain. Luckily for us, he must have had some quite extensive dental work done. There's no doubt it is him."

This is great news and now gives us something concrete to focus on when we interview Eddie. We are just a few miles away from Spalding now and I thank Miller and end the call. Cath smiles and congratulates me.

"You might be a pain in the ass at times, Sean, but your instincts are uncanny. That whole looking into the land registry thing and then searching the last parcel of Eddie's land was genius. It would never have crossed my mind to even think of checking the land ownership. All the BS that Eddie and Joanna gave us about Paul being responsible for the disappearance of Lucy and the death of her mother means nothing now. If it was him, what the hell was he doing burnt and buried on Eddie's land? I'm looking forward to this interview."

I nod my agreement and return the documents to the file. Cath has just confirmed what I was wondering about. Our initial conversation with Eddie and Joanna has changed completely and I am mindful now that I need to be careful not to slip up during the interview.

We arrive at Spalding Central Police Station and are met at reception by DI Miller. After a few minutes of small talk, Miller leads us to one of the interview rooms and we prepare for the arrival of Eddie Wells. My earlier intention had been to start right at the very beginning with the disappearance of Lucy, but with the positive ID on Eddie Wells, this now seems to be the logical starting point for the questioning. I lay out my plan to Miller and to Cath and, apart from a few minor questions, my plan is accepted.

I will introduce and set the scene for the interview and then DI Miller will take over and question Eddie about the discovery of Paul Oliver's body on his land. The plan then is to progress through questioning him about the murder of Father Beale, the attempted murder of myself, and the disappearance of Lucy.

Given the newly found significance of the historic statements implicating Paul in the murder of Beatrice and the disappearance of Lucy, both Cath and I will bounce off each other with the good cop, bad cop routine dependent on any responses given by Eddie to Miller or me. With luck, by the end of the day, we will have Eddie backed so far into a corner that he won't have any other option other than to spill his guts. The real prize, though, will be if Eddie implicates Joanna 'the bitch queen of Colevale Manor.'

We finish our discussion and then Miller shows us to the station canteen to grab lunch. He leaves us to attend to another matter and at just after 1 pm he calls to let me know that Eddie has arrived.

"It's on, McMillan. Bring your A game. They have a big shot London lawyer with them. I've put them into interview room number three."

On the way there, Cath reminds me again to be careful during the interview.

"On Thursday when we found him alone at home, you thought that he might be suffering from some kind of mental illness or dementia. If he is, then anything that we get from him would be inadmissible as evidence."

"Yep, I've been thinking about that, Cath," I reply. "I think if he was suffering from any diagnosed illness, then he wouldn't be here today. Any big shot London lawyer worth his salt would have already filed an objection and we would be back to square one."

"Okay, maybe you're right," Cath says. "But go easy anyway, boss. Don't give the big shot any ammunition to shoot us down with."

I promise to behave.

We arrive outside the interview room just in time to see Joanna wheeling out Sir David in his wheelchair. Neither of them says anything to us, but if looks could kill we would both be dead right now.

Sir David is impassive, but Joanna has a look of absolute disgust on her face. She takes a seat on a bench opposite the meeting room and pulls her father to the side of her to adjust a blanket around his shoulders.

I think for a second to say hello, but then think better of it and go inside. Eddie Wells is sitting next to an immaculately turned out gentleman with thinning gray hair. The first thing that I notice, though, is the faded burn scar on the right-hand side of Eddie's face and a small patch completely devoid of hair above his right ear.

My suspicion that Eddie was caught in the barn explosion seems to have been right. Catherine doesn't bat an eyelid though. So, as I thought, the timeline has only changed for me. For Catherine, Eddie has always had the burn scars.

DI Miller is sitting on the opposite side of the table and he stands up to introduce us to Eddie's legal counsel.

"DS McMillan, DC Swain, this is the Honorable Jeffrey Morris QC."

When DCI Morgan had warned me this morning that the PBs would be wheeling out the big guns, he really wasn't joking. The Honorable Jeffrey Morris QC is about as big as they come. If he was an actual gun, he would be a bloody howitzer. You don't get to be a partner in one of the UK's most reputable law firms and a Queen's Counsel without being a formidable an eminent lawyer.

Whilst the title of QC is purely honorific, the very fact that it has been bestowed by the reigning monarch means that it carries a lot of weight. Morris knows exactly the weight it carries and as we take our seats, he is sizing us up in readiness for his opening statement. With everyone seated and without waiting for an invitation he makes his opening play.

"Detective Sergeant McMillan, I would like to commend you for your work on the Network case. That really was an excellent piece of police work.

"You are clearly a very talented detective, but I do feel compelled to warn you that my client is seventy-two years old and has never had so much as a parking ticket in his life. The work of the Cold Case Squad is no doubt important and I know that under the leadership of Detective Chief Inspector Morgan it has had some considerable success in the last few years, but to suggest that my client had anything to do with the disappearance of his wife's sister forty-six years ago is quite absurd and I will be using all the tools at my disposal to bring this circus to an end."

Wow, that I was not expecting. They seem to be rattled already and I am wondering now if they know that we have found a body on Eddie's land. It certainly seems that way. Cath suggests that we start the interview, but I'm not ready yet.

"Thank you, Mr. Morris. Your point is well noted. Just for clarity, though, I would like to remind you that this case was reopened at the request of your client's father-in-law, Sir David Partington-Brown. As part of our investigation it has been necessary to speak to your client, his wife, and his father-in-law. I hardly think that this constitutes harassment."

"Maybe not," Morris replies. "But entering their property without permission and dragging my client here today without presenting any evidence or just cause in advance certainly is, Sergeant. I hope for your sake that you aren't wasting all of our time on a fishing expedition."

"I can assure you that this is no fishing expedition. By the end of this interview you will have all the just cause that you need. Shall we proceed?"

Morris makes a note of the time in his legal pad and nods. Catherine starts the tape and begins with the opening formalities.

"This interview is being recorded. For the benefit of the tape, the time now is 1:12 pm and the date is Saturday April 21st, 2018. Present in the room are Detective Constable Catherine Swain, Detective Sergeant Sean McMillan, Detective Inspector Patrick Miller, Mr. Edward Wells, and Mr. Wells' legal counsel, the Honorable Jeffrey Morris QC.

"Mr. Wells, you are not currently under arrest, but I must caution you that anything you say during this interview may be used in evidence against you. Do you understand?"

Eddie is smartly dressed in a thick woolen suit, waistcoat and tie. As on every other occasion I've seen him, he is sweating heavily, and his face is flushed.

Cath repeats the question and Eddie confirms that he understands.

"Thank you," Cath replies.

I know my notes like the back of my hand, but I shuffle through them anyway until there is an uncomfortable silence. Annoyed at the unnecessary delay, Morris clears his throat in a display of irritation, and I start.

"Mr. Wells, as you are already aware, my colleague Detective Constable Swain and I are currently assigned to investigate the disappearance of your wife's sister, Ms. Lucy Partington-Brown. We do need to ask you some further questions regarding what you may know about this subject, but before we do, my colleague Detective Inspector Miller would now like to ask you some questions in relation to a young man that went missing shortly after the disappearance of Lucy Partington-Brown."

Morris is about to interrupt, but he stops when Miller turns over a photograph and pushes it across the table to Eddie.

"Do you know who this is, Mr. Wells?" Miller asks.

Eddie is hesitant and now his hands are trembling. DI Miller tells him to think carefully and then holds up the photograph for Eddie to take.

"Go on, take a close look. This is Paul Oliver, isn't it, Mr. Wells?"

Eddie nods and Catherine asks him to confirm verbally for the tape.

"Yes, it's Paul Oliver," Eddie replies.

"You made a number of statements in 1972 implicating Paul Oliver in the disappearance of Lucy Partington-Brown and in the murder of your wife's mother, Beatrice Partington-Brown. Do you remember making those statements, Mr. Wells?"

Eddie looks to his counsel for guidance and Morris asks him to wait before replying.

"DI Miller, may I ask where you are leading with this line of questioning? The statements made by my client in 1972 were corroborated by his wife and, in the case of Beatrice Partington-Brown, by multiple other eye witnesses, as I am sure you well know."

"Yes, I'm well aware of that, Mr. Morris. Recent developments, though, have cast doubt over the legitimacy of those statements."

"You're not a member of the Cold Case Squad, are you, DI Miller? What then is the interest of Lincolnshire CID in this investigation? I assume that some aspect of this case has invoked local jurisdiction?"

Jeffrey Morris is as sharp as they come and within minutes he has already picked up on the fact that DI Miller is leading this aspect of the questioning and not me. Miller had been hoping not to play his hand too early, but now he has no option.

"In March of 1972, your client along with his then girlfriend, Joanna Partington-Brown, gave statements to say that the last time they saw Lucy Partington-Brown was at around 11 pm on the night of March 14th, 1972. They both stated that she had left with the O'Hanlon brothers, the owners of the O'Hanlon Brothers Carnival. Joanna Partington-Brown made a slight revision to her statement shortly after to intimate that Paul might have run away with Lucy and then on April 2nd, 1972, both your client and his wife made a significant revision to their statements. Do you remember what that revision was, Mr. Wells?"

Morris stops Eddie from replying again.

"Di Miller, you haven't answered my question. Is there some aspect of this case that has invoked local jurisdiction?"

"If you allow me to continue, Mr. Morris, I am getting to that."

Morris looks indignant and makes another note in his pad.

"Yes, well, let's proceed and get to the point please, Inspector Miller."

Morris indicates that Eddie can answer the question and Miller repeats the last question.

"Mr. Wells, do you remember the revision that you made to your original statement?"

"Yes, I do," Edward replies.

"And what was that?" Miller asks.

Eddie's voice is trembling badly as he replies and sweat has now left a sodden ring around the top of his shirt collar. His once flushed face is now pale.

"We made a mistake. I mean, I made a mistake. Originally, I thought I had seen Lucy leaving with Tighe and Jed O'Hanlon, but I was wrong. She left with Paul Oliver."

I deliberately and suddenly shuffle my chair forward and scrape it on the tiled floor to get Eddie's attention.

"That's not true, though, is it, Mr. Wells? That's a story that was cooked up by your wife, wasn't it?"

My sudden interruption has shocked Eddie and Morris is quick to object.

"DS McMillan, your tone and your accusation are completely inappropriate."

In line with our game plan, Miller pulls me back and apologizes to Morris and Eddie. Morris continues to scribble in his pad and Miller continues the questioning.

"What my colleague meant to say, Mr. Morris, was that it's a striking coincidence that your client and his now wife both changed their statements to implicate Paul Oliver in the disappearance of Lucy on the very same day that they gave statements to say that they witnessed Paul Oliver murdering Beatrice Partington-Brown. That's all a bit convenient, don't you think?"

"Convenient or not, do you have any actual evidence to suggest that my client lied when giving his statements, DI Miller?" Morris responds. "I really must insist that you get to the point and elaborate on the just cause for questioning my client in such a way more than forty-five years after the events that you are referring to. If you don't have just cause and this is just a fishing expedition, as I first thought, then I must further insist that you allow my client to leave immediately and refrain from any further unwarranted harassment."

Morris makes a show of closing his notebook and readying himself to leave, but he stops in his tracks when Miller pushes another photograph across the table and flips it over for Eddie and Morris to see. The first photograph of Paul Oliver was the creased and stained one from the case file, but this one is crisp and new. Morris looks perplexed, but Eddie knows exactly what he is looking at and his complexion grows progressively whiter as he stares at the charred bones of Paul Oliver.

Morris pushes the photograph back across the table and then hands a glass of water to Eddie.

"DI Miller, may I remind you again that my client is seventy-two years old and in poor health? These kind of shock tactics will not be accepted. Do I make myself clear?"

Miller ignores the rant from Morris and indicates for me to take over, which invokes a further protest from Morris.

"Gentlemen, these tactics are reprehensible. My client is an old ma..."

"Old man or not, your client is a liar," I interrupt. I push the photograph back across the table and tell Eddie to look down at it. "You know who that is, don't you, Mr. Wells?"

He looks towards his counsel and Morris whispers in his ear.

"I don't know who it is," Eddie replies. "Why are you showing that to me? I don't know anything about it."

"You're lying, Mr. Wells," I insist. "You know exactly who it is, don't you? Look again!"

Eddie keeps his eyes firmly focused ahead and then blurts out, "I don't know who she is. Take it away please."

We all immediately realize the significance of what he has just said, and Morris' face turns nearly as white as Eddie's.

"What was that you said, Mr. Wells?" I snap. "Why did you say, you don't know who she is? I didn't say this was a female. Why did you say 'she', Mr. Wells?"

"My client was mistaken, Sergeant. It was a turn of phrase, nothing else," Morris insists. "Move on please."

Morris knows that he is clutching at straws, but for now I let Eddie's slip of the tongue pass and I bank it for later use.

"Thank you, Mr. Morris, your point is duly noted."

I turn my attention back to Eddie. To allow him to compose himself slightly, I pull the photograph away and turn it over.

"Mr. Wells, I asked you if you knew who it was in the photograph. This is your chance to be honest with us. Are you sure that you don't know who it is?"

"I already told you I don't know who it is," he replies.

"Okay, Mr. Wells. That's fine. Let me ask you a different question. Where do you think this body was found?"

"DI McMillan, how on earth would my client know the answer to that question?" Morris answers.

I flip over the photograph again and throw it across the table.

"Because the remains that you are looking at were found yesterday evening on a parcel of land belonging to your client and they were positively identified this morning as Paul Oliver. That's why your client might know the answer and he had better start talking or things are going to go very badly for him."

Eddie is trembling so badly that I can feel the table shaking every time his legs or arms touch it and Jeffrey Morris looks momentarily lost for words. Determined to press my advantage, I take another two photographs from the file and hold them up for Eddie to see.

If the photograph of Paul's charred skeleton was shocking, this new pair are stomach churning. The first is a close-up of the back of Father Beale's shattered skull and the second is a picture of Ben's shredded shoulder. Any remnants of color drain completely from Eddie's face and without warning he lurches to the side and vomits onto the floor. As he drops to the floor retching, Morris stands up and demands that we end the interview immediately.

"In all my years as a lawyer and a QC, I have never witnessed such disgraceful behavior from police officers during an interview. I have no idea what you were leading to by showing those photographs, but whatever the reason, my client is clearly unfit to carry on with this interview. As far as I am concerned, you have failed up to this point to provide adequate reason to hold my client any longer. We will be leaving now, and I will be suggesting to Sir David that he asks for the personal intervention of the Home Secretary to have this investigation terminated."

Without waiting for my approval, Catherine ends the interview and turns off the tape, before helping Eddie to stand up. She hands him a box of tissues and escorts him out, leaving DI Miller and me to speak with Jeffrey Morris.

"Your client is free to leave for now, Mr. Morris, but we are far from finished yet," I tell him.

"Based on the way you have just bullied my client, Detective Sergeant, you should be more concerned about whether your career is finished and less concerned about harassing an old man. You might think you are a bit of a superstar because of your last case, but detectives like you are ten a penny. I'll show myself out, gentlemen."

Morris leaves us alone and Miller is the first to speak.

"Not the result you were expecting, Sean?"

"No, it wasn't," I reply. "We were on a roll, though, and the slip up by Eddie put them both on the backfoot. Morris must have thought all his Christmases had come at once when Eddie puked. QC or not, he nearly shit himself when Eddie said 'she'. With that and with the discovery of Paul's body on Eddie's land he knew we had the advantage. I can't believe I screwed it up. We could have got Eddie to roll over today, I'm sure of it"

Cath has come back into the interview room and has caught the tail end of my comments.

"It's not your fault, boss. Your bull-in-a-china-shop tactics usually pay off. The day hasn't been a total disaster, though."

"What do you mean?" I ask. "One of our main suspects has just walked out with one of the top QCs in the country and they now have a key piece of information that they didn't have yesterday. Not to mention the fact that he will be working on the Home Secretary to have us closed-down. If that's not a disaster, I don't know what is, Cath."

"You've heard the analogy about a broken clock, boss?" Cath asks me

"What? What are you talking about?" I reply.

"A broken clock, boss. They say that even a broken clock is right at least twice a day. Well, consider yourself a broken clock, Sean. You were right about the first body being Paul Oliver and now you are also right about there being a second body in that hole."

She hands me her phone and shows me the message from Dr. Mason.

"This just came in two minutes ago."

'DS McMillan was right. The search team have located a 2nd skeleton. It was around four feet below the first one and it also shows signs of exposure to fire. We are still excavating, but with what I can see already, this one is a young adult female.'

"Fucking yes!" I exclaim. "Those evil bastards are going down, Cath."

"You think it's your missing girl, Sean?" Miller asks.

"It is her," I almost shout. "I mean it has to be," I correct myself. "For the body to be buried below Paul Oliver, it must have been put in the ground before he died. Eddie is the link to both Joanna and Lucy, who were both close friends of Paul Oliver's. The discovery of Paul's body and now a female body below his on Eddie's land is just too much of a coincidence for it not to be her."

"Shall we get going then, boss?" Cath asks me.

"Of course, it would be good to know if it's her before we drag Eddie back in again."

"What about calling Morgan to update him, boss?"

"No, not yet, Cath," I reply. "He will want to know how the interview went and I'm not ready for that yet. He will probably hear soon enough anyway if Jeffrey Morris follows through with his threat to reach out to the Home Secretary. I would rather have some more good news to offset the bollocking that I am likely to be in line for."

We leave Miller in the room to secure the interview tapes and Cath puts on the blue light to clear our path for the trip back to Meadow Farm.


At just after 3:40 pm, Cath pulls up outside the guest house and a few minutes later, DI Miller arrives in a squad car accompanied by a uniformed Inspector. Miller makes the introductions.

"Sean, Catherine, this is Inspector Mark Bradley from Spalding Traffic Division. I bumped into him on my way out of the station. He has something you might want to see."

Bradley places a laptop computer on the bonnet of his car and plugs in a memory stick.

"As you both know, the original search of the traffic cameras drew a blank regarding your mystery dirt bike. So, at your request we widened the search. Unfortunately, this also came up empty, but then one of my officers spotted this."

Inspector Bradley clicks on a video file and we all lean in for a better look. The video is dark, but the image is of a Range Rover parked in front of the vicarage. An elderly woman gets out and the Range Rover drives away.

"This was taken yesterday morning at 3.08 am," Bradley tells us. "We can't make out the registration, but if you look closely, you can see the woman goes through the gate. The vehicle drives to the rear of the vicarage and we lose coverage from the traffic cameras at that time."

"That has to be Joanna," Catherine says.

My mind jumps back to yesterday morning when we had arrived at the vicarage and I had seen an elderly woman getting onto a bus at the end of the street.

"Shit, we were right, the whole thing was a setup. Nobody ever rode that bike. They bloody brought the bike here in the Range Rover. They killed the priest and then Eddie must have come to Tyevale and followed us from the hotel to Meadow Farm, leaving Joanna here with the bike engine running until just before we arrived. I bet if we search Colevale we will find that Range Rover and the quad bike that Eddie made his escape on.

"What about the mud on the dirt-bike tires, Sean?" Cath asks me.

"Eddie probably took it for a burn up on one of the estate fields before they got here," I reply. "Have you got any footage of her leaving, Inspector?"

Bradley nods and opens another video file. The time stamp is 9.32 am yesterday and the image is of the same elderly woman walking along the road and getting onto a bus.

"Unfortunately, as you can see, she has pulled her headscarf down low and is deliberately hiding her face."

"Sneaky bitch," Catherine exclaims.

"Not that sneaky," Bradley interjects. "It's clear that she hasn't used public transport for a while. She wasn't reckoning on there being a camera on the bus. Look at this."

He opens a third file. The footage is taken from a camera located above the bus driver's head and the image of Joanna-Partington Brown's face is crystal clear.

"Is that your suspect?" Bradley asks us.

"Yes, it is," both Cath and I reply in unison.

"I think we have just found our just cause for bringing Joanna in, Cath," I add. "Thank you, Inspector. This is extremely helpful to us."

Bradley hands me the memory stick and I thank him again as he packs up his laptop and gets back into the squad car. As he leaves, Cath asks me again if we should call DCI Morgan.

"This is a major development, boss. We really need to let him know. He won't be pleased if he finds out from someone else."

Sensing my hesitation, Miller also urges me to call him.

"Look, this is your investigation, Sean, but Catherine is right. The interview was a setback today, but you've made significant progress in other areas. I don't personally know DCI Morgan, but I would be majorly pissed off if one of my team was holding out on me."

Under pressure from both directions, I agree, but only after we have spoken to the pathologist.

"Okay, you're both right. I want to speak to Dr. Mason first, though. I'll call him straight afterwards."

None of us had noticed before, but as we turn towards the forest, we are all thinking the same thing. It is Cath that expresses our thoughts.

"I think you might want to give Morgan a call now boss. How the hell did the press get wind of this?"

The cordon at the entrance to the forest is still in place, but it is now manned by half a dozen uniformed officers who are struggling to hold back a growing crowd of reporters and camera crews.

As we get closer, the answer to Catherine's question is answered when we see Peter Jackson, the owner of the guest house, being interviewed by a young woman with long blonde hair. As we approach, Jackson looks in my direction and points to me. This causes a flurry of activity and soon we are surrounded by reporters pushing digital recorders and cameras in our faces. All are desperate for quotes and the questions come thick and fast.

"DS McMillan, is it true that a second body has been found?"

"Is it true that this is the work of a serial killer?"

"Sean, is this connected in any way to the Network?"

"DC Swain, is there a connection here to Sir David Partington-Brown? Didn't he used to be the MP for Spalding? Is he a suspect in these killings?"

Ignoring the questions and with the help of two uniformed constables, we clear a path through the throng of journalists and push our way through the gap in the fence.

"Boss, you need to call DCI Morgan now," Cath tells me again. "If by some chance it doesn't make the evening papers and news, you can bet your life it will be headline news tomorrow morning."

"Yep, got that, Cath," I reply sarcastically. "DI Miller, would you mind going with DC Swain to the search site? I'll call Morgan now and join you in a few minutes."

Miller leads Catherine away and I take a deep breath before dialing Morgan's number.

Part of me is hoping that he is busy and won't answer, but as always he picks up within a couple of rings.

"Detective Sergeant McMillan. Tell me – what's going on?"

Addressing me so formally puts me on the defensive immediately and I suspect that he probably already knows what is going on.

"Some good progress on the one hand, sir, and a slight setback on the other."

"I assume by setback you're talking about the interview of Edward Wells today?" Morgan asks. Clearly, he has already been called by the Home Secretary or by Jeffrey Morris himself.

"Yes, sir. It didn't quite go to plan, but ..."

"That's a slight understatement," Morgan interrupts. "You shoved some horrific images under the nose of an elderly man without any lead in or adequate warning. I understand that your tactics are less than orthodox, Sean, but there is only so much that even I can do to protect you."

"I'm sorry, sir. Wells had just slipped up when we were questioning him about the death of Paul Oliver, and it seemed important to strike while he was still rattled. I do appreciate your support, sir."

"That's my job, Sean. Anyway, leave the Home Secretary and Jeffrey Morris to me. You just said that you were questioning him about the death of Paul Oliver. So, you got a positive result on the ID?"

"We did, sir. It's Paul Oliver without a doubt and that's not all. The search team have located a second body. A young adult female."

"Lucy Partington-Brown?" Morgan asks.

"We don't have a formal identification yet, but it must be. Our colleagues from Spalding have requested her dental records and then we can get working on it. There is also something else."

"Go on, Sean. What is it?"

"We have camera footage placing Joanna at the scene of the murder of Father Beale.

Irrespective of whether we get a positive ID on Lucy tonight, I need your permission to pull them both in for questioning tonight. With what we have now, we are way beyond just cause or reasonable doubt. Can I go ahea ..."

"Sean, hold your horses," Morgan interrupts me. "Under normal circumstances, you are right, but these are not normal circumstances. The Partington-Browns and Jeffrey Morris have an extensive network of extremely powerful and influential friends. In order to pacify Morris and the Home Secretary, I had to agree to giving at least twenty-four-hours' notice before any further interviews. You also need to provide Morris with all the evidence that you are intending to present during the interviews."

"Christ, sir! We are near to breaking this case. Any delay in bringing them in swings the advantage back in their favor."

"Sean, I understand. But if you issue the notice now, you can get Wells back in by 5 pm tomorrow. From what I understand, he seems to be the weak link. Get him to spill his guts and he will take Joanna down with him."

It's frustrating, but as always, Morgan is right. I thank him again for his support and we end the call. I rejoin Catherine and DI Miller and share the advice from Morgan.

"It's not ideal, Cath, but we are where we are. Head back to the hotel and make a copy of the memory stick – or better still, mail the files to Jeffrey Morris along with a summary of what we are accusing his clients of. I want Eddie Wells back in for interview by 5 pm tomorrow."

"What about Joanna?" she asks.

"You heard Morgan's advice, Cath. We stand down on her, until we get Eddie to rollover."

Catherine looks as pissed off and disappointed as I feel, but she doesn't say anything else. We agree to meet later at the hotel, and she leaves with two uniformed officers to assist with navigating a path through the waiting press.

Dr. Mason has been waiting patiently to the side of us and now leads me to the excavation site. To the untrained eye, the skeleton looks no different from the first one, but Mason points to the pelvic bone.

"This one is most definitely a female, DS McMillan. There is absolutely no doubt."

"And what else can you tell us, doctor?" I ask.

"Not a lot at this stage, I'm afraid. The condition of the bones is consistent again with a burial between forty and fifty years ago and as you can see the bones have been exposed to fire. We haven't turned up any clothing fragments, but if you look closely at the right wrist there does appear to be the remains of molten steel and glass."

"A wristwatch?" I ask.

"Yes, I believe so. Sean."

I turn to DI Miller and ask him about the dental records.

"The request is in, Sean. But it's the weekend. My boys are working on getting hold of them, but it may take some time to track down someone who can release them. I doubt very much if we will get them today and tomorrow is Sunday."

This is another unwanted blow, but it makes no difference. We already have more than enough to bring Eddie in. We also have enough to bring Joanna in, but I will play the game and remain patient.

"Do you still have your medical examiners on site, Dr. Mason?"

"Yes, they are both waiting at the guest house."

"Good," I reply. "Keep them here. Once those dental records arrive, I don't want any delays in the identification."

Technically, Dr. Mason and his team work for Lincolnshire Constabulary and therefore don't take instruction from me. He turns to Miller for advice and Miller confirms my instruction.

"Sorry, doctor. DS McMillan is right. If you could speak to your team and ask them to remain on site a while longer, I will follow up with my own guys to get a hustle on with those records. Just another twenty-four hours hopefully."

I thank the doctor and then walk back towards the entrance to the forest. The crowd of reporters has grown even bigger and Miller asks me if I am ready.

I smile and tell him that I was born ready.

"You lead the way, though, and I will tuck in behind you."

"Agreed," Miller says. "There is a car waiting to take you back to your hotel"

One of the constables on duty pulls back the barrier and Miller leads the way through the crowd. As before, we are immediately surrounded and are hit with a new barrage of questions from all sides.

"DS McMillan, have the bodies been identified?"

"Who owns this land? Do you have any suspects? Is Sir David a suspect?"

"DS McMillan, can you give us a statement?"

"Are you expecting to find more bodies? Is the search continuing?"

"Sean, you need to call Clive Douglas. He needs to speak to you."

I stop in my tracks and scan the crowd for who made that last statement.

"Who said that? Who mentioned Clive Douglas?" I shout.

Nobody responds and all I can see are reporters eager for me to speak and the flash of cameras blinding me. Realizing I am not with him, Miller turns back and pulls me forward. We break through the throng and two more constables stop the reporters from following us.

We get to the waiting squad car and Miller asks me why I stopped.

"The first rule of dodging press packs is that you keep on moving, Sean. What happened back there?"

I explain the comment I had heard, and Miller promises to check the credentials of everyone on site.

"If there is anyone there without proper press accreditation, I will let you know. Now, go on. It's been another full-on day and tomorrow is going to be the same. I'm going to stay around here tonight and will let you know if anything else happens. My officer will take you back to Tyevale and unless there is anything else urgent, I will meet you back at Spalding Central tomorrow afternoon."

On the way to Tyevale, I message Maria to check on the condition of Ben. Five minutes later my phone vibrates, and I am pleased to see Maria's response.

'He is much better today, Sean. He is fully awake and was able to eat something a few hours ago. He's sleeping again now, but the doctors are hopeful that he can be transferred to a hospital closer to home in a couple of days.'

Knowing that he is on the mend is a huge relief to me, but selfishly I'm still worried about what he might have told Maria about why he was there in the woods. I send another message asking if he has managed to say anything about what happened. For a few minutes, I can see that Maria is typing a reply and then it comes through.

'Yes, he did. I'm sorry that I thought you might have encouraged him in some way. He told me that it was entirely down to him and that he spoke with your mother to find out where you were. I'm sorry, Sean. I was just so worried and didn't know what to think.'

I reply to reassure her that it doesn't matter, that the important thing is for Ben to make a full recovery. Then I promise to visit again when I am back in London.

Shortly afterwards, I get another message.

'I would really like that. You're a good man, Sean xx'

Now maybe I am reading too much into it, but I'm left wondering if she meant to say, 'He would really like that', instead of, 'I would really like that.' I am so wrapped up in thoughts of taking Maria in my arms again, I don't notice that we have arrived at the hotel until the driver taps me on the leg.

"We're here, Sergeant. Is there anything else you need from me tonight?"

"Um, no, thanks for the lift," I reply.

The driver leaves and for a few minutes I stand outside the hotel pondering the possibilities before going inside. Maria is nearly twenty years older than me and I have no idea how Ben might react if I was to hook up with Maria in the real world.

The sensible part of me says that it is playing with fire, but deep down, I know it is going to happen regardless of the consequences. Maria is a recurring itch and sooner or later that itch will need to be scratched.

"Penny for your thoughts, boss?"

Catherine has appeared at the entrance to the hotel and her question snaps me out of my daydream.

"Oh, nothing much, Cath. I was just taking a breather. It's been quite an interesting couple of days."

"You can say that again, Sean! Come inside, the bar's open. I think we both deserve a drink."

For the next two hours we discuss the recent developments including the Clive Douglas comment over a few drinks and a meal sitting at the bar. Despite the comment from person unknown and the way in which the interview with Eddie ended today, we are both in good spirits and confident that by the end of the day tomorrow, this case should be more or less wrapped up.

If we had been able to carry on today, I'm convinced that he would have caved in. Now that we have a second body and the footage of Joanna arriving at the vicarage in the early hours of yesterday morning, it is a virtual certainty. By 10 pm, I wish Catherine a good night and I get up to leave.

"No particular rush to get up in the morning, Cath. It's Sunday tomorrow and unless there are any new developments, have a lie in. Meet me back in the reception at midday. We're due to catch up with DI Miller again at one-thirty."

Cath sarcastically thanks me for my generosity, and I head to my room to work out my final moves.

For most aspects of this case, I now either know for certain what happened, or I at least have a good idea. I take a sheet of the hotel stationery from one of the dresser drawers and I note down each of the main questions along with the answers or my assumption.

1. What happened to Lucy? – Killed by Eddie Wells, albeit unintentionally. Provoked by JPB.

2. Was the killing of Lucy a deliberate act? – No. From what I saw, the killing of Lucy was unintentional, but there was almost certainly a plan to blackmail Eddie into at least paying off Sir David's debts to keep the estate in family hands.

3. What happened to Paul Oliver? – Not certain, but he seemed to know or suspect something about Lucy's disappearance and for this reason he was murdered by Eddie Wells at the instruction of JPB.

4. Who killed Beatrice Partington-Brown? – Murdered by Eddie Wells at the instruction of JPB. Not sure why yet.

She possibly also discovered something about Lucy's disappearance.

5.   Who killed Father Beale? – Most likely, Eddie Wells, assisted by JPB.

6.   Who tried to kill me and unintentionally wounded Ben Pinto? – Almost certainly, Eddie Wells.

7.   Does Sir David Partington-Brown know about any of the above? – Most likely not. I struggle with the idea that he could know about the death of his daughter and the murder of his wife and accept it, let alone demand for the case to be re-opened.

This then only leaves one major unanswered question. Point number 8.

8.   What is the connection of Sergeant Henry Cuttler, if any, to any of this and why was he protecting the loan sharks? Sir David must surely have known Cuttler well, so why didn't he mention this in his interview statement? And what about his brother DI Alan Cuttler? Is he involved in any way? Were either of the brothers pressured by Joanna into cooperating with the original investigation or closing it prematurely? She knew about her father's debts, so did she also know that Henry Cuttler was somehow associated with the debt?

Proving any involvement of the Cuttlers to the case is irrelevant and not really needed at this point, but it's annoying me that I don't really have much idea of the answers to my questions. My main focus is Eddie and Joanna, but I can't speak to either of them until at least five tomorrow afternoon.

I have a good few hours to burn until then and with my mind made up, I prepare myself to travel again. My seventies suit is in desperate need of a dry-clean, but hopefully this is the last time that I will need to use it. I quickly run an iron over the pants and the shirt and then I dress. I pour myself a small drink and knock it back in one. At just after midnight, I lie down and close my eyes. With the village of Tyevale and the image of Sergeant Henry Cuttler clear in my mind, I begin my now familiar chant and am once more transported back to March of 1972.

# The Past – Tuesday, 7th March, 1972

When I feel how cold it is, it makes me wish that I had my turtleneck jumper on again instead of my suit. On the other hand, it's an absolute blessing that I'm wearing regular shoes and not those bloody platform boots. Sensible shoes will make it far easier for me to negotiate the slush-covered streets without running the risk of breaking my neck.

As before, the O'Hanlon Carnival is spread out across three fields in front of me. I watch for a couple of minutes to see if anything has changed. Satisfied that everything is as it was before, I turn and make my way to the newsagent's on the high street.

Inside, I'm pleased to see that my accuracy has been good again. I pick up a copy of the Daily Mail and take it to the counter. I don't really need the paper this time. I already know the headlines from March 7th, but I figure it will make me less conspicuous in the pub while I'm waiting for the girls, Sir David, and the loan-sharks to show up. Donald Cuttler will probably have a few papers on the bar, but I'd prefer not to take the chance that he doesn't.

Today, I have remembered to bring a few coins with me and without waiting for her to ask, I hand over five pence to the young girl behind the counter. This time around she returns my smile with one of her own, before taking me by surprise by asking me if we have met before. For a second, I have a mild panic, but then she calls back to someone in the stockroom.

"Beryl, get yourself out here. There's a bloke that looks a bit like David Cassidy. You know, that lad from the Partridge Family."

Relieved that that there is nothing more to it than her thinking that I look like someone from a seventies sitcom, I turn to leave just as Beryl appears at the counter. As I walk away, Beryl loudly and completely without shame tells her friend.

"Nah, I don't think he looks much like David Cassidy. Nice ass, though."

Both girls erupt into fits of giggles and I leave the shop as quickly as I can without looking back. Tyevale seems to be the nymphomaniac capital of England and I can't wait to get back to the relative normality of London.

I cross the street and head into the Tyevale Arms. The same drinkers are supping on their pints of bitter at the bar and Paul Oliver and his friends are standing next to the jukebox. I politely tip my hat to the pensioners playing dominoes and the two old men politely return the gesture.

Donald Cuttler is in his usual place behind the bar and after taking a few seconds to pretend to scan the beer options, I order myself a pint of John Smiths Bitter. After handing over the payment, I take my seat next to the fire to warm up and to watch the comings and goings.

Whilst I wait for the arrival of the girls, I absentmindedly flick through the newspaper and smile to myself when I see the article about the IRA bombing of Aldershot Barracks. It makes me think about Ben again and how relieved I was to find out that he is recovering well from his injuries. I had been feeling guilty about giving him a hard time for trying to help me but seeing him so badly injured has put everything into perspective.

He had only been trying to help and it is all down to me that he was ever there in the first place. For the first time, it really hits me that I have a family and, I'm looking forward to getting home and to seeing Ben and Maria again.

I finish reading the newspaper and stand up to get another pint. Whilst I wait for Donald to pour it, the door opens. On cue, the sisters walk in with Abigail Whitchurch and head towards the bar.

Also right on cue, Paul Oliver puts his hand to his mouth and lets out a wolf-whistle and a compliment.

"Looking good, Lucy."

All three girls pretend to ignore his comment and keep walking towards the bar. They don't look back, but Lucy has a huge smile on her face. I hadn't noticed before, but she is wearing a Rolex watch with a silver band and a cream-colored dial. The heat from the fire that killed her must have been incredibly intense. I shudder slightly when I remember the remnants of steel and glass fused to her wrist bone.

While Lucy orders the drinks for herself and Joanna, I am momentarily lost in my own thoughts of a wasted young life. It's not until Lucy asks Abigail what she wants to drink that I am jolted back to reality by the obvious innuendo in her response.

"Unfortunately, they don't serve what I want here, so for now I will settle for a gin and tonic."

The now familiar spark of mischief is glinting in her eye and she follows her first comment with a second one that leaves anyone listening in no doubt as to what she means.

"Maybe one of the lads can sort that out for me later."

Donald frowns and tuts to himself. He turns away to get the drinks for the girls and Paul calls over to Lucy to join him at the jukebox.

"Hey, Lucy, this one is for you. Come and join us."

The mechanical arm in the jukebox selects the next record and Lucy turns to face Paul. As the song starts to play, she teases him about his efforts to attract her and then tells him about the threat from her father.

"My father has threatened to send his gamekeeper after you with his shotgun if he sees you with me. Doesn't that worry you?"

Clearly unfazed by the threat, Paul flashes Lucy the whitest of smiles to win her over. She picks up her drink and all three of the girls join the guys next to the jukebox.

From here on, everything plays out exactly as before. Donald rings his hand bell and loudly declares last orders. I order myself a second pint of bitter and take a seat closer to the jukebox. At 3 pm exactly, Donald is about to pull the bolt across the door when his brother Henry steps in and stamps his feet on the doormat.

"Afternoon, Donald, get me a pint in and a large scotch. It's bloody brass monkeys out there."

Sergeant Cuttler takes his drinks from the bar and Donald continues to serve other customers. I watch as Cuttler makes himself comfortable by the fire and then I turn to face Abigail Whitchurch, who is now sitting next to me. Before she can say anything, I smile and take her by surprise with my own flirtatious comment.

"Wow, to what do I owe this pleasure?"

"Um, sorry, I thought you were somebody else," she replies.

"Really, is that your best chat-up line?" I tease her.

I follow this up with another smile and she visibly relaxes and joins in the banter.

"I knew it as soon as I saw you – you're a London boy. You are way to flash and arrogant to be from around here."

"Not arrogant, darling," I correct her. "I prefer self-confident."

"Okay, whatever you like, Flash Harry. My name is Abigail. What do they call you in wherever it is that you come from?"

I introduce myself and then order a fresh round of drinks. Over the next half an hour, we chat about a fictitious sales job in London and as Abigail gets progressively drunker, I once again find myself fending off her wandering hands. At three-thirty I brush her hand away from my crotch for the third time and get up to leave. Abigail stands up to follow me and, worse for wear, knocks the edge of the table. I already know what is coming, though, and I grab her glass before it can fall.

"Where are you going, lover boy? It's still early," she slurs.

I hand her the glass and smile.

"You're right, it's still early, but maybe you might want to consider making that your last drink and having an early night."

She dismisses my comment with a shrug of her shoulders and sits back down at the table. Before I even get to the front door, she has already been joined by one of Paul's friends and I am quickly forgotten.

I reach the front door and Donald holds it open for me to leave. Before I can step through, Sir David appears and pushes me aside as he comes in. He approaches the jukebox and I watch as he pulls Lucy and Joanna away from the rest of the group so that they can talk in private.

He gets more and more agitated, until finally Joanna shakes her head and walks away. Lucy hands him the two ten-pound notes, which he snatches and thrusts into his jacket pocket.

Without another word, he leaves as quickly as he came. I follow as he makes his way towards the alley at the side of the pub. This time, I have no intention of getting involved. Not yet anyway. Today, Sir David will need to take his beating like a man. I know that he won't be beaten too badly anyway.

I pass his MG sports car and then I cross the road to a spot where I can observe the entrance to the alley. I'm too far away to hear anything properly, but I can see well enough.

I already know it's coming, but I still flinch when the younger thug slams his cosh into the side of Sir David's head.

The two heavies lift him to his feet and push him back against the wall. They talk for another few seconds and then Scarface pushes him to the floor and screams in his face. This time I can make out a few words. The bits that I miss, I fill in through memory.

"You don't bloody have a few more weeks, you toffee-nosed bastard. I want my bleedin' money now, or we make a deal for that car and house of yours."

At this point, I know that Sir David is struggling to breathe. I also know that they have no intention of hurting him badly, so I don't worry unnecessarily. Soon, Scarface releases his grip and lifts him up for a second time. The voices have lowered again, but this is the point where Scarface makes the comment about taking Lucy and Joanna for a walk in the woods.

Sir David takes a swing and Scarface skillfully sidesteps the punch and lands his own in Sir David's stomach. He then nods to his companion and, without the benefit of my intervention this time, Frankie boy brings the cosh down on the top of Sir David's skull. At the same moment, Sergeant Cuttler steps out from the pub and walks to the top of the alleyway.

He stops briefly to check that he is not being watched, and then he joins the two loan sharks at the end of the alley. A few words are exchanged before Cuttler helps Sir David stand up and then all three of them help him to straighten his jacket and tie.

The conversation continues for another five minutes until Cuttler gives Scarface a friendly pat on his back and shakes his hand. With the business seemingly done, Sergeant Cuttler escorts Sir David out towards his car and helps him into the passenger seat.

He checks again that he is not being watched, then he goes back inside the Tyevale Arms, leaving Scarface and Frankie boy still discussing something at the end of the alley

I need to speak to them to find out what is going on between them and Cuttler, but Scarface could return at any second. I'm wondering why he has left Sir David in the passenger seat of his car, when the pub door swings open and my question is answered.

Cuttler is standing in the doorway talking to Lucy. She nods and then gets into the driver's seat of her father's MG. Cuttler watches them drive away and then he closes the pub door behind him, and I hear the metallic clunk of the bolt as it is pulled across from the inside.

Taking my chance, I cross the street and enter the alleyway. As I get closer, Frankie boy turns around, but he makes a massive mistake in misreading my intentions and in underestimating my ability. His cosh is safely tucked away somewhere and, confident that I am no threat, he steps forward with his arms by his sides.

My fist slams into his solar plexus and as he lurches forward my knee connects with the end of his nose with a sickening crack.

Scarface turns just in time to see Frankie drop to the floor. He's not quick enough, though, to dodge the blow to the side of his leg from my extendable baton. His legs buckle under him and he drops to the floor. Frankie tries to stand up and I send him tumbling backwards with a well-placed foot in his chest.

"Stay down, fat boy, if you know what's good for you."

I point the end of the baton at Scarface and gesture for him to get up.

"You. On your feet, baldy, but keep your hands where I can see them."

He had been reaching for something in his jacket pocket, but now thinks better of it. He slowly removes his hand from the pocket and without taking his eyes off me, he painfully stands and sizes me up.

"Steady on there, fella. What's this all about then?"

"Tell me about Sergeant Cuttler," I demand.

"What? I don't know any Sergeant Cuttler. I think you've got the wrong man, pal."

I pull out my warrant card and thrust it into his face.

"Listen, numbnuts, I don't give a shit about you and your boyfriend here, but I do want to know what Cuttler's connection is to you and Sir David Partington-Brown. You can either talk to me here or I can have you both banged away for illegal money lending, assault, and corrupting a police officer."

Scarface laughs at my comment and I ask him what is so funny.

"Corrupting a police officer? That's bloody hilarious! Cuttler is as bent as a nine-pound note. It was him that came to us, not the other way around. I'd never even heard of this shithole until he called me."

"So, it was Cuttler that introduced you to Sir David?" I ask.

"You're a smart lad," Scarface replies. "Cuttler was given my details by another copper. He called me to say that Sir David was in urgent need of a less-than-kosher injection of cash and could I help."

"And?"

"And I helped. I spoke to my boss and it was done."

"Is that as far as Cuttler is concerned?" I ask him.

"That's it. He took a small commission for the introduction and since then he's been looking out for us whenever we come here to collect our payments."

"And he doesn't intervene when you're dishing out a few slaps?" I ask.

Scarface smiles and then shrugs.

"He doesn't give a monkey's now that he's got his money. And Sir David's an educated man. He knew the cost of doing business with us. He should consider himself lucky. We wouldn't be as lenient with anyone else. Are we done here?"

He steps forward to leave and I push him back with the end of my baton.

"Just one more question, do you know Cuttler's brother? He's a detective inspector in Spalding CID."

"Hang on, let me think for a minute, nah I don't know him. I never thought to ask about Cuttler's family tree. It didn't seem important."

Laughing, he turns to face Frankie and asks him if he did.

"What about you, Frankie, did you ask Cuttler how many brothers and sisters he had?"

I've seen and heard enough already to understand the connection. Henry Cuttler is just a mildly corrupt chancer who stumbled across an opportunity to make a few quid for himself. Lucy and Joanna both seem to know about their father's dealings with the loan sharks along with Sergeant Cuttler's connection. DI Alan Cuttler on the other hand seems to play no part in this.

Satisfied that I won't get anything else useful from Scarface and Frankie, I retract my baton and tuck it away in my inside jacket pocket.

I tell them both they can leave, and Frankie stands up. Both are still wary, though, and they wait for me to step to the side. I gesture for them to pass and as they do, I reach across Scarface's shoulder. Before he can react, I pull out the small revolver concealed in his pocket and point it at his face.

"I've got a license for that," Scarface protests.

"That's commendable," I reply. "Ask me if I give a shit."

"What is this then?" he asks. "You're not gonna shoot me. Come on, Frankie, we're leaving."

There is no fear in his voice and he clearly thinks that I am bluffing, until I smile and pull back the hammer.

"You're not a copper. What is this, a bloody shakedown? You're not gonna shoot."

I step closer and put the barrel of the revolver between his eyes.

"Oh, I am going to shoot – and I never miss. Not from this range anyway," I add with another smile.

Frankie is slowly edging away from us, but Scarface is frozen to the spot and his previous confidence has deserted him. I watch as a bead of sweat runs from the top of his head to the base of his chin using one of his scars as a track. He is concentrating hard on the revolver and I know that he is weighing up the odds of disarming me before I shoot him in the head.

The standoff continues for another ten seconds until I deliberately look away for a split second and he makes his move. He lunges for the weapon, but I am way ahead of him. I jump back out of reach and scream for both of them to get down.

"Do it now, get down on your knees, or I will shoot you both dead, I swear to God."

They comply without question and, convinced that they are about to die, Frankie starts to quietly sob when I tell them that this is the end. I suggest that they might want to say a final prayer and Frankie shuts his eyes and clasps his hands. Scarface is not ready to give up just yet and pleads with me not to kill them.

"Just tell us what you want. You don't need to kill us. Please, you don't need to do this."

I move closer and lean in.

"Unfortunately, I do need to do this. I've missed the last bus and I really need to get home."

Frankie stops praying and opens his eyes. He turns to Scarface and asks him what I am talking about, but Scarface looks equally as confused.

He looks back to me to ask the question, but the end of the revolver barrel is already near to my mouth.

"It's been nice knowing you chaps, but I must run."

The words "What the hell?" are barely out of Scarface's mouth when the back of my skull explodes, and my brains splatter across the alley.

# Present Day – Sunday, 22<sup>nd</sup> April, 2018

Well that was fun and, as long as I don't need to go back to Tyevale 1972, no serious harm should have been done to the case or the timelines. I doubt very much whether my loan-shark friends will be running to the police to tell tales anyway and, even if they did, who would believe them?

I rub my eyes and then reach for my phone. There are no messages or missed calls and although the sun is already shining through the gap in the curtains it's only just after seven-thirty in the morning. Hopefully, Cath will have taken my advice and will still be asleep. I'm wide awake, though, and to waste some time, I dress in my running gear and take the lift down to reception. Apart from the night porter manning the desk, reception is completely deserted. I politely nod as I pass him.

After a quick warm up and a few stretching exercises, I jog down the high street, past St Benedict's Church and out onto the country roads. The outward leg of my run is dull and uneventful. A couple of times, I am passed by cars heading in one direction or the other, but otherwise the roads are deserted. I use the time to reflect on everything that has happened in the last few days.

When I reach the three-mile point, I turn back towards Tyevale and concentrate on the day ahead. Lost in thoughts of the interview with Eddie Wells, I don't register the sound of the approaching motorbike until it is almost behind me. The road is more than wide enough for most vehicles to pass a pedestrian without any problems and so I keep on running, but as a courtesy I tuck in closer to the side of the road.

The motorbike doesn't hit me, but as it passes, one of the passenger's legs catches me behind the knees and I fall painfully onto the road.

Fortunately, I'm not hurt badly and I'm back on my feet immediately. The motorbike keeps going and if I was in any doubt as to whether this was an accident, the lack of a registration plate answers that question. But if this wasn't an accident, then what was the point? I'm not badly injured and it would have been all too easy to have run me over without witnesses. So maybe, it's a warning. But from whom?

I watch as the bike continues and then disappears out of sight. When I'm sure that it's not coming back, I continue back to Tyevale. Back at the hotel, I consider waking Cath up to tell her about the motorbike, but there is nothing either of us can do about it right now, so I leave her sleeping and I take a shower. Other than scraped knees and a bit of grit on the palms of my hands where I fell, I am otherwise unscathed.

For now, I put the episode out of my mind, spending the rest of the morning working on my notes. At midday exactly, I put on my jacket, straighten my tie, and give myself a final inspection in the mirror. Today is going to be a good day, I tell myself.

"Looking good, Detective Sergeant McMillan, and it's a beautiful day for putting bad guys away."


Catherine is waiting for me next to her car and she is looking much better for having had a decent night's sleep.

"Good morning, Cath. You look a lot better today. I take it there were no calls last night?" I ask her.

"Thanks, boss. Nope, a nice peaceful night, thankfully," Cath replies. "I did get a message from Miller, though. Lucy's dental records have been tracked down and they should be with the doc and his team sometime this afternoon."

"That's great news, Cath. If we can get a positive ID on Lucy before the interview with Eddie Wells, then that should be the final nail in the coffin for both Eddie and Joanna."

"What about you, boss? Anything new to report?"

In response, I hold out the palms of my hands to her.

"What the hell! What happened, are you okay?"

I reassure her that I am okay and then I explain to her about my run-in with the bikers this morning.

"You think it's connected to this case?" Cath asks.

"No, I don't think so, Cath. If anything, I think this is a warning from someone connected to the Network case and most likely connected to the comment for me to call Clive Douglas. Let's not even worry about it for now, though. Douglas is going nowhere, and we have bigger fish to fry today."

"Okay, but let's not get complacent," Cath warns. "That guy has a long reach and nothing to lose."

We hit the road and arrive at Spalding Central station by one-fifteen. Thirty minutes later, DI Miller joins us in the interview room, and we get down to work. The upcoming interview tactics are our primary focus, but I'm also keen to know if Miller was able to check out exactly who was amongst the press pack at Meadow Farm yesterday.

"Any luck on those names, sir?"

"Sorry, Sean, no. Everyone came up clean. They all had legit press credentials and none of them remember anyone mentioning anything about DS Douglas. To be honest that's no great surprise. They were all fighting each other to get a quote from you. Do you think that you might have been mistaken?"

"I did consider that, until this morning," I reply.

I show Miller my hands and repeat the story of the motorbike.

"Someone is definitely trying to send a message to me, sir."

Miller takes down the description of the bike and the riders, but we all know that he's wasting his time. Whoever they were, they were professionals and they and the bike will be long gone. I thank him anyway and we continue with our preparation.

By 4:50 pm, Eddie is yet to arrive, then at 5 pm exactly, DI Miller takes a call from reception to say that he is here.

Miller leaves us to escort him to the interview room and Catherine prepares the tape.

"Make sure that the machine is working properly, Cath. We can't afford for any screw-ups today."

"Boss, take a chill-pill. We've got this in the bag," she replies. Then with a grin on her face, she adds. "Speaking of bags, will we be needing any sick bags this time?"

"Ha-ha, very bleeding funny, Cath. Point taken. Go on now, get yourself ready. I can hear them coming."

Thirty seconds later the door opens, and Miller shows Eddie Wells and the Honorable Jeffrey Morris QC to their seats. I open the meeting by asking Morris if he has received the camera footage and other materials and if he has had adequate time for review.

"Adequate time is extremely subjective, Detective Sergeant," Morris replies with a raise of his eyebrows. "If you're referring to the minimum requirement by law, then yes I have. If, however, you want my personal opinion, then no I haven't. We all know, though, that my personal opinion has no bearing on this point, so let's proceed, shall we?"

Catherine starts the tape and, as always, leads off with the formalities.

"This interview is being recorded and for the benefit of the tape, the time now is 5:08 pm and the date is Sunday, April 22nd, 2018. This interview is a continuation of an earlier interview with Mr. Edward Wells on Saturday, April 21st, 2018. Present in the room are Detective Constable Catherine Swain, Detective Sergeant Sean McMillan, Detective Inspector Patrick Miller, Mr. Edward Wells, and Mr. Wells' legal counsel, the Honorable Jeffrey Morris QC. I must remind you again, Mr. Wells, that you are not currently under arrest, but I caution you that anything you say during this interview may be used in evidence against you. Do you understand?"

Eddie confirms that he does, and I start the interview by asking Morris if there is anything that he would like to say before I begin my questioning.

"Thank you, DC McMillan. Yes, I would. Yesterday I was provided with three video files that show an unknown female walking in the street and boarding a bus on the morning of Friday, April 20th. I would like to have these exhibits removed from today's questioning on the basis that they do not show my client. Nor does he know who the woman in the video footage is. Therefore, I would suggest that they have no bearing on today's interview."

"Has your client seen the video footage?" I ask him. "Because if he has, I'd be very surprised if he didn't recognize his wife. Her face is very clear in the footage taken on the bus."

Although the second part of my statement was in response to Jeffrey Morris, my answer was directed to Eddie who is now avoiding me by looking at the floor.

"You do recognize your own wife, don't you, Mr. Wells?"

Eddie sheepishly raises his head, but Morris holds him back from answering.

"You don't need to answer that question, Mr. Wells. Sergeant, McMillan, we are all perfectly well aware that even if that was Joanna Partington-Brown in these video clips, under law, Mr. Wells is under no obligation whatsoever to answer questions or give evidence against his spouse. Come, come, Sergeant. This is a lesson from criminal law 101."

We all know this, of course, but we had agreed to chance our arm anyway. It's not a problem, though. There is more than one way to skin a cat. Miller suggests that we leave the video footage out of today's interview. Catherine and I both agree, and he confirms for the tape and asks for me to continue.

"Mr. Wells, yesterday, Detective Inspector Miller showed you a photograph of a skeleton that had been discovered on a piece of land owned by you. When you were asked if you knew who it was, you first replied to say that you didn't know, but then when you were pushed you said that you didn't know who 'she' was. Why particularly did you say 'she'? Did you think that we had found Lucy Partington-Brown?"

"Don't answer that, Mr. Wells. DS McMillan, my client already answered that question yesterday. He was nervous and his reply was nothing more than a slip of the tongue."

I don't respond to Morris and nor do I push the point. Still staring at Eddie, I ask my next question.

"Later, you were told that a skeleton had been found on your land and had been positively identified as Paul Oliver. You know who Paul Oliver is, don't you, Mr. Wells?"

"Yes," Eddie replies.

"And would it be fair to say that he was a friend of yours?" I ask.

"Not so much a friend. He was friends with Lucy mainly."

"So, you didn't like him, Mr. Wells?"

"You need to rephrase that question," Morris interjects. "My client was only loosely associated with Mr. Oliver through his wife's sister. He neither liked nor disliked him. Please refrain from trying to twist it in any other way."

"Point noted, Mr. Morris," I reply.

"So, what did you think when I told you that it was Paul Oliver that was buried on your land, Mr. Wells? That must have been a shock to discover that he hadn't run away with Lucy after all."

Eddie looks to Morris for advice and while they confer I ask another question.

"Did you really think that he had run away with Lucy or was it your wife that convinced you to say that? We can all see that she's a strong woman. You don't need to take all this onto yourself, Mr. Wells."

Morris is livid at my interruption and lets his feelings be known. My intention had been to make Eddie angry, but it works just as well if it's his legal counsel. I know from long experience that anger leads to lack of control and lack of control leads to mistakes. I offer half an apology and then I play my next card.

"Please ignore my last statement, Mr. Wells. For the benefit of the tape, this can be removed from the written transcript. Now, I'd like to show you something that you haven't seen before."

I point to the folder in front of Jeffrey Morris and indicate for him to open it.

"Mr. Morris, please refer to the item marked as exhibit AF46 in your evidence pack. This is a copy of an original photograph taken yesterday afternoon."

I slide my own copy across the table for Eddie to see.

"Mr. Morris, I'm showing your client a photograph of a second skeleton that was discovered directly below the first on a tract of land owned by your client. Whilst we are not yet in possession of a positive identification, it has been confirmed that this skeleton does belong to a young adult female."

I've barely finished the sentence before Eddie turns white and tears start to well up in the corner of his eyes. I wait to let him compose himself, before talking again, but he takes us all by surprise when he speaks first.

"Is that her? Is that …"

Morris interrupts Eddie before he can finish his question and then he hands him a folded piece of paper. While Eddie reads it, Morris tells me that I can carry on.

"Your client asked, 'Is that her?', Mr. Morris. He was also about to ask something else. Why did you stop him?"

"I'm his legal counsel, Sergeant. I should have thought that was obvious by now. It's my job to ensure that he is protected."

"And does he need protecting?" I ask. "Mr. Wells, were you going to ask me if that was Lucy Partington-Brown?"

"I've advised my client not to answer any further questions regarding either of the skeletons discovered on his land," Morris responds. "My client vehemently denies all knowledge of the identities, or indeed of how they came to be buried on his land."

"Really, Mr. Morris? One of them has already been positively identified as a person very well known to your client and the second is almost certainly Lucy Partington-Brown. Mr. Wells knows this very well."

I turn back to Eddie and ask him why he kept that particular piece of land. "We checked the records, Mr. Wells. You sold your farm and most of your land on March 20th, 1972. Why did you sell up less than a week after the disappearance of your wife's sister and why did you keep this piece of land?"

Eddie is struggling to speak, so I keep going and intensify my attack.

"You sold the land because you were being blackmailed by Joanna into paying off Sir David's debts. You killed Lucy after luring her to your farm and Joanna found out about it. You sold your land and handed over everything to your wife and Sir David, but you kept one piece of land. The piece of land where you had buried Lucy's body!"

For emphasis I stand up and slam my hand down on the table as I say the word 'body'.

Eddie has tears in his eyes again and Morris is on his feet protesting, but I'm not done yet. Ignoring Morris, I throw the other photographs of Paul across the table again.

"You killed Lucy, you lured her to the woods, and you killed her in cold blood. And what about Paul Oliver and that cock-and-bull story about him murdering your mother-in-law? That was all rubbish, wasn't it? Paul and Beatrice both found out what you had done, so you bashed Paul's head in, and you smothered Beatrice with a pillow. How could you do such a thing to your own wife's family and friends?"

Morris is demanding I stop, and Miller pulls me back into my seat.

"Gentlemen, let's just calm things down a bit please. DS McMillan, let's move on please."

My attack could not have gone any better and I am pleased that Miller has gone along with the plan without interrupting my flow. I've no idea how much Jeffrey Morris knows about what has really happened, but it is written all over Eddie's face. He is stunned with just how close I am to the truth.

Morris has also retaken his seat, but his annoyance is obvious.

"Before we move on, DI Miller, and for the benefit of the tape, I would like to warn DS McMillan that he is sailing very close to the wind with his confrontational interview style. My client has come here willingly and is prepared to assist in your enquiries, but if he continues in such a way I will have no option but to advise Mr. Wells to withdraw his cooperation."

"I'm actually done for now, Mr. Morris," I reply. "DC Swain will now take over, if that's acceptable to you?"

Morris is no fool and knows only too well that I am far from done, but he knows that Catherine will be less aggressive. Not that we need it, Morris gives his consent and Cath takes over with a far subtler approach.

"Mr. Wells, yesterday, DS McMillan showed you two quite graphic photographs that caused you to get quite distressed and physically ill. Upsetting you was not the intention, but I do need to ask you some questions about those pictures. Is that okay, Mr. Wells? If we can do that, then we can move on and try to end this interview as quickly as possible. I know how stressful these things can be."

Catherine follows up her opening statement with a smile and, pleased that it is no longer me, Eddie smiles slightly himself and agrees.

"Thank you, Mr. Wells. That's good," Catherine replies.

Morris already has copies of the photographs in his pack and for the record Catherine confirms the exhibit numbers, before sliding our copies across the table for Eddie to see.

"Mr. Wells, the first photograph is of a young man who was shot in the shoulder with a shotgun on the morning of Friday April 20th. Is there anything that you can tell us about this?"

Eddie shakes his head and Cath tells him, "For the tape please, Mr. Wells."

"No, I don't know anything about it. Why would I?"

"Perhaps because the young man wasn't the intended victim, or perhaps because the attack took place on your land, Mr. Wells. He was shot in exactly the same place that the skeleton of Paul Oliver was found."

As with me, Eddie is now trying to avoid Cath's gaze. Realizing that he is not going to answer anytime soon, Catherine continues.

"Okay, well I'm going to tell you what I think happened and then you can tell me if I'm wrong. I think that after DS McMillan and I came to your home for the second time, Joanna arranged for you to follow us. You were both worried that we were getting close to the truth about what happened to Lucy. So, you followed us from our hotel to Meadow Farm and into the woods with the intention of killing us both. Unfortunately, this young man spotted you and was shot trying to warn us. You then made your escape back to Colevale Manor on a motorbike or a quad bike. How am I doing, Mr. Wells?"

"That's not what happened," Eddie protests.

"Really? Then what did happen, Mr. Wells? Tell us what happened, and we can help you. Help us to help you," Catherine implores him.

"I don't know anything about this, I wasn't there."

"Well, if it wasn't you, Mr. Wells, then it must have been Father Beale. Our witness does say that he saw the shooter wearing a dog collar. Was it Father Beale, Mr. Wells? You know who Father Beale is, don't you?"

"Yes, it was. I mean, yes, I know him. It could have been him. I don't know, I don't know."

Clearly panicked and vulnerable, I point to the second picture and pick up where I left off.

"It wasn't Father Beale. How could it have been? When this young man was attacked it was after seven in the morning. Father Beale had already been dead for at least four hours by then. Look at the picture, Mr. Wells. No wonder it made you sick. What was the worst part about killing him? Bashing his head in or blowing his brains out?"

"No, please. I didn't kill him. I didn't want any of …"

"Mr. Wells don't say anything else. DI Miller, we need to adjourn so that I may speak with my client," Morris interjects.

"All in good time," Miller replies. "Carry on, DS McMillan."

"This is not looking good for you, Mr. Wells. How many more are there? You're never going to see the light of day again if you don't start cooperating. Tell us what you have done. Tell us about Joanna. Did she put you up to all this? Was she blackmailing you?"

"DI Miller, DS McMillan, I demand that we adjourn immediately."

Morris stands up and I tell him to sit down.

"We will adjourn when we are ready to adjourn and not before. Your client is suspected of multiple murders and he needs to answer our questions, so I suggest that you advise him to stop playing games."

Reluctantly, he takes his seat and allows me to continue.

"Mr. Wells, did you kill Father James Beale at Beckhampton Church in the early hours of Friday April 20th, 2018?"

"No, no, no. I didn't kill anyone," Eddie protests.

"You're a liar," I shout. "Your prints are all over the weapon!"

Tears are streaming down Eddie's cheeks as he turns to Morris.

"He's lying. I never even touched the weapon. It was Joanna. It was her idea, not mine."

Morris looks stunned and Eddie looks beaten, but I feel jubilant. I look to Miller and suggest that now might be the right time to take an adjournment. Catherine notes the time and turns off the tape.

Before we leave Jeffrey Morris alone to speak with Eddie, I give him some advice.

"Mr. Morris, based on what your client has just told us, it is our intention when we reconvene to arrest your client for the murders of Lucy Partington-Brown, Beatrice Partington-Brown, Paul Oliver, and Father James Beale. Additionally, we will be arresting him for the attempted murder of myself and DC Swain, as well as the wounding of Benjamin Pinto. I don't think I need to tell you that Mr. Wells is looking at a mandatory life sentence without parole if convicted. We're going to give you ten minutes alone. I suggest you use that time wisely."

And then to Eddie as we leave, "Mr. Wells, listen to Mr. Morris. You don't need to take this all on yourself. Do the right thing and tell us about your wife's involvement. Anything you do to help us will be considered later and might help in greatly reducing your sentence."

Leaving them alone to speak in private, we walk to the end of the corridor so that we can't be overheard.

"I've got to hand it to you, Sean. That was crude, but it was effective. This is big news," Miller says. "You need to get Joanna in before anything leaks to the papers. With the multiple murders and the connection to Sir David, it's only a matter of time before the press gets wind. When that happens, this is going to be front-page news."

"Yes, I know, sir," I reply. "We need to bring DCI Morgan into the loop as well so that he can brief the Home Secretary and the Chief Constable of Lincolnshire. Not just yet, though. Other than implicating Joanna for the murder of Father Beale, Wells hasn't actually admitted to anything else yet and I don't want to jump the gun."

"You think that Morris will be advising him to play ball, boss?" Cath asks me.

"Yes, I do, Cath. Morris won't risk his reputation trying to defend the indefensible. He will throw Joanna to the wolves and defend Wells on the basis of Joanna's blackmail and manipulation. Undoubtedly, if Eddie cooperates, Morris will get him a greatly reduced sentence. Whether his clients are found guilty or not, he will still be a winner. This will be another case that dominates the headlines for months and there is no such thing as bad publicity for guys like him."

We chat for another five minutes and write up a shortlist of questions, then Cath checks her watch and confirms that their time is up.

"That's their ten minutes, boss. Let's get back in there."


We take our seats again. I ask Morris if he is ready to continue. He confirms that he is. Catherine starts the tape.

"This interview is being reconvened following an earlier adjournment and, for the benefit of the tape, the time now is 5:47 pm and the date is Sunday April 22nd, 2018. Still present in the room are Detective Constable Catherine Swain, Detective Sergeant Sean McMillan, Detective Inspector Patrick Miller, Mr. Edward Wells, and Mr. Wells' legal counsel, the Honorable Jeffrey Morris QC. I must remind you again, Mr. Wells, that you are not currently under arrest, but I caution you that anything you say during this interview may be used in evidence against you. Do you understand?"

"I do," Eddie confirms.

"Thank you, Mr. Wells. Have you had a chance to speak with your legal counsel?" I ask him.

"Yes, I have, thank you," he replies.

"Good, in that case DC Swain is going to ask you a series of questions and we need you to answer them honestly and to the best of your ability. Is that clear?"

Eddie nods and then verbally confirms. I pass the list over to Cath and she gets to work.

"Mr. Wells, before the break you told us that it was your wife that killed Father James Beale. Is that true?"

"Yes, it is."

Morris encourages Eddie to say more.

"Go on, Mr. Wells, the more you can tell the police, the more it will help you."

"We knew that you were planning to visit him, and we were worried about what he might tell you about how Lucy died. Joanna came up with a plan to make it look like it was him that had attacked you."

"The dog collar you mean?" Catherine asks.

"Yes, but also by making it look like he killed himself afterwards," Eddie replies.

"I stole a motorbike and then I drove Joanna and the bike to Beckhampton church. Joanna had called him to say she was coming, so he wasn't surprised and let her in willingly. I parked at the back of the church and Joanna let me in through the gate. He was already unconscious when I went inside. I helped Joanna put him into the chair, but I didn't kill him. I couldn't do it. I'd had enough. She was the one that put the gun in his mouth and pulled the trigger. After that she gave me the dog collar and told me that I should follow you and try to scare you off. I never intended to hurt either you or that boy. Is he okay?"

"Fortunately, yes," Cath replies. "He was very lucky, but don't worry about that for now. I need you to keep talking. Did you kill Lucy Partington-Brown? Is hers the second skeleton?"

"It was an accident. I was fighting with Father Beale and I hit her by mistake. She fell into the fire."

Cath makes a note on her pad before continuing.

"So, Father Beale witnessed her death and that's why he was killed. What about Paul Oliver and Beatrice Partington-Brown. Did you also kill them?"

His voice is shaky and low, but Eddie confirms that he did.

"I didn't want any of this, but Joanna kept saying that if I didn't do exactly what she wanted that she would go to the police and tell them that I had deliberately killed her sister."

"How did you kill them both?"

"Joanna brought Paul to Meadow Farm. I'd sold it, but I hadn't moved out yet. I waited in the woods for them and I smashed his head in with a shovel."

"And Beatrice?" Cath asks him.

"Joanna wanted it to look like natural causes, so we poisoned her with small doses of foxglove. It was taking too long, though, so Joanna insisted I smother her with a cushion. I smothered her. There was someone else there, though, I swear to that. We chased a man out of the house, and he got caught in a trap. I left him to fetch Joanna and when we got back he was gone."

The memory and the pain of the trap is still fresh in my mind, but it has all been worth it. There will need to be many more interviews with both Eddie and Joanna, but today's admissions are more than enough to formally arrest him and to bring Joanna in.

We go through the formal process of placing Eddie under arrest and then Miller calls for the duty sergeant to assist in escorting him to one of the holding cells. I ask Morris if he would mind waiting to speak to me and once Eddie is secure all three of us rejoin Morris in the interview room.

"Mr. Morris, we're going to hold Mr. Wells overnight and will push to get him in front of a judge tomorrow. Given the seriousness of the offences, we will be opposing bail, but I'm sure you know that already."

Morris nods and asks about Joanna. "I'm not sure that she's going to be as cooperative as Mr. Wells, but if it helps I could call her and ask her to come here willingly. I'm sure she would consider that preferable to being dragged in by the police."

"Please, go ahead and call her," I tell him.

We all step out of the room to allow him to make the call and after a few minutes, he calls us back in. His hand is over the phone, so that Joanna can't hear him speaking.

"I've just briefly explained to her what has happened during her husband's interview. She completely denies any involvement, but she is willing to cooperate."

"So, she's coming here?" I ask.

"Not exactly, Detective Sergeant. She would like to speak with you first."

Morris hands me the phone and I put it to my ear.

"Ms. Partington-Brown, this is DS McMillan, I understand that you want to speak to me. I'm at Spalding Central station. Come here and tell us your side of the story."

"I would prefer for you to come here, Sergeant. I want you to take me in," Joanna says.

"Okay, let me send a car for you. It can be there in …"

"No, I don't want a car. I want you personally to come and take me in. If you agree to that, I will cooperate fully."

"Okay, agreed. We can be there in just over an hour. Is that okay?"

"Yes, I'll be waiting for you. Only you should come in, though. Your partner must wait outside."

I agree to the request and hand back the phone to Morris.

"I suggest that you take a break, Mr. Morris. Joanna has asked me to personally bring her in, but it's at least a two-hour round trip. Make yourself comfortable in the canteen. We'll call you when we are back.

Morris leaves and I relay the rest of the conversation to Catherine and DI Miller.

"There is no way you are going on your own, boss. The shotgun that injured Ben Pinto is still unaccounted for and a house like that is probably filled with guns. This has to be a trap."

"I know that, Cath. You can come with me, but you need to wait outside until I call you in. She was insistent on that point. DI Miller can back us up with an armed response team. Sir, you can follow us in and then hold at the entrance to the estate. I don't want to spook her needlessly."

Miller agrees to my suggestion and twenty minutes later we are thundering down the motorway towards Colevale.


At just after seven-forty in the evening, we drive through the gates of Colevale Manor leaving DI Miller and his team outside to await my instructions. The upper floors of the house are in darkness, but the lower floor and the garden are fully illuminated. The front door is wide open.

"Boss, you really shouldn't be doing this," Catherine warns me. "That bitch is dangerous – and you're not armed. Send the armed response team in first."

"You worry too much, Cath. I've got my vest and my truncheon. What more could a British bobby ask for?"

In truth, I'm as concerned as Cath is, but the alternative is an armed stand-off. I know that Joanna will not come in without a fight if the uniformed boys show up for her.

If there is a chance to take her in peacefully, then it's a chance worth taking.

"Just go carefully, Sean. If anything doesn't seem right, get your ass out of there and call for the cavalry."

I thank Cath and then I walk towards the steps to the house. I cautiously enter, but I know already where she will be. Just outside the study, I announce my arrival.

"Ms. Partington-Brown, it's Detective Sergeant McMillan, may I come in?"

"Are you alone?" Joanna responds.

I reply that I am. She tells me that the door is unlocked and to come in.

I slowly push open the door and peer into the room. Joanna is sitting on the edge of one of the leather sofas and the same silver tea service she used during our first visit is laid out on the table in front of her. She invites me in to sit down and then quite nonchalantly lifts the veil on the wedding dress she is wearing and politely offers me a cup of tea.

"Don't look so confused, Sergeant. The last time I wore this was more than forty years ago. It's such a beautiful dress, but it was completely wasted on my excuse for a husband."

I'm listening to her talking, but I'm also staring at the Webley revolver on the tray next to the sugar bowl.

"That was my father's service revolver," Joanna explains when she sees me staring at it. "He was a Captain in the Lincolnshire Yeomanry during the war. He served in North Africa and I remember him telling me how reliable it was."

The comment about reliability is a clear warning and despite Joanna's age, there is no chance of me getting to the revolver before her. I ignore the comment and ask where her father is.

"Joanna, we are going to need to arrange for someone to come and look after him. Can I call DC Swain to arrange that?"

"That won't be necessary," she replies. At the same time, she turns to face the corner of the room and the significance of her words hits me. What I had first taken for a pile of laundry piled onto Sir David's wheelchair is in fact a blanket thrown across his head and body. A small stain of blood is starting to soak through, and Joanna cuts me off before I can speak.

"Did you really think that I was going to leave him all on his own to spend his final years knowing what we have done?"

"So instead you execute your own father in cold blood. This needs to stop right now," I shout.

Joanna tries to justify the killing by telling me that he was asleep and knew nothing about it.

"Save it, Joanna, you're wasting your breath. Murder is murder, whichever way you try to spin it," I tell her.

"You think you're very smart, don't you, Sergeant? You think you've got it all figured out, but you still can't see what's staring you in the face," Joanna taunts me. "The really smart ones figured it out but look what happened to them."

I've heard enough and ignoring the fact that she has the revolver, I start to read her, her rights.

"Joanna Partington-Brown, I am arresting you for the murder of …"

I'm cut off by the sound of my phone ringing in my pocket and I ask Joanna if I can take it out to answer it.

"It could be something important, Joanna. Maybe some news about Edward."

She nods, but then picks up the revolver.

"Answer it, but don't try any tricks please, Sergeant."

The call is from Catherine and instead of saying hello, I tell her that everything is fine and that we are having tea in the study.

Catherine will know immediately what to do and will be already sharing this information with Miller and his team.

"Boss, the dental records arrived on site a couple of hours ago. Doctor Mason just called me."

I interrupt to tell her that the identification is not needed right now.

"It's irrelevant for now Cath, we know that it's Lucy. Eddie already admitted to killing her accidentally and ..."

"Boss, you're not listening. You need to keep quiet and listen," Catherine insists. "The second skeleton, it's not Lucy."

"What, that can't be!" I respond. "If it's not Lucy, then who the hell is it?"

"I would have thought the answer would have been obvious by now, Detective Sergeant," Joanna says.

The revolver is now pointing straight at my chest and she tells me to put the phone down on the table. I do as she asks but I leave the call connected so that Catherine can listen in.

I'm kicking myself for not figuring it out sooner, but her wristwatch confirms it. I picture the photograph of the two girls with their parents standing next to the Christmas tree.

Two beautiful and near identical sisters apart from one small detail, Joanna is wearing her watch on her right-hand wrist and Lucy is wearing hers on the left. The skeleton had the remains of the watch on the right wrist.

Lucy notices me staring at the watch on her left wrist and she smiles.

"Bravo, Sergeant McMillan, finally, the penny drops. As I said, the truth is staring you right in the face. It's almost a shame that it has to end like this."

"Why, Lucy, why did you do it?" I ask her.

"Does it matter now?"

"Of course, it matters. Your husband told us that killing Lucy ... I mean Joanna ... was an accident. Nobody else needed to die and I don't understand why he still persists on saying Lucy if he knows full well that it was Joanna that died."

"Let's face facts, Sergeant, my husband is an imbecile. It was almost a year until my mother figured it out and it was only then that he finally discovered the truth. Even when Paul Oliver found out, I still managed to convince him that I was Joanna."

"Convince him?" I ask. "How could he not know? Joanna was his girlfriend."

"As I've just said, my husband is an imbecile and it was important for me to keep up the pretense. Despite the fact that I was blackmailing him, if he had known that I was not Joanna, it might have made him think twice about marrying me.

"The same goes for my father. He was also a fool. Don't get me wrong, he played the grieving father for a while, but he was never particularly close to either of us and with his finances back in order he soon got over it. It never occurred to him for a second that I wasn't Joanna. And then of course there was Joanna herself. If she hadn't been so weak willed, then none of this would have ever started."

Lucy explains about her father's debts and how she had begged Joanna to ask Eddie to lend them some money to pay off the loan sharks to keep the estate within the family. When Joanna had refused to involve Eddie in their family problems, Lucy had devised another plan to get her hands on his money.

"I persuaded Joanna to play a trick on Edward. On the night of the carnival we swapped places and pretended to be one another. It was never going to be hard to fool Edward, but we were so convincing that we even managed to fool everyone else including Paul, the O'Hanlon brothers, and James Beale.

"Joanna wasn't entirely comfortable with playing along with me. But as I said, she was very weak willed. It was easy to persuade her we were just going to have a bit of fun. When she realized that the O'Hanlons and Paul had no idea about the switch, she was only too happy to go off with Jed and Tighe to see how far she could push it. After the carnival we all went to Eddie's Farm."

"Who is all?" I ask her.

"Myself, Joanna, Edward, and James Beale."

"Why was Father Beale there, Lucy?"

"I needed him as a witness," she replies.

"A witness to what?" I ask her.

"A witness to Edward assaulting me. I was trying to provoke Edward into hitting me, so that I could blackmail him into paying off my father's debts.

James was so infatuated with me that all I had to do was snap my fingers and I knew he would come running. I needed James as a credible independent witness.

Edward was so confused, he lashed out thinking that he was hitting Lucy. In the woods, things just went too far. I think you know the rest. Nobody was meant to die. I loved my sister."

"And what about …"

"No, enough, Sergeant," Lucy cuts me off. "I'm tired now. This is where it ends."

"Okay, well just give me the gun, Lucy. Nobody else needs to get hurt and if you come in willingly, I will make sure that it's taken fully into account. Edward is cooperating fully with us. Do the same and do the right thing, Lucy."

"I can't do that, Sergeant," she replies. "I did what I did to protect this family and to protect this estate. This is all I know."

She pulls back the hammer on the revolver and points it at her head.

"Goodbye, Serge…"

"Now, now, now!" I scream.

My outburst momentarily distracts her and a millisecond later a sniper's bullet shatters the window and smashes into

Joanna's shoulder. The impact throws her into the back of the sofa and the revolver drops to the floor.

I snatch up my phone to call for back up, but Catherine is already on to it. The shot has barely even been fired before the study door flies open and Miller charges in with two armed officers. The response team secure the weapon and, satisfied that there is no further danger, they call to Catherine who has been waiting in the corridor with a paramedic team.

Miller asks me if I am okay. I assure him I am and then I point to Lucy.

"Don't worry about me, sir. Just don't let her die. There has been too much blood spilt already in this case."

The paramedics go to work, and we leave DI Miller and his men to secure the scene.

Catherine leads me outside and asks me again if I am okay.

"That was pretty scary stuff, boss. Are you sure you're okay?"

"Honestly, Cath, I'm fine. I did have a bit of an ass-clenching moment when I saw the gun on the tea tray, but all things considered, it probably ended as well as it could. Were you listening in the whole time?"

"Yes, I was. I also patched you through to the command center, so they should have recorded the whole thing. You know what this means, don't you, boss?"

"Go on."

"It means that we will need to de-arrest Eddie for the murder of Lucy and re-arrest him for the murder of Joanna. It also means I was wrong about her being a bitch. She's not just a bitch, she's a bloody sneaky bitch! And what was that with the wedding dress? Did she think you were coming to propose?"

We both laugh and Cath leads me to her car.

"Come on, boss, it's beer o'clock and it's my round."

Things moved pretty fast after that. On the way back to Tyevale, I called DCI Morgan to update him. To say he was shocked at the latest developments would be an understatement and, suffice to say, I spent the rest of the night on the phone explaining myself to Morgan, the Chief Constable of Lincolnshire, and finally the Home Secretary himself.

Despite Cath's promise of a beer, we never quite made it to the bar that night. By the time everyone had been fully apprised of events to their satisfaction it was nearly three in the morning and after, slumping into my bed, I slept soundly for the first time in nearly a week.

We then spent three more days in Spalding assisting DI Miller with his inquiries including five further interviews with Eddie Wells. The news that his wife was in hospital was the final straw for Eddie and over the course of those interviews he gave a full and detailed account of everything connected to each of the charges.

The final piece needed to close our case was a confession from Lucy herself. In the afternoon of the third day and with confirmation from her surgeon that she was well enough to be interviewed, we visited her in Spalding General Hospital.

Despite her age and condition, it had still been deemed necessary to cuff her to the bed. Even with a bullet wound, she was as arrogant and aloof as ever.

We questioned her for nearly thirty minutes, but she steadfastly refused to speak to us. Despite her refusal to speak, this made absolutely no difference to the result. The transcript from my phone call to Cath was more than enough for Catherine to arrest her. With that done, and with a final confirmation from DCI Morgan, our case was formally marked as solved after forty-six years.

From that point, DI Miller and Lincolnshire constabulary assumed full control for the investigations pertaining to recent events and Cath and I were finally able to head back to London.

# Present Day – Wednesday, 25th April, 2018

After more than a week of thinking about nothing else but the case, it is great to be back in my own apartment and in my own bathroom. After a long hot shower, I dress in casual shirt and trousers and splash my face with a handful of cologne.

Ben has been transferred to a hospital in Hounslow and Maria has confirmed that the evening visiting time runs from seven until nine.

I'm keen to see Ben, but I also want to see Maria, so I time my arrival at the hospital fifteen minutes before the end of visitation. Ben is sitting up in bed and Maria is sitting to the side holding his hand.

"Hey, Ben, you look a lot better than the last time I saw you. Sorry that I'm late. I had a bit of last-minute business. You know how it is."

Ben gives me a knowing look and then tells me not to worry.

"Yep, I know how it is. Thanks for coming anyway, Sean."

Maria gives me a smile and stands up to shake my hand, but the gesture is awkward. I feel myself blushing slightly.

"Hi, Maria. Good to see you again. You must be relieved that he's on the mend. It can't be much longer before he's able to go home."

"Actually, the doctor is saying that it might be tomorrow. We're hoping to get the all-clear after the doctor's round tomorrow morning," Maria replies.

"Wow, that's great news!" I reply "You must be happy, Ben. It can't be much fun in here. You must be bored out of your mind."

"Yep, it is pretty boring. There is only so much sleeping you can do. I just want to get home and then get back to work. You know how it is, Sean."

Maria picks up on the look between us and asks if she has missed something.

"No, nothing, Mum. I'm just looking forward to getting back to my studies. Sean promised me that he would give me a few pointers on criminal law. I'm considering specializing in investigative journalism. Isn't that right, Sean?"

"Um, yeh. Absolutely," I reply.

If I had any doubts before about Ben's recovery, I can stop worrying. The little shit is on top-form and has made it clear that I am far from off the hook. I divert the conversation and for the rest of the visit we make small talk and I give them a potted version of the case as the clock counts down to nine.

At nine exactly the duty matron goes from cubicle to cubicle to tell the visitors to say goodbye and when I offer to give Maria a lift home, Ben knows exactly what I am up to.

"That's okay, Sean. Mum has an Uber booked. No need to put yourself out. Isn't that right, Mum?"

Maria is about to speak, but I interrupt and assure her that it's on my way home anyway.

"Cancel your Uber, Maria. I'm going your way anyway. It's really no problem."

"Okay, as long as it's not putting you out. Thank you, Sean."

Maria turns to face Ben and leans over to kiss him on the cheek. We say our final goodbyes and as I escort Maria away, Ben calls me an asshole under his breath.

Maria turns back and asks him what he said.

"Nothing, Mum, but go safely and have a nice evening. You too, Sean," Ben replies.

I look back over my shoulder and answer with a smirk.

"Thanks, Ben, I will. Sweet dreams."

The journey from Hounslow to Feltham is less than three miles, so ordinarily should be no more than a ten-minute drive. We are so engrossed in chatting, though, that Maria doesn't notice that I am taking an unusually long route and by the time we arrive outside her house it is nearly nine-thirty. Maria thanks me for the lift and when I get out to walk her to the door, she insists that it is not necessary.

"That's okay, Sean. I'm sure I'll be fine from here."

I ignore her and get out anyway. I follow her to the front door. She turns to face me and catches me off guard.

"Was there something you wanted to ask me, Sean?"

"Um, what do you mean?" I awkwardly reply.

"I think you know what I mean," she replies with a smile. "I got the feeling that the small talk in the car was building up to something. Is that what the magical mystery tour was about? I've lived in this area my entire life and it has never taken me that long to get from Hounslow."

I laugh at how easily she has sussed me out.

"Sorry, Maria. Was it that obvious?"

"Just a bit, Sean. So, go on then, spit it out."

With all need for subtlety gone, I take a deep breath and blurt it out.

"You're a beautiful woman, Maria, and I know that there is a bit of an age difference between us, but … well, what I mean is …"

Maria is now smiling. She reaches out and takes my hand.

"Take a breath, DS McMillan, I'm not that scary."

"Thanks. So, what I'm trying to say is that I would be honored if I could take you out for dinner one evening. If that would be okay with you, I mean?"

"That would be lovely," Maria replies.

She then takes my other hand and pulls me closer.

"And would you like to come in for a coffee?" she asks.

Her voice is low and seductive, and I fall for it hook line and sinker. I tell her that I would love a coffee and I put one of my hands around her waist.

Maria laughs and removes my hand.

"The last time I invited a guy in for coffee, I ended up as a single mother nine months later. There's a Starbucks in the petrol station at the end of the road. Call me tomorrow and we can take it from there, Sean."

With that she leans forward and kisses me full on the lips, before turning and leaving me feeling like an idiot staring at her front door.

It could have gone a whole lot worse, though. A kiss from a beautiful woman is better than nothing. I walk back to my car happy to be back on home turf and happy to have a date with Maria to look forward to.

I'm about to open my door, when I notice the motorbike on the opposite side of the road. The bike is different from the one that knocked me down in Tyevale, but the leathers and helmets of the driver and passenger are the same.

I cross the road expecting them to drive away, but they don't. The passenger gets off the bike and meets me in the middle of the road.

"Who the hell are you and what do you want?" I ask.

"I want you to do what I asked you to do at Meadow Farm," he replies. "You need to call Clive Douglas."

He throws me a cell phone and then turns back towards the motorbike.

"I've got nothing to say to Douglas," I shout. "What does he want?"

The passenger turns back to face me.

"Just call him, McMillan. His is the only number in the directory."

He gets back on the bike and without another word the driver guns the engine and they disappear out of sight.

I stare at the phone for a second and then I scroll to the address book. There is no name, but as I was told there is one saved number. I touch the call button and after two rings the call connects.

"Sean, so good to hear from you."

The sound of Douglas' voice sends a shiver down my spine and when I don't answer immediately, he speaks again.

"I guess this is a bit of a surprise to you. I can understand that."

"You know possession of a cell phone in prison is a serious offence," I tell him.

"Whatever, McMillan. I'm already looking at a mandatory life sentence, so ask me if I give a shit about having a few more years added on."

"What do you want?" I ask him.

"I want your help to reduce my sentence."

"Are you bloody kidding me? I wouldn't piss on you if you were on fire, Douglas. This conversation is over."

"Whoa, whoa, McMillan! Don't be so hasty. I don't expect your help for nothing. I have information about another major cold case that could be of use to you. You help me and I help you."

"You're full of shit, Douglas. I don't bloody need your help. I'm doing well enough on my own, thank you. Don't contact me aga.."

"You would do well to listen, McMillan," Douglas interrupts. "The Network might be all but done, but I still have reach, Sean. I still have influence, even in here."

"And what's that supposed to mean?" I ask him.

"It means, Sean, that I can get to you whenever I want. I can also get to DC Swain, but more importantly for you, I can also get to your bitch and her son. Think about that tonight. Think about that boy all alone and unprotected in hospital. Goodnight, Sean."

# ABOUT THE AUTHOR

Ernesto H Lee, is originally from Coventry in the UK, but has mixed Spanish and German heritage and now commutes regularly between his homes in London and Madrid. Previously, he was working in Abu-Dhabi and other areas of the Middle East for more than twenty years as an Electrical Engineer, but he has recently now retired and is a full-time author.

The first book in this series, *Out of Time* was launched in August 2018 and was the first in a planned series of books that focuses on the exploits of Detective Constable Sean McMillan — The Dream Traveler.

*The Network* is the second book in The Dream Traveler series and is the concluding part of the story started in *Out Of Time*.

*Finding Lucy* is the third book in the series and is a one part story.

For questions or enquiries, he can be contacted via email at:

ernestohlee@gmail.com

Made in the USA
Coppell, TX
06 October 2021

63559370R00144